The World Below

THE WORLD BELOW BOOK ONE

VIVIENNE LEE FRASER

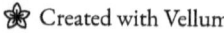

For Sandy for the kick ass girl hero who likes designer clothes;
Selina for the sneak thief; and Serene for the witch in the woods.
Amazingly, between you you sparked a book and a series
—thank you.

CHAPTER 1

The World Below

S hadows darken the dappled sunlight warming my body. I lazily roll onto my back and stretch, moving out of the boy's shadow to recapture the sun. My eyes droop closed, only to flick open as a bee gently lands on the flower by my nose. Ears twitching, I swipe and miss, scaring the annoying buzzy thing into going on its way.

I close my eyes and imagine I am on my sun-soaked cushion on the window seat. Buzzing by my ear ruins the illusion, and I am back in the noisy, busy street with the boy my mistress sent me to watch. I had argued with her, of course, but it didn't work. It never does. I replay the argument, wondering if would I still be here had I done something differently.

'*All I want you to do is follow the boy, Snake, and report back to me each evening.*'

'*Must I?*' *I ask, not even bothering to open an eye.*

'*It is only for a couple of days. I promised his mother I would look out for him.*'

Why don't you go do it, then? The thought pops into my

mind, but I do not speak the words. Instead, I studiously lick my paw and rub it over my head, hoping she will take the hint.

'Come, my friend. I think you have become too comfortable by that fire.'

I ignore her.

'Please. I ask so little of you, and this is such a small thing.' Her fingers scratch behind my ear and I lean into her hand.

When the pleasure gets to be too much, I stand and stretch my back into an arch. 'Will I be home in time for dinner?'

'Perhaps.' She flicks her hand as if sweeping me outside, and I instantly find myself on the front doorstep. 'Thank you,' I hear her voice say in my head.

After a couple of false starts, I had found the boy waiting outside a school— Edgington Elite Academy for Girls. He has been standing across the road, half hidden by a tree, for hours. We have been here for so long, I am beginning to wonder if his mother wanted him watched because he was likely to do something unseemly to one of the girls.

I lift a paw and check for dirt. I turn it this way and that, cleaning it with swift flicks of my tongue. Out of the corner of my eye, I see the boy tense. I pause and follow his gaze. He is interested in a group of girls chatting outside the gates. I can tell which one he is here for. Her essence shines so bright I cannot bear to look directly at her.

Her power is like a magnet attracting all my attention, and the boy is halfway down the street before I realise he's even moved. I rise to my feet, take one last swipe at the bee before creeping through the bushes lining the path as I follow the boy who follows the girl.

'Come on, P. It's only afternoon tea to celebrate the end of school. You'll regret it if you don't come,' Agatha's voice rises above the others as I turn to head home.

'I've gotta go. Mum will make my life a misery if I miss tennis, especially as this is my last lesson.' I fling the words back over my shoulder as I keep walking, hating having to say them, hating that my parents have never allowed me the same freedoms my friends enjoy.

'You're eighteen, P—time to cut the apron strings,' Jeanna says with a sneer. She is one person I will not miss seeing after this week.

Still, she is right. I *am* eighteen, and after the summer holidays, I will begin university. I should be able to do what I want now, but a deal is a deal, and I did promise my parents I would toe the line until after our family holiday in a couple of weeks' time.

The early summer sun warms my arms through my blazer. I want to take it off, but there are still three more days of the school year—three more days I need to wear this horrid, old-fashioned uniform. Then one more week away with my parents—which adds up to ten more days until I can begin making my own decisions.

As I walk along the main road, traffic crawls past me, and I chant, 'No more tennis, no more karate, no more French, no more piano.' Okay, maybe I would still do karate, but piano was definitely going.

I am so engrossed in my personal end-of-school celebration that I don't notice the hairs stand up on the back of my neck until a cold shiver down my spine finally gets my attention. I pause outside a bookshop, stretching out my awareness, trying to identify what is different.

I am used to watching out for attacks. I mean, I live in London, so it is part of keeping yourself safe in a large city.

And this would not be the first time someone has followed me home.

Using the window, I search for the source of my unease. All I find is a black cat across the road. It idly flicks its tail before darting under a rose bush.

The hairs on my neck still warn me that danger is close by. It is not just my parents' constant reminders about the level of violence making me hyperaware. Someone is definitely following me. I glance over my shoulder as I straighten my straw boater, but I still see nothing out of the ordinary.

I warily continue on my journey, and when I am waiting at the crossing, I spot him. A male in jeans, a black Led Zeppelin T-shirt, and a hoodie has stopped at the bookshop. He appears normal enough, but there is something about him I can't quite place my finger on. When he glances surreptitiously in my direction, our eyes meet briefly and my nerves go on high alert; if I had hackles, they would be raised.

As the signal changes, I walk briskly across the road; no Edgington Academy girl would ever run in public. I take the first left and rush the half block to the right turn that will take me into my street.

I risk a quick glance behind. The man is just turning the corner. Now I run. I reach up to hold my hat in place, causing my backpack to bounce awkwardly against my back. I run until I reach the steps leading to my house.

As I climb I let go of my hat and reach round, fumbling in the pocket of my backpack to pull out my keys. My fingers behave like they belong to someone else. The keys slip from them and clatter to the ground. Bending to pick them up, I find myself staring into two green cat eyes.

Keeping the cat in my line of sight, I slowly straighten up. At the last minute, I break the connection and shove the key firmly into the lock just as my pursuer reaches the steps next door. The lock snicks, and I yank at the knob.

I fling the door closed, and it slams behind me with a bang. Leaning my back against the solid wood, I sag with relief. Then I tense. Mum hates the door being slammed. I wait for her to shout from wherever she is inside. The house is silent. That's odd.

I slip my school bag off my shoulder, and it drops to the floor. I pick it up again. Untidiness is frowned upon too. I drag myself up the stairs, listening to the sounds of the house so I can work out where Mum is.

Everything is eerily quiet. No one is home. Not even Susan, my used-to-be nanny, now sort-of housekeeper.

I drop my bag on the bedroom floor and throw my straw boater on the bed. Chewing my bottom lip, I try to remember when I last saw my parents. They had left for work before I got up for breakfast today, but that is normal. In the weeks leading up to a holiday, they often work longer hours.

Yesterday? No. I had gone round to Tanya's after school. By the time I got home, they were out somewhere, and I ate dinner with Susan and went up to bed.

Monday? Yes, I saw them early Monday morning. When I pulled the curtains, I had seen Mum opening the passenger door of the car, and watched as Dad leaned over to say something to her as she got in.

I wander along the hall to their bedroom and opened the door, scanning the room for anything that would tell me why Mum is not here. I skim my gaze over the huge bed to the right, past the two wingback chairs on either side of the window, and round to the doors of their dressing room and ensuite.

Their bedroom is immaculate, but then, it always is. As a child I wondered if they just kept this room for show, and they actually slept somewhere else. I had spent hours looking for their secret hideout, but had never found it.

Today I go left, open the door to the closet, and walk in.

Mum never leaves home for any length of time without taking at least one case, and her luggage is sitting in its usual place. My brow draws into a frown. Only one pair of shoes is missing from the colour-coded shoe wall—the pair she had on when she left for work on Monday.

It is Wednesday today. Mum is always here on Wednesday to take me to my tennis lesson. I am capable of getting there myself, but Mum says she would never miss our mother-daughter time. I often tease her, saying she only comes because she fancies my coach.

I have no talent for tennis at all, but it is fun, and it is better than some of the other edifying things my parents have signed me up for over the years out of guilt because I am an only child and because they travel so often for work.

A quick check of my father's closet, with its rows of suits, shirts, and shoes, shows nothing that would indicate he has been called away either.

As I wonder what is going on here, a loud bang jolts my mind back to the present. It is the noise made when somebody forgets to hold onto the doorknob and it swings into the table behind.

'I shut the door,' I mutter as I speed along the hallway, stopping just before the landing. If I closed the door, then it would have locked automatically.... I peek around the corner and check down the stairs. The front door is wide open, revealing a view of the terraced houses across the street.

It slammed shut. I heard it. How can it be open now?

On silent tiptoes I rush down the stairs and into the living room before screeching to a halt. Standing in the middle of the room is the man who followed me home. Up close he is younger than I had first thought, perhaps only around my own age.

I eye him warily. Standing more than a head taller than me, he is lean, but his loose hoodie makes him appear bulkier. As he takes a step towards me, his hand outstretched, I automatically begin assessing his weaknesses as I move into ready stance. I have learnt from experience that good looks and a friendly smile are no guarantee he will not attack me.

'Don't move. I'm a black belt in karate.' Okay, I'm almost a black belt, but he doesn't know that.

Standing still, he flicks shaggy brown hair out of sea green eyes and laughs as he raises his hands in the universal sign of surrender. 'Don't hurt me. I come in peace.'

'Who are you? Why are you following me? What are you doing in my house? Wait a minute.... How did you even get inside?' I add the last question as I remember the fancy burglar-proof lock on the door Dad is so proud of.

The guy's grin widens. 'Which one of those do you want me to answer first?'

Glaring at him, I'm opening my mouth to give him a piece of my mind when he says, 'Snake Fieth, at your service.' He lowers a hand towards me as if he wants me to shake it, but my hands turn in to fists, and he returns it to its original position.

'What sort of a name is Snake?' I snort.

'A better one than Priscilla Crown.'

He has me there. If there is a name worse than Priscilla, I would love to hear it.

'You may call me Pris.' The response is automatic.

'I thought your friends called you Princess P.'

Hold on. He knows my name and my nickname? Who is this guy? 'You're not a friend,' I spit at him.

He takes a step back and starts to lower his arms. 'Look, I don't have time for long introductions or—'

'Why? You got somewhere better to be?'

His eyes widen as if he is surprised by my question. 'Yes, of course.'

'Then why did you follow me? Why did you break into my house?' I narrow my eyes at him and try to look tougher than I feel. Blood is pounding in my ears, making it difficult to hear his answer.

'Because I thought your parents might be here, or that you could at least lead me to them.'

'Sorry? What? My Parents?' My eyes narrow even more. Does he know my parents aren't here? I eye him warily. 'Why do you want them?'

He ignores my questions, runs his hand through his hair, and glances around the room. There is something kind of desperate about him. 'They're not here, are they? I'm too late.'

My stomach tenses, and I frown, hoping the expression disguises the fear racing through my veins. 'What makes you think that?'

'Are they home?' His voice is barely more than a whisper.

'They're at work, but they should be home soon,' I bluster, but my voice is uncertain even to my own ears.

His arms drop all the way down and his shoulders slump. 'Really? I don't think they will be.'

He raises his head, and his green eyes rake over me as if they can somehow drag the truth from me. Finally, he says, 'I am too late. I had hoped because they were last on the list....'

'List? What list? What's going on here?' I take a step forward. What game is this guy playing?

'Your parents were taken by the.... You are not going to believe this... but there is no other way to say it. They were taken by the Bad Fairies.'

'Bad fairies?' I scoff. 'You mean bad fairies of the "it was the bad fairies" fame?'

He stares blankly at me.

'You know, like when you trip over something and your mum says, "That must have been the bad fairies."'

As I speak, my mind is whirring. I have a right one here. A real lunatic, and I'm alone in the house with him. I plot my escape route in case things get tricky, but I still think I can take him, unless he is on drugs or something—which is a definite possibility given the way he is acting.

Snake glares at me. 'No, not those ones. Well, yes, sort of those ones. They are like the police for creatures like us.' He chuckles, 'I guess they would more correctly be named Fairies for the Bad.'

He is speaking gibberish. This is worse than I thought.

I toss my plait over my shoulder and attempt to placate him. 'Creatures? That's not a nice way to speak of anyone. Do you need one of my parents to help you with something?'

My mother is a human rights lawyer, and my father is the Chief Exec of Homeless London. They deal with some troublesome clients, they talk about them all the time, but this is the first one who has come to our home.

Snake shakes his head, and those lovely eyes look at me with disbelief. He turns and picks a backpack up off the floor.

'Wait, where are you going?'

I can't let him leave if he needs help—that is not what our family does. Besides, he might be crazy as all hell, but he worked out that my parents aren't home, and he believes they have been taken somewhere. And whether I like to admit it or not, I'm worried—quite worried.

I mean, I can go days without seeing my parents when they are on a work trip. But they usually tell me where they are going and when they will be back. And their wardrobes appear not to have been touched since Monday.

He stops but doesn't turn around. 'I thought you knew,' he whispers, and I am not quite certain I hear him correctly. 'I can't be doing this,' he says, louder this time.

'Doing what?'

He turns to face me. 'I can't be teaching you about our world. I need to focus on stopping this nightmare'

'I am sure my parents can help, if you would just wait until—'

'They... are... not... coming... home.' He forces the words through gritted teeth. 'If you want to see them again, you need to come with me.'

The more the intruder talks, the more my stomach churns, and I begin to wonder if something really has happened to Mum and Dad. I am now torn between not letting on that I know my parents won't walk through the door any moment now and asking him what he knows about where they are.

In less than a blink of an eye, he is by my side, grabbing my arm and pulling me towards the door.

I don't think. I just react. I twist my arm to break his grip and sweep my leg to throw him off balance. Next thing he is on the floor, and I am on top of him, my knees pinning his biceps.

I look up into piercing blue eyes that are common in her kind but are all the more startling with her olive skin. She is quick—quicker than I expected—and that is saying something because I am no stranger to creatures with enhanced speed. Through half-closed eyes, I assess her, wondering what abilities she has and how they might help us.

'Don't look at me like that,' she hisses.

I start, then frown. 'Like what?'

'Like you've just been served a delicious dessert.'

I grin. I can't help it. I know it will only make her angrier, but she just described the trickle of sensation forming in the recesses of my mind. It is buried beneath the fear and worry that have been my constant companions for the last couple of days, but it is there all the same.

My smile fades as she presses her boney knees more firmly into my arms. I gasp and grimace. I can probably push her off me, but I just broke into her house, and I want her help. So if this is what it takes for her to be comfortable around me, I'm okay with that. Besides, if she feels any more threatened, she may break something, and I need everything in working order for what is to come.

When she has my attention, she speaks slowly and clearly. 'My parents aren't lost. They are away for a couple of days, and will be back on the weekend.'

I study her face for telltale signs of a lie. Their names were on the list. I saw them when I snuck it out of the fairy's pocket.

Had they disappeared to evade capture? It was possible. Still, they will not be returning. The Bad Fairies always get their creature.

Calling on the voice I use to make a good impression on adults, I say, 'I think you'll find that if they have not been taken yet, they soon will be. Once they are, I can help you find them.'

Her lips press firmly together. I have not managed to convince her... yet.

My hands are starting to go numb. I wiggle my fingers and say, 'If we can just go and sit down—' I nod towards the sofa, hoping she will take the hint. '—perhaps we can talk this out.'

'Who *are* you? And why do you believe my parents are lost?' She leans forward, pinning me with an intense gaze. 'And why are you so sure you can help me find them?'

I need to try something different or I could lose my hand. 'When did you last speak to your parents?'

Her eyebrows twist into a frown, and she appears a little less certain. 'I remember seeing them on Monday morning.... What's it to you?'

'Two days ago?' I'm surprised. 'They were taken that early?'

Her head tilts to the side as she peers at me, making her appear a little less threatening. Perhaps I should push her a bit harder now. 'I think I may be able to find them, but it would be better if one of your kind is with me.'

She instantly tenses, and I lose any ground I made with her. 'What do you mean one of my kind? How does being Black make a difference?'

I can't help it—a laugh escapes, and I try to swallow it, but I can't. I splutter, 'Not being Black—being an elf. Having an elf with me will open doors I can't even knock on.'

That look she had before comes back over her face, the one that tells me she thinks I'm stark raving mad.

The pressure on my arms increases. 'Can I call someone for you? Someone you trust who can come and pick you up?'

Then it dawns on me. 'You have no idea what I'm talking about, do you?' Confusion takes over her face for a moment before she schools it back in to reflect professional concern.

'How can it be possible that you don't know who you are?' This is going to be way harder than I thought if she doesn't even know she has elf blood running through her veins.

She takes a deep breath. 'You clearly believe what you are saying—that I'm an elf, and that. So, what does that make you?'

From the tone of her voice, I sense she is placating me. Still, I tell her the truth. 'I'm a gnome.'

'A gnome?' She laughs, and it comes from deep in her belly. 'I thought gnomes were short and round, and elves were tall and graceful. You're taller than me, and where are my pointy ears?'

She must have had training on how to handle the crazy. She is pointing out what she believes to be the flaws in my logic, hoping to bring me back to reality. If only she knew. I sigh. I can't help it. Why am I the one telling her what all creatures learn before they can walk?

'Every creature knows that in the human world we take human form. It is only when we are in the World Below that we can be who we truly are.'

'Is that some sort of law or something?' She sneers at me.

'Yes, actually, it is. Before 1832, when we withdrew from the World Above almost completely, many of our kind would appear as we are, but equally as many took on human form. Then, when we began setting up ministries in the 1890s to ensure balance was maintained between the worlds, we appeared as humans to disguise our presence. It has been that way ever since.'

'You make it sound so plausible, almost like a history lesson,' she says, easing the pressure on my arms a little.

I open my mouth to tell her that it is history, our history, but she carries on before I can even form the first word. 'Okay. If you're a gnome, can you do magic?'

I snort. 'Of course. How do you think I opened your door?'

She glares. 'You must have picked the locks.'

'Too hard to pick. Easier to persuade them to open for me,' I tell her, and I can't help but smirk as I answer. I actually did pick them because I am not meant to use magic except on official business.

Her face is still set in disbelief mode. I lie still and resist the urge to say anything. She doesn't speak for a while, and I think perhaps she's processing. My blood begins to flow again and my fingers prickle with pins and needles.

She gnaws on her lip as she contemplates me a bit longer. 'All right. Let's say I believe you, that we are both mystical creatures. Why were you following me, and why are you so certain someone took my parents?'

Ah, finally, a step in the right direction. I put on my most charming smile as I answer. 'I've been following you because I was unable to find your parents at work. I thought you might be able to lead me to them.'

She nods a couple of times. 'And what made you think my parents would be taken by these... um... Bad Fairies?' She says the words as if she cannot believe they are coming out of her mouth.

'As I said, I snuck a look at the list the Bad Fairy who took my mother had in his pocket. Your parents' names were on it. In fact, they were the only other names.'

She froze. 'Your mother's been taken?'

Okay, not quite the response I was expecting, but maybe telling her about Mum will convince her I'm not a lunatic.

'Yes, on Monday afternoon. Fortunately, I was home to see what happened. I tried to talk the Bad Fairies out of taking her. When I couldn't, I distracted one of the officers, lifted the warrant from his pocket, and discovered that your parents' names were there as well. I hoped with their being more powerful, they might be able to help my mother.'

The expression on her face is more quizzical than worried, and she is no longer glaring at me. I can tell she is not convinced the fairies took her parents, but she seems more open to what I'm saying now and less defensive.

'I believe my parents are missing. I'm not saying I buy into your Harry Potter worldview, but if we put that aside, where would you suggest we start looking for them... and your mother?'

'We need to go visit the Witch in the Woods. She helps London creatures who are in trouble.'

Pris's face freezes, and I wish I could take my words back.

'You almost had me believing you—'

'Look, you don't need to believe she is a witch or anything. But she is a friend of my mother's, and she will probably know where our parents are... or at least be able to tell us where to start searching for them.'

She gnaws on her lip again. I can't tell whether she is assessing me or considering her options. 'Okay. Where do we find this woman?'

'In Wimbledon. We can take the tube and be back here by dinnertime.'

Pris runs a hand over her hair. Dare I hope she is actually considering going with me?

'What will you lose if you come along? An evening of your time?' I encourage her. 'And it's not like you're in any physical danger. You've already proven you can take me down if you want to.'

I can't believe I'm actually considering going to Wimbledon with this lunatic. I glance down at him. He's very relaxed even though his arms must be aching. A brief flicker of fear in his dark green eyes is quickly hidden, telling me his confidence is a mask. Is he afraid of me? Or afraid I won't help him?

I narrow my eyes as I study his face, but I quickly school my features, not wanting to let him know what is going on inside my head. I'm obviously not going to tennis lessons today—no great loss. And then there is the undeniable fact that something odd is going on with my parents.

I don't believe in his magic malarkey, but on the off chance his friend in Wimbledon might be able to give me some information about where my parents are, I should go with him. Besides, if he is in trouble and he believes I can help, it would be the right thing to do.

My right thigh begins to cramp, and I ease the pressure off Snake's arms. As I move, a thought pops into my head.

'If someone took our parents, we should go to the police.'

Snake snorts, and I mean actually snorts! And not for the first time. Who does that?

'You're kidding, right? We're going to go to the police and tell them our parents have been taken by creatures from another world—creatures from fairy tales.'

A wave of anger washes through me. 'If you truly want to rescue your mother, surely you're prepared to drop this charade for long enough to talk to the police.' I dig my right knee in a little for extra emphasis.

Snake closes his eyes. Maybe I really hurt his feelings this time. He takes a deep breath and expels the air slowly before opening them and looking back up at me. 'There's a reason why we're not allowed to show ourselves.'

'Why?' I ask, barely keeping the contempt from my voice.

'Because people no longer believe in us. They banished creatures to the realm of fairy stories a long time ago. Even if we wanted to come clean, no one would listen. I mean, you're one of us and you don't believe me.'

He's right; I don't believe him. But he's obviously invested in this alternate world. Perhaps it's his way of dealing with the loss of his mum, or stress, or something.

'Besides, humans can't go where our parents have been taken. Not without being invited.'

His voice is calm, and he sounds rational. He makes me want to believe him, but he is talking utter rubbish. I decide to test his commitment to this other world idea.

'Won't we need to "pay a cost" as well?' I ask, remembering the tales I read as a child which always told of magical creatures demanding payment.

'Perhaps, but I am sure we will be more than up to the challenge.'

I can't stop the frown this time. 'Do you actually have a plan for our parents' rescue?'

He smiles a crooked smile. He's quite good-looking when he's not acting crazy. I am suddenly very aware of the fact that I am straddling him, and parts of my body are thinking some very inconvenient thoughts. I should move, but I am reluctant to give up my advantage until I am certain of him.

'Not a plan as such.' His shoulders shift in something of a shrug. 'I guess we could always beg.'

My astonishment must be written on my face, because he bursts out laughing, and I knew I had been got.

'Actually, I thought that once we talk to the Witch of the Woods, we will be in a better position to plan our next move.'

Sounds logical, I think, but I am still skeptical. 'How can you be so sure this... woman will help us?'

'She's helped Mum in the past, and I'm hoping she still thinks kindly of her in spite of what has happened.'

Those alarm bells go off in my head again. 'What exactly did your mother do, Snake?' I silently add, *She didn't murder someone, did she?*

Snake lowers his eyes. 'She and your parents have been accused of the heinous crime of profiting from magic in The World Above.'

I can't have heard him properly. 'Profiting from magic?'

A blush creeps up from Snake's neck and over to his cheeks. 'Creatures who live in the human realm are here to help the people of the World Above, and to maintain the balance between worlds. We agree to live as humans do and must only use our special abilities when assigned a task.'

I nod for him to go on, hoping that amidst the mystical explanation, I will be able to figure out exactly what his mother, and therefore my parents, are actually accused of.

'We gnomes are—'

'Good at digging underground?' I offer, *Lord of the Rings*

17

springing into my mind. 'Or are you more like garden gnomes?'

Snake snorts again. 'Garden centres have a lot to answer for, and it's dwarves who dig underground in Tolkien's book,' he says under his breath. Then carries on as if I hadn't said anything at all.

'We gnomes are skilled at finding and taking things. My family was tasked with tracking misplaced magical items and returning them to their true owners. In particular, my parents retrieved magic artefacts so they could be returned to the World Below.'

'Is your explanation going to take long?' I ask. I'm tired of all the magic nonsense, and my leg is cramping again.

'You could let me up and we could finish this in comfort,' he offers.

I chew my bottom lip.

'I promise you on my mother's life, I will do you no harm.'

His voice is encouraging and sincere. I hate to admit it, but I am no longer afraid of him. Besides, as he pointed out, I've already proved I can deal with him if he gets out of line.

I rock back on my heels, stand, and stretch. I then sit back on the floor, cross my legs, and face him.

Snake looks at me questioningly. I nod, and he sits up, crossing his own legs to mirror me, arms resting loosely on his knees.

'When my father returned below, my mother was unable to take on some of the bigger jobs, so our income was barely enough to pay the bills.' Snake glanced around the ostentatious living room, and I imagine he is thinking I have never experienced what it is like to live hand-to-mouth, and he is right, but I can imagine.

'That must have been hard,' I say, urging him on.

'I tried to help out, but with school I could only work on the weekends. There just never seemed to be enough to make ends meet. Mum began stealing food and little things that I needed for school. None of it amounted to much, but, apart from it being illegal here, it's a big no-no using our powers to steal for our own benefit in the human world.'

Snake colours again, as if he is ashamed of what his mother did. I say nothing, hoping he will tell me more. My patience is rewarded.

'It is one of the unbreakable rules we all agree to follow when we live here. It was a long time ago, though, and she paid for her transgression. I don't understand why this is being brought up again now.'

'Why didn't you and your mother return to the other world with your father?'

The boy frowns. 'Why do you want to know that?'

I almost blurt out, 'I want to make sure you're not completely crazy,' but I don't want to make him angry.

'I just want to... know why your father isn't helping your mother now.'

He nods slowly, as if he can now understand my curiosity. 'Mum didn't share all the details with me. All I know is, Dad just disappeared without a word, and I suspect her pride kept her from running after him.'

His voice cracks a little as he says this, and a niggle of guilt for doubting him tugs at me. I'm also angry. His father should not be let off the hook that easily.

'Didn't your father have to look after you? Like here in the human world where fathers pay towards the keep of their children?'

'Of course, but we don't need anything from him. I have been able to help out more recently, so I thought we were doing better, but maybe we weren't. If she did do something wrong again, she did it for me, and... I can't let her be punished for it.'

A tear slides down Snake's face, and I catch my hand reaching out towards him. I snatch it back before he notices.

'Surely your gnome friends in the human world know what's going on and will help your mother,' I suggest.

'As if! They might decide not to help at all because if my mother is found guilty of breaking this law, my father's family will be brought into disrepute. They will have to tread carefully to ensure this doesn't happen. So, it's up to me to rescue my mother, and I will do whatever it takes—whether you're with me or not.'

His expression hardens and all signs of vulnerability are gone. His support of his mother touches me more than anything else he has said, and I want to help him find her.

More importantly, though, Snake's concern has raised my anxiety levels. If his mother has done something wrong and my parents are somehow tangled up in it, they could be in serious trouble too.

I stand. 'Wait here. I'm going to change.'

'You mean right here?' he asks cheekily.

I smirk, and my cheeks warm. 'No, you can wait in the hall or take a seat. I won't be long.'

I take the stairs two at a time and rush into my bedroom, almost tripping over my bag. I walk to my closet and stop. What do you wear when going to visit a witch? Something similar to what Snake is wearing? No, I can't do the scruffy look. I grab a denim jacket, my favourite white T-shirt with the stylised cat on the front, and my purple skinny jeans.

I look down at my feet. High-tops? No. I pick up my white Mollini trainers with the leopard trim—perfect. Once I'm dressed, I pull my unruly hair into a messy ponytail and run some lip gloss over my lips, then rub it off; it's not like this is a date or anything.

Grabbing my wallet, I check to make sure my Oyster card and my platinum Visa—only to be used in emergencies—are safely inside. I shove it, along with my phone and keys, into my favourite Coach shoulder bag. I am ready to face anything.

When I return, Snake is sitting on the second step from the bottom, elbows on his knees, shoulders slumped, head resting in his hands. For all his confidence before, he actually looks lost, almost forlorn.

He needs help. I tell myself I am doing the right thing. Plastering a smile on my face, I say, 'Come on. If we're going to do this, we'd better hurry. I must be home in time for dinner.'

CHAPTER 2

The Witch of Wimbledon

I manage to hide myself away from prying eyes under a bush. I wait patiently in the garden across the road from the house the boy broke into. He has some skills—I will give him that. The afternoon sun warms me, and I'd like nothing better than to sleep, but I must remain vigilant.

He went inside a while ago. Perhaps he is not planning to come back out. Should I go home and report? No, my mistress will want me to find out what his next move is. I glare at the house. I suppose I could make it up to a windowsill. I might be able to find out what is going on if I choose the right room.

A bird twitters nearby, and I rest my head on my paws. It is so warm here. Maybe I will wait a little longer, until the sun goes down.

Just as I settle in for a long wait, the boy emerges with the girl following close behind. She closes the door and puts the keys in her bag before heading off along the street.

Sighing, I stretch. I have no option but to follow. My stomach grumbles as I creep through the bushes conveniently placed in front of the houses. I hope they won't be long. I want to return to my place by the fire and let my mistress reward me with some tasty morsels of food.

Keeping to the shadows, I trail along the street behind them, hoping to overhear their plans. Then maybe I can simply meet them at their destination. They tell me nothing, and I endure listening to that girl ask *the* most stupid questions. How can one who shines so brightly be so ignorant?

'If you're a gnome, and you're not like the garden variety, where do you fit in, say, compared to me?' she asks.

The boy answers her more patiently than I would. I mean, she is clearly an elf, perhaps from the Unseelie court in the north. She should know all about this stuff. I flick my tail in frustration.

'Gnomes are quick of hand and of mind. We love puzzles. In general, we are bound in service to elves, but some of us, like my family, become.... Well, I guess you could call us detectives.'

I mean, honestly, everyone knows gnomes are simply lesser elves—well everyone who matters.

'If there are others like you in London, how can you tell if someone is one of them?'

I groan out loud, and she turns at the noise as I dart behind a car. I must be more careful.

'Our magic causes a glow if we do not know how to contain it. If you watch people carefully, occasionally you can see a shimmer that will tell you who they really are,' Snake explains.

The elf starts to stare intently at people passing by. When someone mutters, 'How Rude,' her gaze drops to the pavement.

'Perhaps you should be a little more subtle,' Snake chuckles.

Honestly, how can he put up with her? Mercifully, I am able to fall behind when increased foot traffic means I have to duck behind a fence, and I no longer have to listen to her inane prattle.

I finally find out what their plan is when we are almost in front of an underground station. They stop by the map outside and discuss their options.

'We're here, at Ladbroke Grove. If we head to Hammersmith and change to the District Line going to Earl's Court, then we can take a train to Wimbledon from there,' the girl says, and the boy nods his agreement.

Oh no, this is going to take a lot of energy. My tummy rumbles again. And on an empty stomach too!

I cast my spell and follow them through the tube station entrance, confident that now no one will see a black cat.

As I enter the nondescript Victorian brick building, I brush past a woman in a floral summer dress. She squeals and stumbles into a tall gentleman carrying a briefcase.

'Excuse me,' she says, turning bright pink.

'Not at all, my dear. These things happen in a busy station,' the man responds and almost steps on me. I jump out of the way. I do so dislike travelling like this.

I keep my eye on the boy and girl as they wend their way through the bustling station, heading for the turnstiles. I rush to catch them up.

A train pulls into the station as I reach the platform. I spot them just as the blips sound. Slipping into the carriage just as the doors close and quickly raising my tail to make sure it doesn't get caught, I find an out-of-the-way spot under a seat and sit down.

I stick close to the humans I'm following so that I know when to change trains. Finally, they find two seats together and sit. I don't let go of my spell though. It wouldn't do to let people see a cat travelling with them. Imagine the chaos!

Just as I am getting comfortable, the driver calls our stop, and we are on the move again. I sigh with relief when we leave the Underground and it is again all right for me to be seen.

· ·*· ☽ ·*· ··

I loathe taking commuter trains. They are always packed, you never find a seat, and the carriages reek of stale sweat. When we finally get out at Wimbledon, I heave a sigh of relief as I gulp in the fresh air.

As I follow Snake through the meandering paths of Wimbledon Common, I sneak a sideways glance at him. He hasn't spoken a word since we entered the Underground. His jaw is tense and though his hands are now shoved deep into his pockets, during the train trip they had fiddled incessantly with the cord of his hoodie.

He catches me looking at him and I turn away, suddenly interested in a group of dog walkers standing around chatting. I am so intent on avoiding looking at Snake, I forget to check my surroundings. Normally when I find myself in a new place, I scan the area for potential hiding places for attackers. This evening I am so off balance, I completely forget my father's training.

We are almost at the edge of the common when I realise my mistake. I catch a movement in the bushes, and I don't react immediately. This small hesitation is a mistake. I jump and am almost pulled off balance as a hand roughly grabs my arm, and moments later, I am held tight against my attacker's chest.

A sharp point sticks me around kidney height. I gulp back a gag as I am engulfed in the scent of cheap beer and cigarettes clinging to the fabric encasing the arm around my neck. I struggle briefly before muscle memory takes over.

I allow my body to go limp. A smile curls his lips, the only bit of his face I can make out under his hoodie, and I catch a glimpse of the knife as he raises it to strike. This is my cue to act. I twist out of his grasp, then use my momentum to swing back around and punch him in the jaw.

I don't stay to see the effects of my handiwork. Grabbing a hold of Snake's sweatshirt, I pull him into a run. Moments later, we are off the common and in relative safety on North View.

'What the hell was that?' he gasps when we finally slow to a walk.

'It's Wimbledon Common, so I guess it was a mugger,' I respond as I check behind to make sure we are not being followed.

He stops, and a few steps later I do too, turning to see what is delaying him. I find Snake staring at me as if I have gone bonkers.

'What?' I ask.

'A mugging? In broad daylight? When you are walking with someone?'

'Of course.' I shrug. 'What else could it be?'

His eyebrows shoot up. 'Does this happen to you often?'

'Probably only as often as it happens to other Londoners,' I respond.

'You don't think it has anything to do with who you are?' he asks, his brows forming a frown.

Who I am? I'm no longer exactly sure. Wanting to change the subject, I say, 'Where does the witch live? These houses must cost a bomb. I can't believe the residents are happy about a witch living on the common.... It's so close to their homes.'

Snake's frown deepens, and he doesn't answer for a moment. I am sure he is going to say something more about the attack, but then he relaxes, and I hope he has decided to let our previous conversation go. 'She doesn't live *on* the common.'

He begins walking again, checking off house numbers before turning into the drive of a three-story, semi-detached house. Taking the steps two at a time, he knocks firmly on the door.

I remain on the driveway, not wishing to waste energy climbing the six steps only to be turned away.

A boy of about four or five years old with a mop of curly black hair opens the door. He looks like he's stepped out of a Gap Kids catalogue, further confirmation that Snake must be out of his mind. Witches do not live in Victorian mansions on the edge of Wimbledon Common or dress their kids like that.

'Yes?' the boy asks as a black cat slips through the opening. The boy's eyes follow the animal as it disappears down the dimly lit corridor. 'Nan, someone is at the door for you,' he yells after it.

He leaves the door open and returns to whatever he was doing before we interrupted him. My mouth drops open in shock. Who leaves their door wide open with strangers on the doorstep in the middle of London?

Snake catches my eye and, as if he has read my mind, he says, 'I don't think anyone would dare enter this house without an invitation.'

I close my mouth and join Snake, trying to brush off the ominous undertone of his words. Moments later, a woman appears in the doorway. She is tall and graceful with long black hair caught in an untidy bun. She is obviously related to the boy, as they have the same piercing blue eyes.

I grab Snake's arm, an apology for disturbing the family this close to dinner ready on my lips. I pause when the woman's face breaks into a smile as she catches sight of Snake.

'Snake, finally,' she says pulling the door open wider. 'Come on in.'

She leads Snake along the hallway to the back of the house. As I follow, I catch glimpses of a dwelling tastefully decorated with what I assume are all original Victorian features. The woman raises her hand, and I jump at a bang behind me, and I half turn to find the door has closed by itself. A shiver runs up my spine. Was that magic or the wind?

The kitchen at the back of the house is bright and modern, and as I enter, the woman moves in behind a butcher block and begins chopping carrots.

'I expected you earlier, young Snake. You know you are always welcome here. Although, now that I see who you are with, I can understand why you delayed your visit. Having an elf on your side will make things a little easier for you.'

I stand in the doorway. This whole thing is surreal, and I can't quite get my head around it. 'You're a grandmother?' The thought pops into my head and out of my mouth before I can stop it.

The woman who Snake claims is the Witch of Wimbledon smiles at me. 'Yes, my dear—many times over. Carlos is just the youngest. He stays with me while his mum works in the health food shop on the High Street.'

She turns her attention back to Snake. 'You know you are welcome to stay here through this troubling time, but I sense you want something else from me.'

Snake shuffles his feet a bit, as if he is trying to make up his mind what to say. 'Ma'am, I was hoping your friendship with my mother means you might help me rescue her from The Court—and of course, Pris's parents too.'

The last bit about Mum and Dad was definitely an afterthought. I try not to mind too much. I mean, it is not as if I believe in any of this.

'I am sure that the last time we met, I told you to call me Eleanora.' Her piercing gaze swings round to me. 'They took your parents too. I can't say I'm surprised.'

I nod, unwilling to speak because I am not sure I've bought into all this other world stuff yet. Still, this woman is talking as if she knows my parents. Perhaps she is a part of whatever my parents are involved in, and she might be able to tell us where they have gone.

Eleanora cocks her head to the side and stares at me for a long moment before turning her attention back to Snake. I get the feeling I have been assessed and found wanting. I stiffen as anger at being so readily dismissed threatens to make me lose my cool.

'I expected you to come and ask for my help when I found out your mother was taken,' Eleanora says to Snake.

'Does that mean you will help us?' Snake's voice is so eager, it almost breaks my heart. Not waiting for an answer, he rushes on. 'I believe there are ways to wrangle an invite to The Court, I just don't know how. If you could set us on the right path, I'll do whatever it takes to attend and plead my mother's case.'

My jaw drops. I know I must look like a moron, but I can't help it. Snake is talking to this woman as if the subworld he talked about is real. At best, this urbane woman will laugh at his flight of fancy, and at worst she will throw us out. This last would be bad because she did offer to take Snake in, and he could do with somewhere to stay and get his head straight.

'And what about you, Priscilla?' I flinch at the use of my full name. 'Will you do whatever it takes to help your parents? Even if it means suspending your current beliefs and committing to attend spring court in the World Below?'

'I.... But surely....' I don't know what to say. She sounds like she believes this nonsense is real. Perhaps it's code for some sort of nefarious activity. Is someone listening in on our conversation? What are my parents mixed up in?

The woman's mouth curls with amusement. 'Yes, my dear, I do believe in all this stuff. I am a witch, as I am sure Snake already told you. He and his mother are indeed gnomes, and you are an elf.'

'But—'

'Perhaps if your parents spent more time with our community, they would not be appearing before The Court now. Then again, I must thank them because now Snake has a high-status elf to help him on the journey he must undertake.'

I am speechless, and that is something that doesn't happen often. The whole world has gone mad. The anger I have been holding in check bubbles inside of me, and flashes of red distort my vision. I glare at the elegant woman Snake told me would help us, annoyed I have wasted my time.

'You seriously expect me to believe my parents were abducted because they used magic for profit?' I sweep my hand around the room. 'Apart from the fact the very idea is absurd, we are no wealthier than you. Why weren't you taken too?'

Ice-cold blue eyes stare at me, and for a moment, I wonder if I have gone too far. All warmth has gone from Eleanora's voice as she says, 'My family and I have been working on the surface for centuries. One of my ancestors fell in love with and married a human. He left this house to her when he passed. We never, ever use our skills to gain from humankind, and it is the greatest insult for you to even hint at it.'

Eleanora's eyes pierce my soul, driving home her words. Even though my stomach is curdling, I meet her gaze unflinchingly.

· · * · 🌙 · * · ·

Great. The one person who can help us get to The Court and Pris has pissed her off. I must have been out of my mind to bring her here. I mean, sure, her elf blood will open doors, and she has as much of a stake in this as I do. On the other hand, she has shown she knows nothing about our world, and she just demonstrated how much of a liability that can be.

I insert myself between the two women, holding up my hands, palm outwards, and saying, 'I am sure Pris didn't mean any offence.'

Pris's sharp intake of breath makes me pause—just for a second though. Clearly, she doesn't like anyone speaking for her, but at the moment, her injured pride is the least of my worries.

'She doesn't know much about our ways, but she shouldn't be punished for her parents failing to teach her,' I finish.

Eleanora's shoulders relax a little. 'The Queen should never have let her parents choose this path,' she says, followed by, 'If it were not for Petunia....' She returns to chopping her vegetables, although the aggressive way her knife rises and falls has me wondering if she has actually let go of her anger.

From behind, I hear Pris mutter, 'Who's Petunia, and what has she got to do with this?'

I ignore her. 'I would appreciate your help getting to the Midnight Court,' I say, hoping to distract Eleanora and gain her support at the same time.

She vigorously chops a few more carrots. Her ferocity makes me think she is imagining Pris on the chopping board. Finally, the knife pauses, and she places it on the worktop. Wiping her hands on a towel, she says, 'All right. I guess I do not get to choose who comes to me for help or how they behave when they get here.'

Pris shuffles behind me, and I sense her moving to the side. I take a step, keeping myself between her and Eleanora. She does not realise the massive insult our hostess is choosing to overlook.

'A creature who is not a member can attend the Seelie Court if they receive an invitation from the Queen or if your attendance is endorsed by four senior members of The Court. Above ground, that means you must approach the senior creatures of four races and ask them to approve your attendance.'

It sounds too easy. There must be a catch. 'So, if you endorse us, then we only need to find three more,' I say, feeling Eleanora out.

She laughs. 'You of all creatures should know that nothing in our world is ever that easy. I may be a member of the Seelie court, but I am a minor representative. If you want the witches to endorse your entry, you must speak to the most senior of our kind in England. Only she can grant what you desire.'

'You're saying it can't be just any court member, but the most senior of each kind living in the human world?' I ask.

Eleanora nods, then adds, 'And they must be approached formally at the source of their power in the World Above.'

Damn it, this makes things more difficult. Instead of being able to approach their representatives in London, we must travel to find the creatures we need to speak with.

'Can you give us an idea of who is most likely to support our petition?' I ask, hoping to save some time by only calling on those most likely to help.

'I am sorry, Snake, but the witches gave me leave only to tell you how you might gain entry to The Court. If I help you directly, you may not be allowed in.'

'Can you at least tell me where and when The Court will be held?'

Sighing, Eleanora again wipes her hand on the towel and reaches into her pocket. Her hand emerges, clasping a piece of paper. 'You must solve this riddle to find The Court and to gain entry.'

I take the piece of paper and open it. I read the words and

splutter, 'You're joking, aren't you? How are we supposed to decipher this?'

Pris moves behind me, and I turn so she can see the paper.

"When the old man's face looks down on earth, and two hands meet in the dead of night, the underwater ball begins.

"Pass the gatekeeper the token and the gold, heads up tails down, before speaking the word for that which needs our breath but cannot breathe to prove your worth."

'Two hands meet in the dead of night. That must be midnight. And the old man's face. That's what my dad calls a full moon,' she says.

I look to Eleanora to confirm Pris's guess, and although she is trying to remain impassive, a smile tugs at the corner of her mouth.

'That's amazing,' I tell Pris. 'If only the rest were that easy.'

'I'm sure that with a little time, we can work out the rest of the riddle,' Pris says.

My stomach clenches. 'If you're correct about the when bit, then there isn't much time for us to figure the rest out—the full moon is in seven days.'

I point at the calendar hanging on the fridge, then look at Eleanora. 'Is that right? We only have seven days to get four endorsements, solve the riddle, and make our way to wherever they are holding The Court?'

Sadness clouds Eleanora's eyes as she answers. 'As that is part of the riddle, I cannot answer your question. All I can say is, your knowledge of our law will help you.'

My knowledge of the law? My mind is spinning as I look at the paper again. Nothing is coming to me.

Fingers gently squeeze my arm, and a hand takes the riddle from me. 'We don't need to work this all out now. Why don't I put this somewhere safe, and we can figure it out later?'

I allow Pris to fold the paper and put it in her bag. I'm

numb. In my mind, the Protector of London was going to invite us to The Court as her guest and all we would have to do is count down the days. This wild goose chase is completely unexpected. Then again, it was obvious if I stopped to think about it—nothing to do with the Seelie Court is ever that easy.

'I have done all I am able. With so little time for you to complete your quest, you had best be getting started.'

I slowly shake my head to clear my thoughts. Eleanora has done the best she can to help us under the circumstances. Remembering my manners, I say, 'Thank you, Eleanora. You have been a great help. And yes, we must get going now.'

Pris opens her mouth, and the cross set of her face tells me she is not thankful at all. I grab her shoulders and turn her around, bundling her through the door before she can say anything to anger Eleanora further. She may only be a second-tier member of the Seelie Court, but she is a powerful witch.

'Good luck to you both, and I hope to meet you again when The Court convenes,' Eleanora calls after us.

The door opens as we reach it, and I push Pris through before she can say what is on her mind.

As we walk back across the common, Pris turns angrily. 'How can you be so polite to her? She gave us a riddle and told us to seek out endorsements, which means she gave us very little.'

I stop and stare at the ground, wondering again why I had thought bringing Pris along was a good idea. Sure, as an elf she can go places I can't, but how helpful will she actually be if she doesn't know a thing about our world? I raise my head, ready to tell her I will continue on my own and do what I can to help her parents as well as my mother.

I can't say the words. My gaze follows the line of tears trailing down her cheeks, and I find my own fears and worries reflected in her face. She roughly brushes the tears away as I realise I can't leave her like this.

'Lesson one about the Seelie Court. Invitations are issued by the Elven Queen. Only those with invitations or a royal appointment can attend, and in some instances, they can invite another creature. I had hoped Eleanor might have made arrangements for me at least to attend with her.'

Pris opens her mouth to respond, but before she can say anything, I rush on. 'For some reason Eleanora was not given leave to invite us. Instead, she found a way for us to enter by ourselves... and that means she must have called in a lot of favours.'

Springs of black hair blow across her face. She pushes them away distractedly as she processes my words. Her anger slides away as quickly as it came, and a blush colours her cheeks.

'Oh my goodness, did she really go out on a limb for us? And I was so rude to her....'

I grin at her. 'Yes, you were. I would not be asking any favours of her for a while if I were you. And next time when you are talking to her, try and remember she could turn you into a toad with a thought.'

Laughter dances in her eyes as her smile lightens my heart. 'Okay, I'll try.' Her eyes suddenly go dark, and she says, 'All this is new to me, Snake—this other world you talk about. I am not sure I quite believe in it yet, and I certainly don't understand it.' She draws her bottom lip between her teeth. 'But I am trying, really, because I want to find my mum and dad.'

· · * · ◗ · * · ·

Standing on the doorstep with my mistress, we watch Snake and the elf talking. In spite of her rudeness, I am still attracted to the girl's shining magic. Then again, that is always the way with elves. They are rude and entitled, but everyone is drawn to them.

'He has his hands full with that one,' my mistress says. 'And I am not sure whether she will be more of a hindrance or a help.'

Something moves in the bushes beside them, and my mistress stops speaking. I catch the flash of a knife, and my mistress mumbles something and points. There is a tingle of magic in the air, and the figure falls to the ground with the barest rustle of leaves.

'They are safe. He will sleep for a long, long while,' my mistress says before turning her attention back to the two figures. 'I wonder if they know the full extent of what they are up against.'

My stomach is full, and all I want to do is to go back into the lounge room and curl up in my basket over the radiator and sleep off my meal. I fear it will be a long time before I am allowed such luxury, as I can guess what is coming next.

My mistress pulls in some magic and casts a spell so we can speak.

'I promised Ginth that should anything happen to her, I would take care of Snake.'

'You have. You gave him a way to rescue his mother.'

She considers my words for a moment, and I allow a small flicker of hope to warm my gut. Then The Witch of Wimbledon sighs, extinguishing that flame.

'It is not enough, my lovely. Other forces are at play here. Someone wants to make sure the Crowns are no longer a part of The Court, and that someone must be powerful if they are prepared to take on royalty, however distant they are from the throne.'

'I thought we were helping Snake.' My tone is petulant, but I can't help it. I just want to go inside.

'Ginth being taken is obviously meant to sow seeds of disorder in the higher echelons of gnomes. Her husband's family are as close to the royal line as their kind can get.'

I say nothing. I don't think I am expected to. Eleanora is merely processing her thoughts out loud.

'What I cannot work out is whether someone is making a play for dominance here in the human world, or are they making a power play in the World Below. I fear these two young creatures may be in more danger than they realise.'

With her words my fate is sealed.

'My lovely, I hate to ask this of you, but I need you to stay with them and report any unusual activity to me.'

'What can I do if someone comes for them?' I ask, still hoping beyond hope she will relent and let me stay.

'Maybe nothing, but there may also be something.'

'If it is your wish, then I will go.'

I pause a moment in case she changes her mind. No, nothing. I stretch and start down the steps.

'I will contact you on the tenth hour each night.' I throw the comment over my shoulder.

I reach the bottom step as she says, 'Percival.' I pause. 'Please be careful.'

I am grumpy, but it is hard to stay that way when she sends such love and gratitude with her words. I glance back, but she is already inside.

Dodging the evening traffic, I reach my travelling companions in time to catch the elf girl saying, 'I'm tired, and we need to figure out where we go from here. Let's go home and see what Susan is making for dinner.'

She slips her arm through Snake's and leads him towards the tube station. Instead of following them, I close my eyes, and cast one of my favourite spells.

When I reach my destination, I creep around the side of the house and jump up onto the window ledge. Peering in to a large open-plan kitchen and dining room, I find them empty. I thought the Susan person was supposed to be making dinner.

Not my problem, I think. My problem is that I will be seen if I remain here. I find a hiding place under the garden furniture and nap while I wait for the others to join me.

CHAPTER 3

There Are Elves. And Then There Are *ELVES*

The train carriage rocks gently back and forth as it makes its way back to central London. Dusk is settling, and I catch Snake's and my reflections in the window across from us. His hands are shoved into his pockets and his face reads as despondent.

I study my own reflection. Do I look different after the revelation that other life-forms share the world with us? Hold on—not *us*. If Snake is to be believed, and I am starting to believe he should be, I am not human. I am an elf.

I don't look any different. Same corkscrew hair and copper brown skin as my father, and the ice blue eyes I got from my mother. The face staring back at me is mine, and it shows nothing of the inner turmoil finding out about my origins is causing.

Moving my gaze to the other people in the carriage, I try to find the 'glow' Snake spoke of before. There is nothing. Part of me hoped to see a small sliver just to confirm I am not going mad. My eyes slide sideways to Snake; surely, he must have it. I think I almost catch a glimpse of... something, then it slips away as he raises his head to look at me.

'You can stay in our spare room tonight. We can eat and decide what to do next,' I say to him, and perhaps I can take some more time to get my head around all this.

He turns his head slightly so his eyes meet mine in the window opposite. 'Or we could go to Mayfair and meet with the Regises.'

'Who?'

'Giles and Amandine Regis—the most senior fey in the upper world. If we visit them tonight, and if you convince them to endorse us, then we will only need to find three more races to help.'

My stomach roils. The inner turmoil I had begun to tame by planning our evening rears its head again. 'Oh, so we just knock on their door and ask them to give us an invite? It's as easy as that, is it?'

'I didn't say it would be easy.' Snake turns in his seat so he can look directly at me. I want to meet his gaze, but I concentrate on the houses rushing by out the window. 'None of this will be easy,' Snake says. 'But if we can convince the Regises to endorse us, then that will hold some sway with the others.'

'How about you go, and I head home and let Susan know we will have a guest tonight.' I cross my arms over my chest.

Snake snorts. 'You think they would let the likes of me inside their home?'

My head pivots round. 'Why wouldn't they?'

'Because they are fey, because they have royal blood, and because I'm a gnome. They won't even speak with me without you.'

This time I turn round to face him. 'And what makes you think they will speak with me?'

'This is so strange, me teaching you about this,' he mutters.

I blush, suddenly ashamed of my lack of knowledge of this other world I am a part of. All those years I accepted Mum and

Dad's tales of how they both had no family and so we had to be there for one another. What if even that is a lie?

I want to be angry at them, but I am too worried about where they might have been taken. Then a thought hits me—what if the reason they kept everything secret is because something bad happened in the past?

Snake takes my hand, sending a tingle of electricity up my arm. I look up in surprise. I did not expect that. I mean, he's cute and all, but we only just met. Besides, this other world thing he has introduced me to is just plain weird, and I don't quite know what to make of him. His next words tell me Snake obviously did not feel the same frisson.

'I'm sorry, Pris. Getting your head around everything must be difficult.'

I draw a deep breath and try to concentrate on the task at hand. 'Okay, explain exactly why you need me to go with you.'

'The Regises will at least listen to you because you are an elf—one of the fey. They are obligated to ask you in and offer you hospitality by the rules of our society. Also, the rules that operate in the World Above make them responsible for those of their kind who work here.'

His tone is patient and his explanation is logical, but it does nothing to make the situation less surreal. How can people I have never met be obliged to offer me hospitality? It's too strange, like something out of Greek history. I'm not sure I can face any more strange people.

'I just want to go home. I feel... overwhelmed. I'm not at my best, and I don't want to be with strangers who know more about who I am than I do.'

My words are cross and sharp, and Snake flinches, but he keeps hold of my hand.

'This is hard, but it will be harder if you are left up here alone, trying to deal with the disappearance of your parents. Don't you want to do everything you can to find them?'

Harsh, I think. Before I lash out, returning the favour, I stop myself. Although he must be worried about his mother's disappearance, there is genuine concern for me in his eyes. And, frustratingly, he is right—I want to find my parents.

'Perhaps,' I say, buying some time to process my swirling emotions.

Knowing my parents have lied to me my entire life makes me simultaneously want to hit something and hide under my duvet and forget this ever happened. Unfortunately, self-indulgence is not a luxury I can afford. With only seven days until the solstice, I need to put on my big-girl pants and do something to save them.

Snake must have read my change of heart from my face because he lets go of my hand to pull his phone from his hoodie pocket. 'Okay, if we get off at Bond Street it's a short walk to Grosvenor Square. If we change onto the Circle Line—'

'Hold on.... How do you know where the senior elves live? I mean, is there some sort of online directory, or an app?'

He laughs so loud, the elderly couple down the other end of the carriage turn and stare at us. Their glare sobers Snake up, and his laughter subsides to a chuckle.

'Our kind are not that tech savvy, and besides, they would be worried the information would fall into the wrong hands. A lot of our rules about living in the world above are to ensure our presence remains a secret.'

This is like talking to a politician—I ask one question and he answers a completely different one. 'You still haven't said how you know this,' I point out impatiently.

He looks sheepish. 'Sorry, I didn't want to rub your nose in something else all creatures know.'

I forgive him instantly. After all, it isn't his fault my parents didn't teach me these things. 'So....,' I prompt him.

'Yeah, well, because the senior members of each race of

creatures are responsible for their kind in the World Above, there is a designated place for us to contact them. Sometimes it's where their kind come and go from this world, sometimes it's their base of operations. All creatures learn these contact points much like human children learn the address and phone number of family they can call on.'

'And you're telling me that the contact point for elves is in Grosvenor Square?'

'Yeeesss.'

The word is drawn out, almost like he can sense what is coming.

'So, I am guessing in this instance the elves actually live there?'

'I believe so. In Blackburn Mews.'

My temper explodes again, although, recognising I am in a public place, I spit my next question out in a whisper. 'How is it my parents are accused of using magic for profit when the senior members of our race live in one of the most expensive, exclusive squares in London? How can they do that without using magic?'

Snake answers in the same tone teachers use when dealing with recalcitrant children. 'They don't own the house as such. Well, on paper they do but only because humans would become suspicious if they didn't. But it's perhaps best to think of the house as an Elven Embassy. When the current family are recalled, ownership will be transferred to the next inhabitant. It has been this way for generations, since long before Grosvenor Square became a sought-after address in London.'

My head is spinning. I have gone from thinking Snake insane talking about elves and fairies and gnomes, to beginning to think it may all be true, to finding out they built up a whole infrastructure aimed at keeping their identity secret during their hundreds of years of residing in England.

Snake takes my hand in his again, and I find his touch strangely calming.

'You know, it wasn't always like this. Once our people mingled with humans, coming and going as they pleased.'

'What changed?' I ask, intrigued. History has always been one of my passions.

'Religion changed. When Henry the Eighth started the Catholic-Protestant divide, both religions became more dogmatic. You were one or the other; there was no room for a third category. Those of us who wanted to remain in the upper world changed themselves to appear more human to fit in.'

'And that is why we take human form now?' I guess.

'We?' Snake raises an eyebrow.

My cheeks warm. When had I started to think of myself as one of Snake's creatures? I'm not sure, but somehow, I have.

'Yes, that is why we take human form. But soon even appearing human wasn't enough. In Oliver Cromwell's time, the border between worlds in England was closed to preserve our kind. A few chose to stay above ground, but most creatures returned to the World Below.'

Snake falls silent as the doors open, and a young couple enters. He scowls at them, and they react as you would expect most Londoners to. They immediately head down the other end of the carriage, distancing themselves from potential danger.

'I'm sensing a "but" here,' I encourage once we are alone again.

'That was when we found out that the World Below and the World Above were linked. I guess if the two realms were people, you could say they are linked by a common aura.'

'Only if you believe in that sort of thing,' I say under my breath.

Snake frowns at me. 'Magic and auras and world energies

may be a leap of faith for you, but they are as real to our kind as air and water are to humans.'

He pauses as if waiting for me to make another facetious remark. I bite my tongue, wanting to hear the rest of what he has to say.

'Anyway, when things are in turmoil up here, there is turmoil below. You get the idea?'

I nod. I may not believe it all, but I do understand what he's saying.

'In 1690, the Seelie Court called a full council and decided to open the border and allow a few of our kind to come here and keep the humans on the right track. Rules of interaction were drawn up to keep our secret, rules we still follow today.'

I appreciate how this potted version of his history fits with English history as I know it, but it still feels a little like Snake is telling a story. Notting Hill Gate is announced. We jump off and head to the Circle Line platform.

As we travel the three stops to Bond Street, I feel Snake's eyes on me, as if he's making sure this new info dump hasn't broken me. I want to reassure him that I am fine, but I'm not. When I think about this new world I am a part of, everything keeping me anchored to who I am slips from my grasp, my head spins, and I no longer know who I am.

My hands shake and I clasp them together. I take a shuddering breath as I make a decision. The only way I can cope with my parents' disappearance at the moment is to deal with this other world stuff and who I really am later. If I want to find my parents, I need to focus on the task in front of me, and hopefully it will take me one step closer to my goal.

· · ● · ·

As we exit Bond Street tube station, Pris is still distant. She has disappeared somewhere inside her head. When I found out she knew nothing about who she is, I didn't want to take on the responsibility of bringing her up to speed. Now I'm worried I have broken her.

She walks beside me, hands stuffed in pockets, shoulders hunched and head down, dejected and alone. All I want to do is hug her and tell her it will be all right, that we will get through this together. Not in a romantic way... Not that she isn't attractive.... I mean, I could get lost in those eyes, but she is a bit buttoned down for my tastes.

Still, when she sat on me before... No, I don't want to imagine running my hands up her legs and kissing that mocking mouth. She is an elf, and they are all about the purity of their race. Even my offering her physical comfort would be frowned upon and, this close to the elven stronghold, I don't want to take the risk of being seen.

Damn it. *Focus,* I tell myself. *The objective here is to get all of your parents back, and you can't do that if she is a total mess.*

With my actions suitably justified, I take her hand and give it a squeeze. Okay, it isn't a hug, but I think she needs to know someone is here for her. And the warmth spreading through my body at the contact is totally beside the point.

She smiles wanly at me, and my stomach does a somersault. My body obviously doesn't know what my head does. We turn around the corner into Blackburn Mews and a shiver runs down my spine. Someone is watching us.

I pull Pris to a stop and check out the area. I can't see anything obvious—no shimmers from invisible fairies and no creatures in human form loitering in doorways. Perhaps the attack on Wimbledon Common has set me on edge.

'What is it?' Pris asks.

She is already overwhelmed, so there is no need to burden her with my overactive imagination. 'Just stopping for a quick briefing,' I improvise. In fact, that's not such a bad idea. Things will go more smoothly if she knows what she's letting herself in for.

'You'll need to do all the talking once we're inside,' I carry on. 'I'm only able to speak if the Regises ask me a direct question.'

Her eyes focus on my face, and she frowns. 'You're kidding, right? That sounds so servile and, well, medieval.'

My cheeks warm, and I look at the ground, attempting to hide my embarrassment. This is one piece of creature law I had hoped to avoid for a while.

'Snake, what is it?' She tugs at my hand and I let go.

If I distance myself from her, I won't feel so bad when she realises what gnomes really are, and she no longer wants to have anything to do with me.

Deciding to own who I am, I raise my head and look her in the eye. 'Gnomes are lesser elves. We are those with elven blood who perform the menial tasks true blood elves do not want to lower themselves to do.' There. Finally, it's out in the open.

Pris laughs. 'You're kidding, right? You're not kidding?' She shakes her head. 'You mean other elves treat you like servants.... No, worse than servants—like indentured labourers?'

I say nothing, but I am surprised as her cheeks redden. At first, I think she is embarrassed by being seen with me. I couldn't have been further from the mark.

'That is barbaric, and wrong on so many levels. I.... I....' Her words are angry and a lot louder than they were moments ago.

I can't let her go where she wants to with this. Although it warms my heart that she doesn't buy into the whole lesser creature thing, I need her calm and collected and acting like the elven highborn she is when she meets the Regises.

'Calm down,' I say and immediately regret it when I see a flicker of fire in her eyes.

'Doesn't it make you angry? I mean, in this day and age, to treat someone as if they are little better than a slave—you can't tell me it doesn't bother you.'

I shove my hands in my pockets. 'Of course it bothers me, but I'm not going to be able to change that in the next few minutes. We have to work with what we have, so, for the moment, that means you must behave like other elves.'

She stares at me blankly, as if she can't believe what I'm saying. I don't back down. My mother's life may depend on what happens in the next few minutes, and I will not risk her life to salve my ego. Perhaps Pris's thoughts are running in a similar direction. Her jaw loosens and she takes a deep breath.

'Okay. Tell me what you need me to do.'

'You are elven royalty, but so are the Regises. The only thing we have over them is that you are closer to the throne than they are, since Giles and Amandine are, at best, cousins—distant cousins.'

'I'm royalty? For real?'

'Um... yes?'

She throws her head back and laughs, then stops suddenly. 'Hold on, how royal?'

I shrug. 'I'm not sure exactly. Your mum's a princess, so I guess—'

Pris squeals. 'I'm some sort of a princess.'

Passersby are giving us strange looks, and that's never a good thing in London—especially not in this swanky neighbourhood.

'Calm it down, will you? People'll think you're nuts,' I say.

Pris sobers up but can't wipe the grin off her face. 'I always thought Dad calling me Princess P was a family joke. Do you think I'm actually, like, Princess Anne royalty, or more like Princess Beatrice? No... don't answer that.' Pris chews her bottom lip. 'Whatever this means in the other world, it means nothing here—I am still just me.'

'But—'

'But it matters to them, doesn't it? That's why you told me.'

I nod.

'You want me to play the princess demanding her right to be heard—to be given their endorsement?'

'Exactly.' I grin, happy I don't need to explain the details.

'And what about Plan B?'

'No. What? Why would we need that?' I am confused.

'Because it is my experience that people who love wielding power are not so keen when others use their authority against them.'

That stops me in my tracks. I have never been in a position of power. Can this really be how it works?

'My experience of bullies is that when someone bigger and stronger fronts up to them, they back down,' I argue.

She nods. 'True, but they will always find a way to hit back. I wonder if we might get a little more from them if we try stroking a few egos?'

'But—'

'How about we try it my way first? If it doesn't work, I can go all imperious.'

Argh, she's good at this. And, of course, she makes a fair point. After you demanded something and get nowhere, it is difficult to back down and then ask politely.

'All right, we'll do it your way.'

She starts down the street. 'Which house?' she asks.

I point to the white five-story affair. As she turns to ascend the steps, I grab her arm. 'Don't forget to tell them I am your bodyguard.'

'My what?'

'Bodyguard. If you don't, they'll make me wait outside.'

'This is madness,' she sighs, 'but I guess you know best.'

She starts climbing, and I follow one step behind. As we reach the door, voices and music drift out into the night. Through the window in the room to the left, I can see figures moving around, mingling in groups, chatting and laughing.

'Sounds like they are having a party of some sort,' Pris says, sending a questioning glance my way before dropping the knocker.

I fold my arms across my chest, standing firm.

'What if they're... you know... a little tipsy? We might not get a fair hearing,' she presses.

I relax a little. 'I guess we could come back tomorrow, although alcohol may—'

'Make them a little more relaxed,' Pris finishes as the thump of the knocker rings out.

Almost immediately, the door is opened, and a petite blonde woman glittering with sequins and diamonds smiles in welcome. Her face soon changes to a frown. 'You're a little... underdressed. Ahh, you're not here for the party, are you?'

'No, we're not. I was wondering if I can speak with—'

The door is wrenched open wider, and another woman appears and gives us the once-over. She is an older, taller, thinner, blonder version of the first woman, and she looks down her nose at us as Pris starts again.

'I am Priscilla—'

'I know who you are. You had best come in. Elodie, could you be a dear and go ask Giles to meet me in the library.'

'Of course,' the younger woman says but doesn't move. She is assessing us, clearly wanting to know why we are here.

'Now!' It's a command, and the younger woman reluctantly departs.

The older woman turns her ice-blue gaze to Pris and says, 'Follow me.'

Pris does as she is bid, and I follow her.

'Not him. He waits outside.'

Pris's eyebrows rise, and I realise she didn't completely believe me when I said I wouldn't be granted entry. *Please just do as I asked*, I plead with her inside my head.

'He's my bodyguard, and he goes where I go,' Pris says. Her tone is firm and authoritative. A smile tugs at the corner of my mouth. She has obviously taken to being a princess like a duck to water.

The woman doesn't even bother to answer. I close the door behind me and heave a sigh of relief at having passed the first hurdle. Squaring my shoulders, I follow Pris down the hallway into the... library?

The room may well have been a library once, and certainly one wall is filled with bookshelves, but there isn't a single book in sight. The shelves are filled with filing boxes. In front of them sits an oak desk with a closed laptop placed in the centre. A sofa and a few chairs are set on a Turkish rug in front of a fire, and this is where Amandine leads Pris.

'Please, take a seat,' the woman directs. 'My husband will be here any minute.'

Amandine Regis is very, well, very elven—cool, aloof, and entitled. All I know about her is her reputation for enforcing the rules of our kind to the very letter, and usually to her advantage.

I take up a position just inside the door and stand to attention, hands behind my back, trying to look like I would know what to do if Pris were attacked. In reality, as she had already demonstrated today, she would have more chance defending herself than waiting for me to save her.

Pris sits in the furthest armchair, where she can see me and whoever comes through the door. Amandine remains standing, silent and imposing.

We do not wait for long. Moments after Pris is seated, an elegant, tawny-haired man enters the room with what most would take as a welcoming smile plastered on his face, only there is no warmth in his eyes. I pray Pris is not taken in, because if rumours are correct, this man makes his wife look like a pussycat.

'Ah, Priscilla, so wonderful to finally meet you. No, don't get up. I am afraid it is my daughter's birthday, and she has friends over, so this won't take long.'

Pris raises an eyebrow at Giles Regis's approach and his lack of introduction. *Stick it to him*, I will her. *Deflate that ego. Go on! Do it!*

'I assume you are Giles Regis, and this is your wife Amandine. So pleased to meet you too.' Without rising, Pris holds out her hand and Giles is forced to shake it.

She looks every bit the princess greeting her subjects, and the slight drawing together of Giles's brows tells me he has noticed this too. A flicker of doubt crosses his face, but it is gone so quickly, I am not totally sure I didn't imagine it.

'I apologise for gatecrashing your daughter's birthday, but it is unavoidable under the circumstances. I learnt today that you are the only person who can help me find out what has happened to my parents, and so I came here immediately to request your help.'

Neither of the Regises moves.

'You do know my parents were taken to the World Below, don't you?'

The Regises share a quick glance before Giles takes a step forward. 'Ah—'

'Oh, but of course you know. You are the most senior elves in the human world. I am sure nothing goes on up here amongst our kind without you hearing of it,' Pris continues.

'Of course, my dear. Tragic for you. But I am not sure how we can help,' Giles says. 'If we had been able to do anything, we would have prevented the arrest itself.'

Giles presents his hands palms up as if to show he has

nothing to hide. I'm immediately suspicious and want to find out what Giles knows but isn't telling us. Pris's face shows no reaction at all.

'Obviously, my parents' situation has hit you hard—'

'And if we can do anything to help you while they are gone, we will, of course, for you are still one of our charges,' Amandine interrupts, the chill in her voice making a mockery of her words.

'So kind of you to offer, and so timely, given that I found out today that if you endorse my bodyguard and I, we can go to the next sitting of The Court and help my parents.' Pris presents this as a done deal, almost daring them to refuse. Well played. I suppress a grin.

The smiles freeze on the Regises' faces. They had not expected this.

Giles looks at his wife and says, 'Well, Priscilla, of course—'

'What Giles is trying to say is, there would be no point. You would still need three other endorsements to gain entry, and as you have never been part of our world, you are unlikely to get any more, and—'

'And it would be cruel of us to give you false hope,' Giles finishes for his wife. 'What we can offer you is our guidance on how to deal with the authorities. Help you with the paperwork pertaining to your parents' disappearance and such. We must ensure no one asks any questions that might shine an unwelcome light on us.'

From my position by the door, I can see Pris stand, drawing herself up to her full height, which isn't very tall at all, ready to put Plan B into action.

'Mother, Father, how could you?'

I jump. The voice comes from right beside me, and I hadn't even heard the girl enter. She is almost an exact duplicate of the woman who had opened the door, except her face openly shows distress.

'If you were taken somewhere I would expect all the elves up above to do anything in their power to help me find you.'

'Verona, you do not understand all the forces at play here.' Amandine strokes her daughter's arm as if to soothe her. It doesn't work.

'Would you be breaking any laws if you gave her your endorsement?'

Giles shakes his head. 'No, but—'

'Then give it to her and come back to the party,' the girl pleads.

'It may be the only one she gets,' Giles says again. 'What good will one do her?'

'What good? Why, it will show her that at least her own kind are prepared to help her,' Verona says. 'Come on, Daddy. It's my birthday.' She takes her father's hand and smiles up at him. 'It would ruin my party if you refused her.' She pouts prettily at him. This girl knows how to get her own way. It's very impressive.

Giles catches Amandine's eye above his daughter's head and sighs. 'What harm can it do?' he asks.

His wife scowls. Clearly, she doesn't agree. When Giles does not respond, she purses her lips. 'I must go and attend to our guests.' She turns on her heel and leaves the room.

'It seems it is your lucky day, Priscilla,' Giles says as he moves to the desk and opens a drawer.

As he reaches inside, Pris mouths, 'Thank you,' to Verona, and the elf smiles in return.

Pulling out a shiny black box, Giles carries it over to Pris. Sitting on the chair beside hers, he opens it. I am so engrossed watching the two, I have forgotten Verona. When her hushed voice sounds from right beside me, I can't help but jump.

Perhaps bodyguarding is not really my thing. Maybe next time I should masquerade as a servant.

'Be careful, gnome. Dark forces are at work here. I have done what I can to help you. It may still not be enough. Good luck.'

Before I can turn my head to respond, she is gone, and Priscilla is walking to the door, escorted by Giles. 'You will each need to gather three other pieces to complete the endorsement—that is, if you want to take your bodyguard with you.'

'Thank you so much, Giles. I will not forget our meeting,' Pris says as he opens the front door to escort us out.

·· ·* 🌙 .* ··

I keep my back straight and my head high as I walk past Giles and leave the Regis house. Our host's face is impassive and his body tense. He hadn't wanted to give me the token of his endorsement. As he passed the two quarter coins to me, his eyes flicked to where his daughter had stood. Seeing her gone, he had hissed under his breath, 'You and your family are no true elves. You are no better than that gnome by the door. Don't ever come back here. You are not welcome.'

I was shocked by the hatred in his voice, but I kept my expression blank and considered how to respond. Remembering Snake's words about our relative stations, as I stood to leave, I said, 'Is that how you speak to someone of high blood? Perhaps my extended family will be interested to learn of this insult.'

The words sounded childish to my ears. The threat was hollow, as I had no idea who my family was. Giles clearly did, though, as he blanched and went all stiff and formal on me.

Who were my family that wielding their name could put someone as high up as Giles in their place?

The door closes behind me and my body relaxes, but only a little. We have what we came for, and we are one step closer to finding our parents. I should feel satisfaction, or at the very least relief, but my stomach is churning as my world continues to spin off its axis.

Snake places his hand on my arm. 'Are you all right?'

His voice comes from far away. I lift my head, and it takes a moment for his face to come in to focus.

'He hates me.' My voice is barely above a whisper. 'I only just met him, yet he despises me.'

I don't know why this upsets me so much, but it does. I want to know why a complete stranger bears me such animosity, but at the same time, I want to go home, curl up under the duvet, and forget this strange new world exists. Unfortunately, that will not help me find my parents.

Snake gives my arm a gentle squeeze. 'Hey, you did well. You got us our first endorsements.'

I shake my head. 'No, *I* didn't. Verona did. If she hadn't intervened, Giles would have sent us away empty-handed. I wonder why she cared?'

Snake leads me down the steps, then helps me thread my way through the people crowding the streets. I look around me, suddenly aware that while my life is in crisis, the world still goes on. Londoners are heading home from work or are on their way out to enjoy an evening's entertainment.

As we turn towards the tube station, I'm suddenly hungry and weary to the core. I can't face the crowded trains. I think this may be time for my trusty emergency Visa to make an appearance.

When we reach Grosvenor Square, I hail a taxi. I give the driver my address, he closes the partition, and I finally relax.

Turning my head slightly, I find Snake resting his head

back against the seat, his eyes closed. He has been doing this for two days already, and the tension doesn't totally leave his face. As if he senses me watching him, his eyes open to meet mine.

'Verona gave me a warning, you know. She said other forces are at play, and we should be careful.'

My stomach clenches. Why would she do that? Especially as her parents clearly did not want anything to do with us. 'Snake, do you trust her? I mean, she had no reason to help us.'

His startled expression tells me he wasn't expecting the question. 'I don't know if she is trustworthy. Rumour has it, she was sent below for a while because she was drawing too much attention to herself. I mean, she was in the society pages almost every week. It might have something to do with that. Perhaps she is hitting back at her parents—or perhaps she has her own agenda.'

'Maybe.' But Verona's skillful manipulation of her father seemed like more than childish rebellion to me. My brain is too fried for me to put this into words, so I stare out the window as familiar streets flash by.

The seat moves as Snake sits forward a little. 'The more important question is, what did she mean? Up until now, I believed Mum was taken as part of a cleanup of above world practices—that's what the Fairy Guard said. Now, I'm not so sure. But I can't think of any other reason why she might have been taken.'

On top of everything else today, this is too much for me to even start to contemplate. My phone vibrates in my pocket, and I am relieved to have something to do that is not associated with this madness.

The text is from Susan. I swipe my passcode and read, 'Sorry Pris, emergency at home. Dinner in fridge. CU tomorrow.'

I stare at the screen, trying to make sense of the words. Susan always lets my parents know her whereabouts, and then they tell me. So why is Susan texting me herself today? Then it hits me—she already knows Mum and Dad aren't coming home. Is she part of this other world too?

'Snake, do you know if Susan, our au pair, is an elf, or someone from, you know, below?'

'What makes you ask that?'

I show him Susan's text. 'She knows Mum and Dad are missing. That's why she sent the text to me.'

Snake looks up from the phone and smiles. 'Pris, remember what I said about elves. No self-respecting elf would take a position as a servant. She may be a gnome, but I can't say for sure.'

My heart starts to pound in my chest, and I can't breathe. And just like that, my brain shuts down. I can't go on like this. Not if I am going to find my parents.

'Snake, I can't do this.' My voice waivers.

Beside me his body stiffens. 'Find our parents?' His voice is tired, uncertain, fearful.

I reach across the seat and entwine my fingers in his. The warmth of his touch gives me the courage to speak.

'No, I want to do that. But I can't deal with all this other world stuff. There is too much I don't know, and the enormity of it is paralysing me. I need to ignore that side of things, otherwise I am going to be no help at all.'

Snake's laugh is hollow. 'How are we going to do that when we must track down three different races of creatures?'

All right, my plan is not foolproof. I draw my bottom lip between my teeth as I think.

'I guess we can't ignore it completely. How about we treat this as a normal human search, and you limit your lessons to what I need to know to get my parents back. Everything else I can sort out later... with them.'

Snake thinks about this a bit. 'Aren't you and I a bit old to play pretend?"

'Perhaps, but I guess even adults can be a little childish sometimes,' I tell him, certain that this is the way to go for me to retain my sanity. My head is already spinning less.

'You do know you must face who you are and where you come from at some stage, don't you?' His voice is gentle as his fingers curl around mine.

'Yes, but I can't deal with being someone else... something else, and focus on finding our parents at the same time. It's too much. Every time I think about being a... you know... elf'—I lean in and whisper the last word in case the driver can over-hear—'all I want to do is hide in my bed. I'm afraid if I don't ignore that fact for the moment, I will fall apart.'

Snake keeps his own voice low as he replies, 'I believe you are stronger than that, but it is totally up to you. We can play at being humans for now, concentrate on finding the endorse-ments, and deal with the rest later... if you're sure that's what you want?'

'It is,' I say as the taxi pulls up in front of my home.

After paying the driver, I resist the urge to rush inside, away from the turmoil of the day. As I open the door to let Snake in, I realise that without my parents waiting for me, this is no longer my safe haven—the place where I can escape the world; either world.

CHAPTER 4

The Grand Plan

O nce inside, the uncertain girl from moments before is gone, and Pris is all business, giving me the impression that she goes into organising mode when she is stressed. Leading me upstairs, she shows me to a guest room that would take up half of Mum's and my entire flat.

'The bed should be made up, and your bathroom is through there.' She waves a hand towards a door to the right.

I drop my backpack on the bed, take a look at the pristine white duvet cover, and move it to the floor. I pull off my hoodie, fold it up, and place it on the chair beside the bed. My T-shirt is a little wrinkled, but there isn't much I can do about it because I'm sure whatever's in my pack is little better.

What I can do something about is the fug of stale sweat reaching my nostrils. I poke around in the front pocket of my bag, then reach under my shirt, spraying my armpits before returning the canister to its hiding place. I pass the bathroom sadly as I head downstairs—I'd love to hide under the soothing water of a shower, but there isn't time.

Sounds of movement from the back of the house draw me

along the corridor. I enter the kitchen in time to catch Pris sticking her head inside the most enormous fridge I have ever seen. Pulling out a large dish covered in cling-film, she asks, 'Lasagne all right for dinner?'

My mouth waters. My last meal was a hasty breakfast before I left home this morning, and I'm suddenly ravenous.

I politely answer, 'That would be great, thanks.' Mum would be proud of me. My stomach voices its approval, and the effect is lost.

Pris chuckles. 'I'll get this sorted quick smart, then.'

I watch her as she moves around the kitchen, feeling somewhat like a spare wheel. I need to be doing something... anything. 'Can I help?'

She stops unwrapping the meal and tilts her head to the side. 'I've got this covered. But... um... I put my laptop in the dining room. I thought we could eat and work in there. The office is next door. Could you grab us some supplies?'

I raise my eyebrows. 'And the dining room is where?'

She laughs. 'Next door. And the office is the next one along.'

I head back down the corridor to the second door and open it tentatively. I can't help feeling like a burglar as I turn on the light and survey the room.

The only window is a thin strip of glass above the bookshelves in front of me. To the left, an antique wooden desk takes up most of the space, and to the right is a comfortable chair by a faux wooden filing cabinet.

On the shelves opposite the door, I spy a world atlas. As I reach out a hand, I find tucked in beside it an old, dog-eared atlas of England and take that instead. From the shelf closest to the desk, I grab one of the legal pads from a neat pile before pulling a couple of pens from the holder on the desktop. I turn off the light and pull the door closed behind me.

Pris is already seated at the dining room table when I

enter, shovelling salad into her mouth with her right hand and logging on to a laptop with her left. I drop my supplies beside a second bowl of salad.

'I'm so hungry, I thought this would do as a starter while the lasagne heats up.'

'Thanks,' I say, sitting down at right angles to her, my back to the door. The salad barely touches the sides as I wolf it down.

'So, how do we do this?' Pris asks.

On the trip back from Wimbledon, I'd been thinking about how to approach the other races, especially as we only have a short amount of time.

'Creature strongholds are dotted all over England. I think we would make best use of our limited time if we decide on a region with a creature cluster, so to speak.'

Pris stops, her fork dripping leaves halfway to her mouth. She places the potential mouthful back in the bowl and stares at me.

'Why don't we just head straight to the gnomes. I mean, if it's good enough for me to go to the elves, why don't we go to them next?'

My stomach lurches, and the salad threatens to reappear. That we would get to this point was inevitable, but I didn't think it would be so soon. I like Pris, in fact I more than like her, if I'm being honest. Still, I'm not sure I'm ready to trust her with something this important—this personal.

'It's complicated,' is all I say.

'So was my going to the elves,' she presses.

How can I put her off this idea without telling her the truth? 'It's political, and you just told me you don't want to know about that sort of thing.'

I hate using her fears against her, but I'm just not ready to talk about my relationship with the gnomes yet. Her eyes narrow, and I can tell she is trying to decide whether or not to press her point. *Let it go,* I will her, hoping my fear doesn't show on my face.

Pris studies me for a moment longer, then says, 'Just out of interest, if we had no other option but to ask for the gnome's endorsement, where are they based?'

I've been let off the hook, or so I think. I catch a glint in her eyes, alerting me to the fact that a plan is formulating in that head of hers. Although I don't want to, I must tell her the truth because this may prove to be important later. Besides, I think I can work out where she's going with this.

We don't want to travel too far away from Cornwall, where the gnomes are, to gather the other tokens because if I am forced to throw myself on the mercy of our leader in the upper world, then we don't want to have to travel days to meet with him.

'Cornwall,' I say.

'And if we were to head towards that part of the country, is there a chance we would find some other creature strongholds on the way?'

Taking a deep breath, I open the atlas and flick to the map of South West England. I study the area, searching for some place names I memorised as a child.

Finding the elves was easy because they're London based, but they are the only race whose stronghold is situated in England's capital.

Although I know the names of the creature strongholds, I've never actually visited them, and my knowledge of England is limited. I'm embarrassed to admit Mum and I never leave London—not even to go to visit the gnomes in Cornwall. Whenever we met with other gnomes, we did so on neutral ground close to our home.

I scan the map and am relieved to find three names I recognise on the way to Cornwall. We can complete our endorsements without having to resort to the gnomes. Phew. I'm reaching for the pad to write down the locations when my eyes are drawn to another name.

'Hey, Pris, do you have the riddle handy?'

'I can get it.'

Her chair scrapes across the floor, and she leaves to return a moment later with the piece of paper. She opens it and places it in front of me. Then she leans over and looks at where my finger is marking a place near Godalming.

'What's that? It looks like some sort of park with a lake.'

'The Underground Ballroom,' I say.

'Underground Ballroom?'

'Yes, I remember overhearing my father talking about attending court.' I think back to the conversation they had while Dad helped me build some Lego. It is one of the few happy memories I have of my father. It hurts to dwell on it, but if it will help Mum, I will put aside my personal feelings. 'He was telling Mum about the amazing ballroom underwater. And see, here in the riddle, it says "under water ball."'

Pris grins 'So we know where and when we have to roll up for The Court.'

And we have our first endorsement, I mentally add. After two days of treading water, today I finally achieved something that could lead to freeing my mother.

.·*◗.*··

I return to my laptop and search for the place Snake believes The Court will be held. I don't want to dash his hopes, but he must have it wrong. The Underground Ballroom is an abandoned folly under a lake?

'The Underground Ballroom hardly looks big enough to host the Seelie—is that the right word?—Court,' I start in gently, 'and it's....' I search for the right word. I want to say derelict, but I go for abandoned.

Snake's shoulders rise and fall in a somewhat unconcerned shrug. 'The World Below is hidden from humans, so things aren't always what they seem.'

'But it's in the middle of a lake that's part of a conference centre. If magical creatures were using it, I am sure someone would have noticed by now—and there's nothing on the internet,' I press on with my objections.

Snake's jaw takes on a stubborn set. 'You didn't know another world existed under your very nose, and now you're an expert?'

Ouch. That hit home. For a moment, I consider hitting back, but we have more pressing matters. 'We can argue where the ball is later, once we wrangle our endorsements from the other three races.' I change the subject. 'So, do any of these places on the way to Cornwall ring a bell for you?'

'Yes. Bodmin Moor in Cornwall is the home of the sprites. Wistman's Woods in Devon is the goblin stronghold. And here, the White Lady Waterfall in the Lydford Gorge is the witch's source of power in England.'

Ignoring the surreal vibe in the room as we discuss witches, goblins, and gnomes in the same way we might talk about people from other countries, I chew the end of my pen. I reach for the legal pad Snake scribbled on.

'That makes four potential sources for endorsements. Should we visit them in any particular order? I mean, we don't want to offend anyone,' I say.

Snake shakes his head. 'The elven token means no one will object to supporting us on political grounds for fear of upsetting them. So, we should be able to do what works best for us, time wise.'

Part of me wants to ask what were the other grounds they might object on, but the minute I think of that, my head starts swimming with possibilities. I need to focus on something more tangible.

The timer on the oven pings, rescuing me. I hurry out of the room and immerse myself in the normalcy of serving dinner. I dish the lasagne onto the two plates, then take them into the dining room. By the time I return, I have regained control of my thoughts.

In my absence Snake has been flicking through the book of maps. As I place food in front of him, he says, 'I hope all these guys are happy to support us, because the next closest race stronghold is the fairies' in North Wales.'

I push my laptop out of the way to make a space to eat. 'I thought fairies and sprites were the same thing,' I say before chomping down on a large forkful of food. I can hear my mother groaning over my table manners, and my cheeks heat at the thought.

'Don't ever say that to a sprite or a nixie,' Snake laughs. 'Think of them as cousins. Fairies get all the good press. Nixies and sprites are sort of the black sheep.'

'So, are you saying I should ignore everything I ever read about magical creatures?' I ask, still trying to find some sort of order in the chaos of this new world.

'Yes and no,' Snake says between mouthfuls.

'Not helpful.' I respond.

My voice sounds tart to my own ears, so I am not surprised when Snake freezes.

'Sorry,' he mumbles. 'The stories you heard were once true. Over the years, humans distorted them, turning the tales into fantasies to explain away things their minds couldn't comprehend—'

'Which means there is always a little truth to the tales,' I finish for him.

He nods and carries on eating. That makes sense in a way.

I push the plate away. My meal is only half eaten, but I no longer have any appetite.

'If the different races can be approached in any order, I suggest we start at the closest and make our way down to Cornwall last.'

I start tapping keys, bringing up train times and making notes on of potential routes. Where I cannot find a train going to where we need to be, I search for local bus routes. My planning stops at Bodmin. I can do no more until Snake tells me exactly where to find the gnomes.

I shut the lid of my laptop before ripping the pages off the pad. On a fresh sheet, I write our schedule and push it across to Snake. While he reads it, I take our dishes into the kitchen and start cleaning up.

I bend to start the dishwasher, and when I stand back up, I find myself face-to-face with a set of green eyes staring through the kitchen window. I bite back an involuntary scream as I twist to look for a knife to defend myself. When I turn back, carving knife in hand, the eyes have gone.

A nervous laugh escapes. This has been a strange day. I must have been imagining things.

'Pris, are you okay?'

I turn at the sound of Snake's voice, wondering what he is on about. I follow the line of his gaze and my eyes land on the knife clenched in my hand.

I smile, suddenly feeling rather foolish. 'Yeah, some animal outside startled me, that's all. Do you want some coffee or tea?' I ask, placing the knife back in the block on the bench.

'Do you have hot chocolate?' Snake asks. 'I might need a little something to help me sleep after tension the last couple of days. Not to mention, your schedule is pretty hectic. I will need all the rest I can get tonight before tackling that.'

I grin. Our train tomorrow leaves Paddington at 6:30 in the morning, so perhaps hot chocolate is in order—the good kind. I grab milk from the fridge, decant some into a jug, and put it in the microwave to heat.

From the cupboard above Dad's super-deluxe coffee machine, I extract two chocolate balls wrapped in cellophane and two mugs. I pour the warm milk over the balls and stir each cup slowly with a spoon before sprinkling some baby marshmallows on top.

Snake picks up the cups, and I finish putting everything away, then follow him back into the dining room. The chocolate moustache over his upper lip tells me he's already sampled his drink.

'This is heaven in a cup,' he says, taking another mouthful.

I have my first sip and I have to agree. 'This is my mother's patented down-in-the-dumps drink,' I tell him. 'She says things are always better after drinking chocolate.'

A wave of sadness engulfs me as I think of the times my mother's made this drink to cheer me up. Memories of curling up on the sofa together and watching girlie movies threaten to overwhelm me.

Snake reaches out and places his hand over mine. 'We will find them and bring them home,' he says.

He sounds so sure we will succeed, but I'm not, so there is little comfort to be found in his words. Still, I am grateful he tried, and his touch helps me feel a little less alone.

I take another couple of sips of my drink as I scan my notes to see if I missed anything. My gaze is drawn to the list of creatures we are to visit, and something occurs to me.

'Snake, in fairy stories you have to give something up to get something from magical creatures. Is this one of those things that has been exaggerated over the years, or is it true?'

Snake is focused on getting the last of his chocolate from the bottom of his cup with a spoon. He suddenly looks much younger than I thought he was, and it occurs to me I am relying on him to lead us on the quest to find our parents when I know nothing about him, not even how old he is.

This thought disturbs me as I reflect on the few "more-than-a-friend" feelings I had for him today. What if he is still a kid? Or do gnomes age differently? Is he actually much older than me?

Unaware of my inner turmoil, Snake continues to scoop melted chocolate from his cup as he answers. 'I'm not sure. I mean, you didn't give anything up for the elven token.'

'Perhaps I didn't need to because Verona asked for it as a birthday gift.'

Snake raises his head, a smirk twisting his lips. 'I wondered if you had realised that. Look, we will have to give something to them, but we have no way of knowing what until we face each creature. So, there is no use worrying about it until we need to.'

I want to ask more, but he is right. You can't plan for the unknown. Which now takes me back to my new problem: finding out a little more about my travelling companion.

My phone vibrates, and I glance at the text. It's from my friend Amalie. It says, 'Do you want to meet for breakfast before school tomorrow?'

School. I forgot about school. I finished my A-Levels last week but had returned to school as part of a community outreach programme supporting potential scholarship kids through the selection process. I enjoyed working with the candidates, and it was especially close to my heart as my best friend Amalie was a scholarship student.

My screen flashes with another text. 'Pris, you home?'

I picked up my phone, reluctant to answer. We only have one more week of school, then Amalie will be working all summer before heading off to Edinburgh University. I, in turn, would have been off on a family holiday and then interning for my mother in the remaining weeks before taking up my place in Cambridge.

I was throwing away my last few days with the person who had been like a sister to me, and I would be damned if I would lie to her about it.

'No can do,' I text. 'Heading off on family trip early. Call u when I am back.'

Okay, not full the truth, but close. This *was* a trip, and it really was for my family.

I scroll through my contact list, find the number I am looking for, then head next door to the office. Using the landline, I dial and, using my best impersonation of my mother honed over years of practice, leave a message for the school, giving the same reason I gave Amalie to excuse my absence for the rest of the term.

My phone beeps. 'Bummer. Why now?'

'Family crisis or something.'

'Cu when ur back.'

I text a thumbs-up as I return to the dining room.

Snake is leaning back in his chair, feet stretched out in front of him. 'Problem?'

'No, well, sort of. I was catching up with my friend before school tomorrow, and it reminded me I needed to tell them I won't be round for the rest of term.'

His eyes narrow as he assess me. 'I don't know why, but I sort of had the idea you were like me, finished A-Levels and finished with school. But that was stupid, of course, since I found you at school today.'

Chuckling at his confusion, I say, 'I am finished. I was just helping out for a couple of weeks until the end of term. They are sticklers for uniform, even if you are technically no longer a student.'

'Good, because this could have gotten tricky if we had to

explain to the authorities why you weren't turning up to classes.'

I nod, aware for the first time that I really am free of school and all the constraints being a child placed on me. I no longer have to answer to anyone. Thump! From the heady heights of freedom, I drop back to reality. The people I usually answer to are no longer here to question my choices.

As if sensing the change in mood, Snake stands and stretches.

'It's late. We should sleep. Let me tidy up while you head to bed.'

He places his hands on my shoulders and steers me out of the room. My feet do the rest, taking me to my bedroom of their own accord. As I reach for the handle, I glance towards my parents' suite, wishing I could simply walk down the corridor, open the door, and find them safely inside.

·· * ☽ * ··

I learn from my mistakes. This time, I wait until the lights are out downstairs before making my way back to the house. I tell you, that girl took away one of my lives, appearing in the window like that. One moment the room was clear, then she popped up out of nowhere.

I should have used a 'don't see me' spell, but I could not help it, I froze. Fortunately, she turned away for a minute, and I was able to escape into the shadows, hiding under the patio furniture again.

Once my heart stops pounding, I begin considering my options. I must find out what Snake and the girl are planning so I can report back to my mistress. I stretch as I ponder, then freeze. There is another presence in the garden, and a tingle in the air tells me they are using magic to cancel themselves.

Fortunately, cat sight has its advantages. In the gloom, I find something crouched in the corner of the stone wall, watching and waiting.

The lights on the ground floor blink out, and the other creature moves ever so quickly. The presence disappears for a moment, reappears, then is completely gone.

I wonder if they found what they were looking for. Regardless, I need to know what they wanted. Keeping to the shadows, I pad to the door, incant a simple spell in my mind, and the lock clicks open as I reach it. I slip in through the smallest of gaps and sniff the air, trying to get a sense of the place.

Snake and the elf did not spend much time in the kitchen. I follow their scents to the dining room. Papers are spread over the table. I jump up, sending a pen clattering to the floor. Freezing, I wait for the sounds from upstairs telling me I have been found out. All is silent.

I walk over the papers, and they move under my paws, no matter how light-footed I am. Then I see it: the faint glow of magic where the other visitor touched the pad just for a moment.

I peer down and read what appears to be travel plans. Ah, they are going after endorsements in the West Country. Smart move. The density of magical creatures in the area should give them ample opportunity to complete their tokens.

I take note of where they are going, ready to relay the details back to my mistress. She will do what she can to help from her end.

For a moment, I think of my bed by the radiator and sigh. I will not be home for some time. My mistress is right; some other force is interested in what Snake and his friend are up to, and I will need to stay close to them if we are to find out who is behind this.

I return to the kitchen, jump onto the bench, and flick on the cold water tap for a quick drink before dropping down and heading to the fridge. I leap up and grab hold of the handle, hanging off it until the door opens.

I jump back onto the bench, and I survey the contents. On the top shelf are two sausages covered in cling film. One of them will do nicely. I leap across and hang from the shelf. It wobbles a bit, unable to hold my weight for long. My back feet find purchase on the door of the freezer.

I make sure I am stable before reaching up to slice the cling film with a nail. I hook a sausage and fling it towards the door before letting myself drop gracefully to all four paws.

Finally, I leap and push the fridge door closed. I take the sausage and leave, using magic to shut the door to the garden behind me. Of course, I could have used a spell to steal the sausage, but it is so much more satisfying going old school.

Back under the patio furniture, I finish my meal before lying down and clearing my mind so I can report to my mistress

CHAPTER 5

The Hag in the Bog

I t is still pitch black when Imagine Dragons blare out "Radioactive" in my ear. Reaching under the pillow, I grab the phone to turn off the alarm. Still half asleep, I stumble to the ensuite and use the shower to fully wake up. After changing into my one clean set of clothes, I fold the dirty stuff into a plastic bag before stuffing it into my pack, followed by my phone and e-reader.

After making the bed and ensuring the room is left as I found it, I can't help but smile. Mum would be proud. My eyes tear up at the thought of her and how far away she is. Swallowing the lump in my throat, I pick up my hoodie and backpack and head downstairs.

Early though I am, Pris is even earlier. She is scraping scrambled eggs from a pan onto a plate, frowning as they tumble onto buttered toast.

'What's up?' I ask.

'I could have sworn there were two sausages in the fridge last night, but when I went to get them to add to the scrambled eggs, I only found one.' She looks at me, eyebrow raised.

I hold my hands out in front of me, palms facing

outwards. 'Hey, it wasn't me. I was stuffed after all that chocolate and lasagne.'

Pris rinses out the pan and places it on the draining board, the frown deepening as she tries to work out what happened to the missing food.

'Look, eggs by themselves are fine,' I tell her. 'In fact, they're more than fine. I have eaten better since meeting you than I have for days.'

The smile she gives me sends heat rising up my neck. *Get a grip*, I tell myself. Spying the large pack by the backdoor, I opt for a change of subject.

'Good, you found some camping gear. Hopefully, you packed a tent?'

Pris plonks a plate down on the counter in front of me.

'You're kidding. That's my clothes.'

Clothes? How many clothes do you need for a week? Fortunately, I didn't let that thought out. 'Oh, okay.' I eat some of my eggs. 'Do you have a tent? I'm happy to carry it.'

'A tent? What for?'

Man, this is like wading through treacle. 'Where do you think we're going to be sleeping this week?'

Pris doesn't miss a beat. 'Motels, hotels, B&Bs.'

I stop eating as I think of the small amount in my bank account. As it is, I will have to work every free hour to pay for uni next year, I probably won't be able to go if I use all my money now. I shake my head. What am I saying? Of course I will use every penny if it means getting Mum back. Still, I may not have enough to pay for accommodation and food for an entire week. 'They cost money, Pris—money I can't afford,' I reluctantly admit.

Pris studies me for a moment before saying, 'My parents gave me an emergency credit card, and I would say this is an emergency.'

'Still, it will have to be paid back.' I am embarrassed at her offering to pay for me, while at the same time a little relieved most of my savings will still be there once this is over.

'Think of it this way: my parents will be happy to cover the costs if we rescue them. And if we don't....' My heart clenches as tears well in her eyes. It nearly breaks when she brushes them away almost angrily. 'If we don't, it will be my money to dispose of anyway.'

This is the first time I allow the possibility of failure to enter my head, and the thought turns the food in my mouth to sand. I put the fork down and take my plate to the bin. Scraping the leftovers into the rubbish, I refuse to think about not getting Mum back. I can't leave her down there alone in the World Below.

Pris grabs my plate, rinses it, and puts it in the dishwasher. I bag up the rubbish and take it to the bin out back. I'm not sure, but I think there is a shadow under the patio furniture. A fox or a cat, perhaps? It is watching me as I return to the kitchen, and the hairs on the back of my neck stand on end at the thought.

Pris is standing with hands on hips, looking at my backpack. Oh my goodness, what is she wearing? The jeans and designer sweatshirt are fine, but the Converse high-tops are not going to be any good for hiking.

'Don't you have any walking boots... something more suitable for rough terrain?' I ask.

She frowns and stares at me like I'm speaking a foreign language. 'I was just about to ask if that is all you brought for the next seven days. We're going to be together a lot, and I don't want to put up with... you know... unwashed boy odours.'

'This is all I need: one set to wash and one to wear. I was hoping to find laundromats along the way.'

'We won't have time to...'

I don't catch the rest because Pris takes off down the corridor. Footsteps thump up the stairs before fading into nothing. I check the time on my phone. We have to move, or we will miss our train.

I pick up our packs and head to the hallway, meeting Pris at the foot of the stairs. She is carrying some walking boots, an identical pack to the one her gear is stowed in, and an assortment of clothes. She dumps it all on the floor before sitting down and unlacing her trainers.

'These are Mum's boots—they should fit. The clothes and pack are for you. Some of Dad's things. They might be a little big, so I grabbed a belt. You can also use his pack. Come on. We have to hurry.'

Still in a daze, I shove the stuff from my pack into the larger one before holding up one of the two pairs of jeans from the pile on the floor. Right length, but Pris is correct, they are at least a size bigger than I would buy. I roll them up, along with a couple of plain black t-shirts, a red-and-black checked shirt, and a zip-up hoodie.

Three packages are left on the floor. Two contain new underwear, and one is an unopened three-pack of socks—all from M&S. I look at them as if they are alien.

'Dad always keeps a few new packs around for when he travels,' Pris explains. 'He won't notice any of this is missing.'

I shove them inside the larger pack and put my own backpack on the top, thinking it might come in handy. As I transfer my phone and wallet to the outside pockets, I can't help thinking how the other half lives. The clothes I am borrowing cost more than my entire wardrobe, and Pris has virtually given them away without a second thought.

Pris shoves her high-tops into the top of her pack and hauls it over her shoulder. Picking up her keys from a bowl beside the door, she looks at me. 'Are you ready? The taxi should be here now.'

'Taxi?'

'Of course. There's no way I am missing the train because of delays on the tube.'

She opens the door and bundles me out towards the black cab idling by the curb.

'Damn it,' Pris says from behind. 'I won't be a mo.'

I head down the steps and say, 'Hi,' to the driver before opening the door into what must be the oldest London cab still in action. The driver obviously isn't a morning person as he doesn't even acknowledge me.

I have just hauled my pack over to make way for Pris, when she jumps into the cab, waving sheets of paper in a plastic document wallet. 'I almost forgot these,' she says. 'Won't get far without our itinerary. And I left a quick note for Susan saying I will be staying at Amalie's for a few days, just in case she isn't, you know, one of us.'

As she shoves the wallet into the front pocket of her pack, she pulls out a D&G cap, pulls it down firmly on her head, and tells the driver, 'Paddington Station, please.'

···•◡•···

I slump into my seat as the train lurches away from the platform. Snake dumps his pack across from me and settles down beside it. I take a moment to catch my breath as he leans forward, arms resting on the table between us.

'I was sure we were going to miss it,' he says, panting.

'Who would have thought traffic would be so busy this early in the morning,' I grumble. 'Still, we were lucky the train was running a few minutes late.'

As we pull out from the station, I relax a little, and Snake sits back in his seat. The trip to Lydford will be over four hours, giving us plenty of time to plan our attack.

Snake reaches into his bag and pulls out his phone and some earbuds. He slips them in, rests his head against the window, and closes his eyes. Clearly, we won't be doing any planning together on the trip.

I, on the other hand, am too keyed up to sleep, and I always perform better when I am prepared for whatever life throws at me. I pull a book from my bag. I found it in Dad's office when I went to look for a plastic folder for our itinerary. The title, *Magical Places of Great Britain*, caught my eye. It was exactly what I needed for this adventure. I put it on the table and search for my earbuds.

As I slip them in place, I look up and find Snake eyeing the cover, his lips forming a smirk. I snatch the book off the table and hold it in front of me, aware I am being overly defensive. Snake double taps his right ear.

'I see you brought some research. Just don't take everything you read as gospel. Things aren't always what they appear to be in the human world.' He taps his ear again and closes his eyes.

I find my pen pal Ausgirl04's playlist she made to introduce me to her kind of music on my phone. I settle down and open the book. As Bic Runga's sultry tones form the lyrics to "Drive", I search the index for White Lady Waterfall, Lydford, flick to the page, and begin reading.

I'm so engrossed I do not realise Snake has moved until he touches my shoulder. I pause my music and look up at him.

'Would you like a tea or coffee?'

'Tea with milk, please,' I say, reaching for my wallet.

He smiles wryly. 'I can run to a couple of drinks.'

My cheeks warm, and I'm grateful my dark complexion is likely hiding my embarrassment.

He disappears down the carriage, and I glance at my phone. How long have I been reading for? Two hours? My eyes slip to Snake's e-reader, which he left still running on the table. I read the upside-down title *Where Science and Magic Meet*. My eyes widen. From what I can gather from the text, this is proper science.

'Just getting in some pre-uni reading,' a voice says from behind me as Snake reaches over and places a cup for life on the table. 'I'm going to need a lot of these over the next few days, so I did the right thing—save the planet and all that.'

Funny, he appeared to be more embarrassed about caring for the environment than reading a science book for fun.

'Thanks for the tea,' I say. As he sits, I ask, 'So you're going to uni? What are you studying?'

'Physics,' he answers before taking a sip from his cup. 'Ahh, coffee. I can't function until I've had my first cup. What?' he asks when he realises I haven't moved. 'Don't tell me you have never met a coffee addict before?'

I'm suddenly conscious that I am staring at him. 'Physics?'

Okay, so words have escaped me. To my eyes, Snake looks like your average guy. If I am honest, a little bit better than average with those twinkling green eyes and the floppy brown fringe he keeps flicking out of the way. And I sat on the guy. He is all muscles and sinew. He is not your regular geek.

'Is there something wrong with that? My background gives me a unique perspective on the energies powering our world, don't you think?'

'You don't seem the type,' I say, floundering out of my depth.

He grins at me. 'No glasses and nerdy clothes, you mean. Things have moved on since the eighties.'

Caught out stereotyping, I resist the urge to look away and am searching for something cutting to say when I stop—suddenly aware he's right; I'm out of touch with the world.

I've had most of the same friends since primary school. I spend my leisure time with them, except when we go on family holidays, always overseas and always somewhere educational.

I've had very little experience of the world at large, and not even London at large.

'Sorry, not many sciency people in my social group,' I say to cover my confusion.

'No magical people, no science people. You're missing out on making some great friends.' Snake grins and picks up his book. 'We're just the same as everyone else, you know. We eat the same food, listen to the same music, watch the same movies.'

He focuses on his book, occasionally taking sips from his mug. I turn my music back on and close my eyes, wondering if he was talking about magical people, science people, or simply people who do not live in my exclusive world.

··*·◗·*··

Lydford Station is exactly what I expected from a country stop. The wooden building stands on one of the two concrete platforms separated by two railway lines—one for each direction. I am surprised to find it staffed, and by one of the most helpful station workers I've ever met. Then again, as I am well aware, my experiences of living in London have not prepared me for the way the rest of England works.

George, as he asks us to call him, is happy to store our packs in a locked room, so long as we pick them up before 5:50 p.m. when his shift ends. We assure him we're only going to walk the Lydford Gorge, and we should be back in plenty of time. Snake pulls his daypack out before leaning his bag up against mine.

'So, you're trekking the gorge,' George says as he locks the door to the storeroom. Walking a few paces to the ticket counter, he then reaches over and scrabbles for something.

Moments later he hands Snake a pamphlet. 'This is the path to the gorge car park and a map of the track.'

'Thank you,' Snake says, shoving the pamphlet in his pocket.

'It is a good two-to-three-hour walk, so you might want to nip across the road to the cafe. Myrtle does a lunch pack for hikers such as yourselves. Reasonably priced too.'

'What a great idea,' I say. 'Thank you so much for your help.'

'My pleasure,' George responds, opening the door to his office, mind already on his next task.

I walk, or more accurately float, out of the station, marvelling at how someone taking a little time to help us out has made my day.

Snake insists on buying lunch, and I let him, realising that this was his way of contributing to our search. He has no idea that his very presence is giving me the courage to travel round the country, so far out of my comfort zone, and that is more than worth any amount of charges on my parents' credit card.

While I wait, I study my surroundings. Lydford is my idea of a typical English village: a mixture of ancient stone houses and modern new builds trying to blend in. Apart from the pub, which doubles as a B&B, I find a post office, the cafe Snake entered, and a local restaurant slash takeaway, which strangely does both fish and chips and Indian meals. I half expect a Miss Marple type figure to pop out of one of the doorways.

As Snake emerges from the cafe, shoving water bottles, sandwiches, and fruit into his pack, I smile at a middle-aged woman jogging by who says, 'Hello' as our eyes meet. It's odd being spoken to by a total stranger, but I feel compelled to acknowledge her friendly greeting.

'Let's get going,' I say as Snake joins me.

'Not quite Kensington High Street, is it?' he says, accurately guessing at my discomfort as he hauls his pack over his shoulder.

'Everyone is so nice and friendly,' I say under my breath as Snake consults the pamphlet.

'Odd, isn't it. It's so quiet, and the people are so chatty,' he says, then points down the street, away from the station. 'The track is this way.'

By the time we reach the carpark, I'm over walking. We take a drink break before we start on the hike, and I ask how much further to the falls.

Snake laughs. 'I would say about an hour or so from here.'

I think he is teasing me until I read the signs at the beginning of the track. The journey here had clearly not been part of the stationmaster's calculations.

As we walk the track through the gorge, I lose myself in nature. Everything is so green and beautiful, and everything smells... fresh. It's the only way I can describe it. Most of the track is boardwalks interspersed with some gravelled sections. As I slip for the third time on the wet wood, I appreciate Snake suggesting a change of footwear this morning.

'If you haven't been out of London much, how did you know about the shoes?' I ask when we stop at a viewing platform for yet another drink break.

'My father used to go and visit some of the other races, and he always kitted himself out like this.' He looks down at his clothes, and shrugs. 'So, I thought it might be a good idea to be prepared.'

Snake turns away and gazes down into the gorge, and the silence is uncomfortable. The way he looked at his feet makes me wonder if his shoes, like mine, were borrowed from a parent. I want to ask him about his father. I also want to ask my parents if their weekend hiking trips were to meet with representatives of the other races.

I can do none of this. Instead, I pop my bottle back into

the side pocket of Snake's pack and say, 'Come on, not long until the top now,' and carry on walking before my body decides it's had enough and refuses to go on.

Near the top we meet an elderly couple who do not look nearly as knackered as we do, and I say an embarrassed 'Hello' as our eyes meet.

'You're almost at the falls, love. Keep it up,' the woman, who must be seventy if she's a day, says as she passes.

I mumble thanks, and not for the first time, I think I really should fit some more cardio into my life. The woman is right though. As I climb, the roar of the rushing waters of the White Lady Falls fills my ears.

I catch Snake up. He clearly spends more time walking than I do, even if he isn't used to country treks. When we arrive at the top of the trail, I pause and take in the view.

The falls are like nothing I have ever seen in real life. I could stand here and watch the water all day, following it as it froths and gushes over rocks and finally calming when it reaches the pool below. The frantic movement of the falls is a counterpoint to the serene greenery surrounding it.

'Up here or down there?' I ask, still almost too out of breath to form a full sentence.

'Down, I think.' Snake leans forward slightly over the railing to get a better look.

'Of course,' I say, glaring at the steps down to the pool at the bottom of the waterfall. I sigh and take a sip of water as I peer down the shadowy path again.

I could have sworn I saw a black cat descending—well, the tail of one at least. When I look again, it has gone. Oxygen deprivation is obviously playing tricks with my mind. I place my foot on the first step—the sooner we get to the bottom, the sooner we leave, and the sooner I can be done with all this walking.

I pause before following Pris down the path beside the waterfall. For the whole morning, I have successfully put off thinking about approaching the White Lady, the most senior of witches above ground. Although I made light of it to Pris, I am worried what toll she will exact from us in exchange for her endorsement.

Will she ask too much? Will we have to turn her down? Will she even come when called? What if she turns up but won't endorse us?

'Snake, are you coming?' Pris calls up.

Standing here worrying won't get the job done. I urge my body down the stairs. When I arrive at the viewing platform at the bottom, I find Pris already there, staring into the water.

'Are you sure this is the right place?' she asks, glancing around.

I follow her gaze upwards to the top of the falls, which now dwarf us, and I nod, surprised she can't sense the magic swirling around us.

'What now?'

I tear my eyes away from the mesmerising flow of water. 'We call the witch.'

Pris turns to me. 'What, just say something like "White Witch, we want to speak with you?"'

'Pretty much,' I answer, and I can't help but laugh as she raises an eyebrow.

'You're kidding.'

'I don't exactly do this every day,' I tell her. 'I'm sort of winging it.'

I wait for a group of school kids and their teacher to head past before lowering my pack to the ground and facing the waterfall. I close my mind and let the magic in the air wash over me until the medallion on the leather strip around my neck warms, signalling that I am at one with the energies of this place.

'I, Snake Fieth, request an audience with the White Lady.'

My voice is loud and clear, and it rings around the gorge. Giggles drift down from the group of kids on the path by the waterfall, and I can't help but be a little embarrassed.

'Nothing's happening,' Pris points out.

'Be patient. She doesn't actually live here,' I tell her, more confidently than I feel.

We wait another five minutes, and still nothing.

'Did I hear you call The White Lady?'

I start at the voice so close behind. Swinging around, I come face-to-face—well, not exactly face-to-face, more like face-to-top-of-hat—with an elderly lady dressed like an advertisement for a walking magazine.

'No, of course not.' Pris colours as she answers, then drops her gaze.

'It's all right, no need to be embarrassed. Many come here to call her, but she doesn't speak to them all.' She waves as she heads back to the track. 'Must be on my way, things to do, people to see. Good luck with whatever you want her for.'

Pris waits until she has disappeared before saying, 'Should we call for her again? Maybe make contact with the water when we do?'

My medallion is still warm, so the magical connection is still active.

'No, I think we should just wait. Perhaps we should eat our lunch.' My stomach rumbles as I lower myself to the ground.

Pris hesitates, starts to say something, then joins me. 'If you're sure.'

I'm not sure exactly. Mum normally handled contacting

the elders of our race and any inter-creature communications. Whenever she did, the medallion given to me by my father's family at my birth always heated up.

We eat our lunch in silence, facing the waterfall. The crusty ham-and-cheese roll is fresh and crunchy, just the way I like it. I'm finishing off my apple when I notice the waterfall begin to ripple. The air around us thrums as I nudge Pris and haul her to her feet just as a face appears in the water.

At first it is a shimmery outline, but in moments it forms into a 3D head protruding from the flowing water, like some CGI thing from a movie.

'I was expecting someone more like the Witch of Wimbledon, not a hag like in the fairy stories,' Pris leans in and whispers into my ear. She is trying to sound casual, but she can't keep the excitement from her voice.

'We don't use the term hag,' a melodic voice says. 'Hag is what men threatened by our power call women like us as they burned my kind at the stake. Some of them even had the temerity to call me the Hag in the Bog—as if this place could ever be a bog.'

'I'm sorry, I meant no offence,' Pris quickly stammers as the image changes to one of a beautiful woman.

'You prefer me like this?' the voice asks. 'Is physical beauty easier to deal with than a visage showing age and wisdom?'

'Is this some sort of test?' Pris asks. Her words are brave, but her voice is uncertain, and her hands are tightly clasped in front of her.

'No, child; merely a comment on what society now values.'

'This is going well,' I say under my breath before taking a step forward. 'Greetings, Eugenia, White Woman of Lydford and Earth Mother of England. Thank you for coming to meet with us.'

'It is a pleasure to meet you again, Snake. You have grown

a little since you and your mother returned my ancestor's grimoire.'

'That was a few years ago now.' I smile, remembering how generous she had been with her thanks. Real diamond earrings for Mum, which had long since gone to pay some bill or other. For me, she brought my first guitar. She told me my family were gifted musicians and she was sure my talent for slight-of-hand was not the only gift I had inherited.

'You summoned me to this place. What can I do for you today?'

So, we were moving right on to the formalities. I had hoped for a bit more time on the catch-up, reminding Eugenia of our shared past before we got down to business.

'This is Priscilla Crown—'

'I know who Priscilla is. I was one of the three of my kind who attended her christening, welcoming the new princess to the royal line.'

'You know me?' Pris splutters, and I place a hand on her arm. I cannot allow a repeat of our audience with Eleanora. For a moment, she tenses, then puts her other hand over mine. I let out the breath I was holding, relieved she will let me handle the audience.

'We are here today to request your endorsement so we might attend the Spring Court to speak up for our parents at their trial.'

'As I already suspected. Eleanora sent her friend to speak on your behalf, and I am inclined to support you both. However, we must follow the correct forms before you receive the tokens.'

'See, I told you we would have to give something up,' Pris whispers, worry creeping into her voice.

'Not give something up, child, but give something of yourselves. I want to be sure you are honest and trustworthy and are prepared to fight for your parents' freedom.'

'What must we give to gain our tokens?' I ask, suddenly wary. Personal information is common currency in the World Below, but one that can have unforeseen repercussions if you aren't careful.

'I want you to tell me what you most fear at this very moment.'

'That's easy,' Pris says, stepping forward to answer. I again grab her arm before she can say anything more.

'Our fears can be used against us. I want your promise that once you assess our commitment, you will forget you ever heard them.'

Pris turns angrily to me, wrenching her arm out of my grip. 'What are you doing? You don't bargain with someone you are asking a favour of.'

'No, child, the boy is correct. Knowing someone's fear is a weapon beyond price, and Snake is right to ensure it cannot be used against you. As it is not my intention to ever use this knowledge beyond today, I agree to your terms. I will wipe my memory of whatever you tell me.'

I move out of Pris's way so she can answer Eugenia.

She states her fear simply and directly. 'I am afraid I will not be able to free my parents.'

The White Lady's lips form a smile. 'Of course you are, but that is not the root of your fear, is it?'

The tension around Pris's eyes tells me Eugenia is right, and my stomach knots —we will not be let off the hook by offering up any old fear. She wants to see into our very core. I begin formulating an answer that will satisfy her without giving too much away, but I am distracted by Pris's next words.

'All right,' Pris almost hisses. 'I am afraid all this nonsense about magic and creatures and the World Below is real, which means my parents haven't prepared me for who I need to be to rescue them. That scares me, but it also makes me angry.' She folds her arms across her chest and glares at the image in the waterfall.

Eugenia glares back, not giving Pris an inch.

Pris's shoulders slump, and she says, almost in a whisper, 'I am afraid I don't know who I am anymore.'

I reach out and place a hand on Pris's shoulder, but she doesn't appear to even notice my clumsy attempt to console her. My hand drops back to my side as the witch finally speaks.

'You are right to fear you have not been prepared well enough to complete your quest, but you are stronger than you think. If you work with Snake, you will do well enough. In the meantime, you might do well to remember that what you are is different to who you are.'

Pris actually humphs as she drops back to the ground. She does not understand that in return for her honesty, Eugenia gave her some useful advice.

'Now, Snake, what is your greatest fear?'

My stomach somersaults. I have been so engrossed in the exchange between Pris and Eugenia, I have not fully prepared my answer.

'I am worried I will not be able to save my mother and I will be left alone in the World Above.' The words tumble out, and before I am even finished speaking, I realise it will not be enough.

'Partially true, but you can do better.'

I gaze into the water roiling at the base of the falls as I consider what to say next. Can I actually say the words that will unlock the fear that built inside me over the last eight years? I worry that if I do, my heart will break and I will be of no use to anyone.

I gulp in air, suddenly unable to breathe.

'Come on, Snake. You can say it. If you don't, it will fester inside you and may prevent you from succeeding in freeing your mother.'

Eugenia's musical voice is gentle, and I can't be sure she hasn't put some magic behind it, because I find myself saying, 'I am afraid I am more like my father than I would like to be, and that I will let my family down when they most need me.'

Freeing my fear is like pulling out a rotting tooth: equal measures of pain and relief. Eugenia's watery figure produces a hand that reaches out to me, as if to offer comfort in the same way I had to Pris moments ago.

I wipe the tears from my eyes. Anger and sadness war inside of me as my head drops and I shove my hands in my pockets.

'There is more to that story than you know, young man,' the White Lady says, her voice compassionate but controlled. 'What happened with your family eight years ago is very likely linked to what is happening now. Do not close your mind or your heart in the coming days or you may fail this mission.'

I worry the coins in my pocket as I consider her words, and I come across some new odd-shaped ones. Drawing them out, I find the witches' tokens.

Pris reaches into my pack and pulls out the two we got from the elves. Taking one of her pieces, I give her one of mine. I then hold my two tokens together, and Pris's eyes widen as they snick into place, forming a half coin. She follows my example and laughs as her pieces do the same.

'Thank you,' I say to Eugenia. I elbow Pris.

'Yes, thank you. We appreciate your help.'

'It is my pleasure. I just hope our support is enough. I fear darker forces are at work here. Good luck on your quest.'

As Eugenia's face merges with the waterfall again, I catch sight of a form behind the water. Is that a cat? I open my mouth to ask if Pris can see it too, just as the image disappears.

As I bend to pick up my pack, Pris asks, 'What does she actually look like, the White Witch? Crone or White Lady?'

'Whatever she wants to,' I reply. 'Witches are amongst the

longest lived of creatures in human years, and they use their magic to shape shift into whoever humans will accept.'

'Cool!' Pris says, clearly impressed.

I check my phone. 'Oh no, this has taken far longer than we anticipated. We're going to have to leg it to get back to the station in time.'

All thoughts of our quest leave my mind as we rush to rescue our luggage.

CHAPTER 6

A Little Bit of Glamour

From my perch above the waterfall, I wait while Snake and the elf leave the clearing. A hand strokes my head, and I arch my back as it moves down my body. Eugenia tickles my ear, and I purr my pleasure.

'Did you like my water show?' she asks, and I shake my head. I think it was showy and unnecessary, as she had to also hold a vision of the waterfall as normal for other passersby. She would pay for that later.

'What else was I to do when they did not recognise me in the flesh?' She gestures to her elderly form encased in walking gear. 'I blame the *Harry Potter* movies. Ever since they came out, everyone expects magic to look like something special effects technicians dreamed up.'

I say nothing, but I think she enjoyed the show she put on rather too much.

'Well, we can't hang around here. I mean, I can, but you still have work to do. If the figure you saw last night was sent by the person behind this, then the goblins may already be considering not supporting Snake and Priscilla. You must go and persuade them otherwise.'

I want to argue that I can do that just as well in the morning. That I will do better on a full stomach and after a good night's sleep, but we have had this argument already. She will remain in Lydford tonight with Snake and that elf, and I will go talk with the goblins.

Nasty creatures, goblins. They are rude and do not respect their betters, so they will have little patience with me, even if I go as Eugenia's representative.

Eugenia reaches into her pocket and pulls out a handful of cat kibble and places it on the ground. Not my favourite food, but I tuck in hungrily.

'I can't let you go on an empty stomach. Come visit me once you speak with the goblins, and I will give you a proper meal.'

I finish the food as she walks away. Before I depart, I clean my face and stretch. I consider a five-minute nap in the last of the sun, but voices drift along the track and I am gone before the walkers turn the corner.

· · ∗˙ 🌙 ˙∗ · ·

George is pulling the station door closed as we rush down the road.

'Wait, please wait,' I yell as I put on a burst of speed.

George grins when he finally catches sight of us. 'Cutting it fine, you two. Another minute and I would be gone.' He nods towards the car idling at the side of the road and raises his index finger to the middle-aged woman driver, indicating he will only be a minute.

'Thank you for doing this,' I say, following him into the station.

We retrieve our packs and hurry out, not wanting to delay the kindly man any longer.

'Next train out of here isn't for an hour or so, so if you want a meal, the bistro at the pub is pretty good,' George says as he locks up.

'We were sort of hoping to stay here tonight,' I say, and he raises an eyebrow.

'Only B&B is at the pub, and they're a bit old-fashioned. They won't take kindly to two young people like yourselves staying without parents. Maybe better to head to a bigger place where they don't mind such things.'

I am about to tell him I am over eighteen and don't need a guardian, but he is already heading towards the car.

With no outlet for my anger, I turn to Snake. 'We need to stay here because this is the best place for us to head out from tomorrow. I can't believe they won't let us rent a room without a guardian. I mean, it's not like we're going to share a bed or....'

Snake smirks and I stop mid flow. 'You didn't think we were sharing a room, did you?'

'It would be one way to save money,' he says.

My heart skips a little at the thought of him that close to me. *Stop it.* We're just... what? Almost friends? The look in Snake's eyes suggests he would not be averse to being something a little more. I haul my pack onto my shoulder. I am not going to go there. 'Two rooms, but it's moot if they won't let us stay.'

Snake shrugs, almost as if to say you can't blame a boy for trying. 'You could just glamour them,' he says, and I actually choke on air.

'Sorry? What?'

'You know, elves have magical abilities. With not knowing you're a creature, chances are no one has helped you discover your unique talents. It doesn't matter, though, because the one thing all elves can do is glamour humans.'

Is he mad? 'You think I can persuade someone to do something against their will?'

'Well, yes. You can't tell me you haven't done it before.'

I turn to face him. He is serious about this. 'Of course I have changed people's minds before, but I did it by persuading them, and eventually they come round to my way of thinking.' Why is he making such a big thing out of this?

His head tilts to the side as he asks, 'And how often does this happen? I mean, do you win most "arguments"?'

He actually air quotes the word argument with his fingers. Really, who does that anymore?

'On average, I win more than I lose, but I am good at building a convincing case,' I tell him.

'Okay, when is the last time you lost an argument against anyone but your parents when it was something you honestly wanted?'

'Just last....' I trail off. I actually can't recall the last time I was not able to persuade someone to do something I believed was right, something I was passionate about. 'You mean, I'm not great at turning people round to my way of thinking?'

My world is starting to shift again as another thing I was so sure about myself turns out to be a lie.

As if sensing my unease, Snake rubs my arm. 'You probably are good at it. I also imagine that when you are passionate about something, you can push a little persuasion behind your words. Maybe you never actually glamoured anyone as such....'

'Oh.' I'm relieved but also somewhat disappointed. I really thought I could use magic. 'If I haven't done it before, how will I be able to do it now?'

Snake frowns and runs his hands through his hair. 'I was taught to use my magic, so I can show you. I am not sure whether it will be the same for you, but it's worth a try.'

I am distracted for a moment by how cute he looks with his hair all messed up. *Focus*.

'When you want to win an argument, do you do anything differently to when you don't care?'

I chew my lip. *Do* I do anything differently? Mum once told me when she was helping me with debate prep that it's important to look a person directly in the eye when you are trying to convince them of something they might be opposed to. My hands tremble a little as I remember her words, and a wave of loneliness washes through me.

I clasp my hands together as I try to concentrate on what she actually said. Ah, that's right—she gave me some speech about people being able to tell if you are genuine or not, and Dad had teased her about being too intense. Now, looking at things in a different light, I wonder if maybe Mum was surreptitiously teaching me to glamour.

'I have an idea,' I tell Snake.

'No harm in trying, if you're game?'

I grin, excitement over the possibility of being able to do magic warring with my fear that this might all not be quite real. 'Sure, why not. Hold on.' My conversation with the Witch of Wimbledon comes back to me. 'I thought we were not allowed to use our magic for personal gain.'

Snake shakes his head. 'Personal gain would be getting the room for free, not talking them into giving us the rooms in the first place. Or, if there was a legal reason for us not to stay, then it would be wrong to persuade them otherwise.'

Nodding to show that I understand the distinction, I force my weary limbs to move along the road towards the pub. It was a typical whitewashed Ye Olde English building, with a B&B sign out the front. As we walk, I notice Snake looking around, checking alleys and scanning the rooftops.

'Is everything okay?' I ask.

'Yes.... Um... I'm not sure. I thought I felt someone

watching us,' he says as he leans round me and pushes open the door. 'But I must have been imagining things.'

Although I am old enough to legally drink, my social life has been limited to cafes and clubs. This is my first ever time in an actual pub, and I am not impressed. The fusty smell of stale beer wafts over me as I enter, overpowering the supposed homeliness of the bright patterned carpet and the heavy wooden furniture. My overall impression is of walking back into a bad eighties sitcom.

It is still early, but two of the tables are occupied by couples, and three men sit at stools in front of the bar, half-drunk pints of ale in front of them. Everyone turns as we walk in. A barman appears from nowhere and starts to ask, 'What can I get.... Sorry, guys, I will have to see some ID before I can serve you.'

Fumbling in my backpack for my driver's license, I offer it to the barman. Snake, one step behind me, does the same. Having checked our ages, the bartender continues, 'Now, what will it be?'

'Actually,' I say, 'we would like a couple of rooms for the night.'

The man freezes. 'You must be twenty-one to book a room.' His tone is terse and dismissive.

'Is that a legal requirement?' I ask.

'House rules,' he says, refilling the pint of the man sitting closest to him.

'Why?' I press.

'Just the way it is, missy.'

'We can pay in advance, if you're worried we will skip out. And you can keep my credit card number and charge any damage we do to the rooms.'

He concentrates on wiping the bar, making it difficult for me to catch his eye. 'Everyone pays in advance. And you don't look like the room-trashing types.'

'We're not,' I agree, perplexed as to why he won't let us stay if we're so respectable. 'We can vote, join the army and fight for our country, and you would serve us at the bar, but you won't let us sleep here?'

Sighing, he raises his head, and I use the opportunity to capture his gaze. 'I can't be responsible for you,' he says, a tinge of sadness in his voice. 'I am the only one here most nights, and I don't have time to check up on children.'

'We are more than capable of looking after ourselves,' I say, but I get the impression there is more to this. 'What is it you are really worried about?' I ask.

Nothing,' he mumbles.

'Tell me,' I say, willing him to speak with all my strength. I feel a little foolish, staring intently at him and trying to push my will through my eyes.

I'm about to break away when he says, 'What if something happens during the night, a fire or the like? I might not be able to save you.'

What an odd thing to say. I search his face and find a real fear in his eyes. 'Has that happened before?'

He nods. 'A young lad stayed here once, and there was a gas leak. The boy almost didn't make it.'

Still holding the man's gaze, I place my hand on his. 'It's all right. We can look after ourselves just as well as any adult staying here. We can get ourselves out if there is a fire, or if something else happens.'

He pulls against my hand as if he wants to wrench away, but I refuse to let him. Throwing all my weight behind the words, I say, 'If you rent rooms to us, everything will be all right, I promise.'

Neither of us moves. It's as if we are frozen in time. I am about to break away, feeling foolish at having even tried this, when the barman relaxes.

'Yes, you're right. Everything will most probably be fine if you stay tonight.'

I bite back a smile and ready myself for one last push. 'So, you will allow us to stay.'

The room is silent and the air around me seems electric as the barman nods slowly. 'Of course. You had best come through.'

It worked. It actually worked! I want to dance and sing as we follow the barman through the door into the hallway, but I contain myself, aware every eye in the bar is on us.

As we pass by the public toilets and a door with a sign saying, "Office", I wonder if the real power of the elves is not to confuse or befuddle people into agreeing with them, but in finding the real reason for their resistance and offering a way out.

I suddenly realise that the barman is speaking to me. 'Sorry, what?' I look around in confusion.

Snake is leaning against a counter, signing his name in a register. 'He said he has given us the two rooms at the end of the corridor, closest to the shared bathroom. Breakfast starts at six, and there is room in the bistro if we want to eat here tonight,' he says as he reaches out a hand for the keys.

'You'll need to sign in.' The barman pushes the register towards me. I add my details below Snake's and hand over my credit card.

'Tap all right?' he asks, and I nod, still a little distracted, trying to work out how my glamour worked.

'Right, top of the stairs and keep going. Bistro is already open if you want to eat.' He slips back through to the bar and asks, 'Who's next?'

The rooms continue the theme of bad eighties decor, but they are clean, when I sit on it, the bed is comfortable. My weary body wants to lay down and sleep, but Snake is already in the doorway.

'Shall we eat?'

I want to tell him all I need is a bath and bed, but he's right, we should put food in our stomachs. Tomorrow will be another long day of walking, and we need to make sure we fuel up.

After eating a surprisingly good meal downstairs of home-made pumpkin soup and fresh bread, I wait while Snake finishes off his steak, eggs, and chips. We head back upstairs, and he offers me first use of the bathroom. I don't argue.

I'm disappointed that there is no bath to stretch out in, but the shower is hot and strong, and as the water washes over me, my aching muscles begin to relax.

After standing in the steam, my hair's turned into a frizzy mess of corkscrew curls. I don't have the energy to deal with it, so I comb through some leave-in conditioner and bundle it into a loose ponytail before slipping into my favourite over-sized Minnie Mouse T-shirt and some cotton sleeping shorts. On the way back to my room, I knock on Snake's door.

'Bathroom's free.'

He mutters something, and I take that as thanks and head back to my room.

Knowing I should not sleep so close to eating, I put my phone and earbuds on to charge and grab my laptop from the bag. The B&B has Wi-Fi, but my laptop is set up to use my phone data, and I don't like the thought of using a public connection.

I bring up a web browser and begin researching the Underground Ballroom, looking for anything that might link it to the magical world. Dad's book didn't mention it, and I want to confirm whether or not Snake is right about it being where The Court will meet.

The first page I open tells me it was built by Victorian industrialist Whitaker Wright on his estate in Surrey. It was once impressive but fell into disrepair after his death.

'He was a dwarf, still is in fact, but he moved back underground. He couldn't take the shame of being forced to lose his fortune; he was drawing too much attention to himself, and The Court decided he should disappear.'

How on earth had Snake opened the door and made it to my bed without my noticing? I had been engrossed in what I was reading, but still.... And I wish he would put some clothes on.

Snake is standing right beside my bed, a none-too-large towel wrapped round his waist. He is all lean muscle, and *omg, get a grip, girl*.

He pulls a T-shirt over his head, and I manage to force my eyes away from the muscles rippling across his stomach and back to the screen. 'A dwarf?' I choke the words out.

'Yep, they are attracted to gold and precious metals. They often became captains of industry in the nineteenth and twentieth centuries. Nowadays, they're mostly merchant bankers, although some of their kind will do almost anything for money, not all of it strictly legal.'

The heat from his body is making it difficult to concentrate. 'You said he had to give up his fortune?'

'Yep. It wasn't the personal gain thing because he used to give a lot away to charity, but he was getting too well-known. Humans think he committed suicide, but he moved back below. Rumour has it, he's a bit of a recluse.'

'So, why don't people, humans, use the ballroom now?' I ask. Snake leans over to get a better look at the screen. As his arm brushes against mine, tingles shoot all over my body and heat rises up my neck. It is all I can do to bring up the next page.

'The ballroom was built on what was once a door between the two worlds. I guess technically it still is, although it's closed most of the time. Whit asked the Queen to place a glamour on it so no one would demolish it or use what he believed was his crowning glory.'

An awkward silence follows his announcement as the tension in the room almost overwhelms me. I'm about to ask why he is here when he clears his throat and says, 'Just popped in to suggest we head down for breakfast at six. I'm not a morning person, so I need to set an alarm if you want an early start.'

I glance up, and there is a twinkle in his eyes, as if he is aware of how his presence is affecting me.

'Six will be fine,' I say, turning back to my screen. 'Sleep well.'

Then he is gone. An hour or so later, my hormones have settled down enough for me to feel drowsy, if a little lonely.

CHAPTER 7

Goblins of Wistman's Wood

The sound of "Love Music, Pt.2" by Ren blasts in my ear through the pillow. I grab for the phone. I struggle to find it, and my fingers fumble as I try to turn off the alarm before it wakes the entire village. Love the song, but it's a bit full-on for first thing in the morning—I guess that's why it works so well as an alarm.

I force my legs from under the warm covers. My body is heavy and still half asleep. I could do with another couple of hours kip, especially because I couldn't sleep last night.

I would love to say my restlessness was due to worry about Mum, but it was nothing that altruistic. No, my mind kept replaying the scene in Pris's bedroom, and try as I might, I couldn't help but wonder what would have happened if I had kissed her like I wanted to when I leaned over to read what was on her laptop.

She looked so cute with her hair all messed and wearing that Mickey Mouse tee.... I almost forgot why I was in her room. I had to force myself to leave before the effect she was having on me became obvious.

Any other girl, and I might have made a move. Not that

I'm any sort of ladies' man, but I do all right. And it's not that I don't like Pris—I do. And there is definitely a physical attraction—very definitely. But she is beyond my reach, both in this world and the other. Especially the other. The powers that be will never allow such a match between the races.

I sigh and dress in the clothes I laid out last night. Before I leave my room, I make sure everything is in my pack, ready to go. I turn from locking the door and almost bowl Pris over.

I suppress a smile. The only thing country walk about her is her shoes. Her denim jacket is lined with a purple-and-black-checked fleece that matches her purple jeans and black D&G t-shirt. Her hair is tucked under a slouchy black beanie.

'Love the hat,' I say to cover my chuckle.

'You know, people have no idea how difficult this type of hair is,' she grumbles as she leads the way down the hall. 'Taming it will take time—time we need for walking.'

'Hey, I loved the look last night, so don't hide it on my account.' The words tumble out before I can stop them.

She half turns to check I'm not taking the mick, then her lips curl into a smile. I follow her downstairs. At the counter, she pulls a pamphlet from the display box as we pass. I catch a quick glimpse of the title: *The Lych Way*.

'We might need this,' she says as she leads us through the bar to the bistro on the other side. The smell of breakfast has my mouth watering.

The only other occupant of the dining room is an elderly lady. She looks familiar, and I realise she was the woman we spoke to on the walk yesterday. And is that a cat under her table? The animal shifts into the shadows as a harried middle-aged woman bustles through the kitchen doors.

'Full English for you two?' she asks.

I nod enthusiastically, and Pris says, 'Yes, please.'

After placing a full plate in front of the other guest, the woman bustles back into the kitchen, and we take a seat.

'Good morning,' our breakfast companion says as she reaches for the pepper shaker. 'Nice day for a walk.'

'Yes,' I respond as Pris opens the pamphlet so we can both study the map.

'According to my book, the Lych Way is also called the Way of the Dead,' Pris says as a pot of tea and two mugs are plonked on the table between us.

'Nice,' I say reaching to pour.

'So, this map confirms what I thought. It's about five hours to Two Bridges, and the route passes through Wistman's Wood. Then it's about another hour and a half from Two Bridges to Postbridge, where we need to catch the bus to Yelverton at 2:30.'

My muscles groan at the thought of another walk today, especially such a punishing one, but I ignore them.

'Is the bus from Yelverton to Plymouth the only option that keeps us on track?' I ask, sipping my tea.

'No, probably not, but time spent replanning is time lost for our walk, and if we are to walk to Two Bridges today...,' Pris says, leaving me to make the connection.

I take her word for it. She is very organised, and I'm sure she has plotted the optimal route.

'I am sorry, but I could not help but overhear.' I start at the voice so close by and turn to find the woman at the next table leaning towards us.

'I am driving over to visit a cousin in Postbridge after lunch and would be happy to swing by Two Bridges to pick you up. Do you think you could be at the end of the walk by about one thirty?'

I am taken aback by the offer. 'That is very kind of you—'

'Hope you don't mind cats, as mine will be with me, but there should be plenty of room for you and your gear for a short trip.'

'It would help us out...,' Pris says, turning a questioning

gaze to me. 'And I for one would appreciate not having to walk the extra miles.'

I am still reluctant to say yes. Growing up in the world of creatures, where nothing is ever given for free, tends to make you suspicious of kindness.

As if sensing my reluctance, the woman says, 'You are right to be suspicious of strangers, young man, but I assure you my offer is genuine, and I am not an axe murderer or anything. Just ask Mable here.'

I turn to find myself face-to-face with a plate piled high with bacon, sausages, mushrooms, tomatoes, and scrambled eggs, topped with a slice of fried bread. My stomach grumbles in appreciation as I take the food and settle it in front of me.

'Ask me what?' Mable asks as she puts Pris's plate down.

'Whether or not I am trustworthy.'

Mable laughs. 'Mrs Wilson has been a regular here for as long as I can remember. She is as honest as they come, even if she does insist on sneaking the odd animal into the dining room.'

'See,' Pris says around an enormous mouthful of mushrooms. 'We can trust her.'

I can't stand the pleading in her eyes. Besides, it would be nice to not have to walk the extra miles.

'Can we pay you for petrol, perhaps?' I offer, still not completely comfortable with accepting help.

'Nonsense, young man. My offer is made without obligation.'

The words she speaks are the formal release from a potential bond, and I start, knocking my teacup. Is this woman more than she appears to be? Is she from my world? Mrs Wilson seems ignorant of my scrutiny as she slips some sausage under the table to her cat. Pris kicks my shin and I jostle the table.

Realising I had better answer before anything else happens

to breakfast, I say, 'All right. Thank you, we would be grateful for a lift. I am Snake, by the way, and this is Pris.'

'I am pleased to meet you both and happy you accepted my offer.' Mrs Wilson stands. 'Well, I have things to do this morning. I will see you at the Two Bridges entrance to the Lych Way around one-thirty.'

'We will be there, and thank you again, Mrs Wilson,' Pris says.

I say nothing as the woman leaves, cat close at her heels. Something about both the cat and the woman niggle at me, but I can't place what it is.

'Are you going to eat your mushrooms?' Pris asks, bringing me back to reality.

'Yes, I am,' I say as I fork a mushroom, shoving it straight into my mouth. 'Delicious.' She rolls her eyes at me, and I smile, digging into my meal.

Talk is limited as we stock up on fuel for the walk ahead. I leave Pris to settle the bill and buy some bottled water and nuts for our trek as I head upstairs to retrieve our packs.

At just after seven, we arrive at the Lychford green and find the start of the Lych Way. As we follow the meandering path, I fully appreciate why it is known as the Way of the Dead. In spite of the warm early spring morning, the air is heavy with morning mist stifling any noise and creating a sombre tone. Pris says the name comes from times past when locals took this route to bury their dead, but I wonder if there is more to the name.

Still, it is a beautiful walk over the moor, and I wonder why Mum and I never came here. She has always been friends with the witches above ground, and a few gnome kin live down this way. Maybe when she is back, we can spend some more time out of London.

The thought is bittersweet and brings with it a nagging doubt about my ability to rescue her from a court I have never attended. I try not to wonder if cutting myself off from my father's family might play against me now. Instead, I concentrate on putting one foot in front of the other—and on getting the next endorsement.

·· *· 🌙 ·*· ··

Trees form misty shadows in the distance as morning dew paints the grass intense shades of greens and browns and reds. The picture is framed by slate grey fences. It is difficult not to be distracted by the beauty of the moor.

Every muscle groans. After yesterday's efforts I suspect they were wanting a rest. The pack on my back is way too heavy, but even as my body protests, I find myself enjoying the experience of walking in the fresh morning air.

When we stop for a drink break, I take off my jacket and tie it around my waist before pulling my pack back into place. By the second stop, I am so hot, I take off my beanie. I grimace as I tidy my hair into a loose braid in an attempt to tame its wildness.

Snake has been silent the entire time and, unusually for me, I don't feel much like talking either. It's almost as though being somewhere less frantic is allowing my brain to slow down and relax, to appreciate the silence rather than feeling a need to fill it.

Three hours into the walk, I check the map. We will soon be at Wistman's Wood, the goblin stronghold. At the very thought of the place, any sense of peace vanishes. I am all too aware that I don't know what to expect and, even worse, I have no idea how to behave. I have spent my life learning what is expected of me in every possible social situation, so this realisation is mortifying.

'What are goblins like?' I ask, breaking the silence. 'I mean, I always imagine them a little like Dobby from *Harry Potter*.'

Snake barks out a laugh. 'You'd best keep that thought to yourself when you meet them.'

'So, what *are* they like? And why is their stronghold so close to the witches'?'

I hate not knowing this stuff, and I really hate relying on Snake so much. But I do want to rescue my parents, and I can't do that if I don't learn more about the creatures we will be meeting.

'Human storybooks got some things right about goblins. They are fast and mischievous. Mostly, though, they are game players. Like gnomes, they are not as well thought of as elves and witches. Even though they aren't a lesser race, they often feel the need to ally themselves with the powerful,' Snake says.

The snarky tone of his voice tells me he doesn't like goblins very much. Which is interesting because he would rather go and ask for a token from them than his own people. I file that away to consider later while wondering what had happened that was so bad, he wouldn't ask his own race for help.

'Actually,' Snake continues, 'we can use that to our advantage. They like flattery, although not obvious flattery. In this instance, because of who you are, you should speak with them.'

I frown, trying to catch up. 'Because I am an elf and you are a gnome?'

'Exactly. And because your family is from the royal bloodline.'

'Does it really matter that much?' I ask.

He stops in the middle of the path and his eyes pin me in place. 'Ever been somewhere in the human world where people speak to your friends but not to you? Where they won't even meet your eyes?'

I'm about to tell him not to be ridiculous, people don't behave like that in civilised society. But I bite my tongue. He is right, much as I hate to admit it. There are enough people who judge me not worthy simply because of the colour of my skin that I know what it feels like. Dad says things are better than when he was a kid, but that doesn't mean racism has disappeared. It's more that most people hide it better.

'And in the World Below, you are treated like that?'

Snake nods. 'Pretty much. Not by the lesser creatures so much, but by the others. And to be fair, most goblins are treated that way too. The only difference is, they are always playing power games, trying to trade into better positions. That earns them respect from some, fear from others, and vilification from most.'

'That's so sad.' I'm liking the World Below less and less. From my current perspective, it makes medieval times sound progressive. Perhaps Mum and Dad had good reasons for keeping me away.

'Is positioning their stronghold close to the witches' a sign of a political alliance? Is that why you think coming here is a good idea?'

'You're catching on.' He turns and starts walking. 'Come on. I think that's Wistman's Wood over there.' He points to the edge of a copse of trees.

My muscles twinge and complain as I force myself to move. I keep fit with karate and tennis, but this walking lark is a whole new ball game. It takes about another half an hour for us to reach our destination.

As we move under the shelter of the trees, I am taken aback by how dark and weird and twisted and tortured they look. I mean, these are right out of every creepy forest in every horror movie, and I can almost hear their cries of pain as we brush past them. The air is cool, and at the same time, oppressive.

Goosebumps prick my skin as I ask, 'Do we need to go right in?' I'm hoping the answer is no.

'A little further, I think,' Snake says.

I try to suppress a shudder. 'How do you know when we're at the right place?'

He takes a few more steps under the trees, stops, shuts his eyes, then slips his backpack from his shoulders.

'Close your eyes,' he tells me.

My natural instinct is to snap at him to stop ordering me around, but I do as he says, trusting he has a good reason for being so bossy.

'What are your senses telling you?'

I peek through a single eye, thinking he can't be serious. His face shows no sign that this is a joke, so I squeeze my eyes shut and describe everything I am sensing. 'I smell damp earth. It is cool here. A breeze is blowing hair across my face. The rustle of leaves sounds so loud.'

'Good. Now hold on to those feelings, listen to the trees, and block everything else from your mind.'

This sounds very new agey, and I cringe as I do as he says. Moments later, the noise in the clearing changes. The rustling is louder, and the air feels almost as though it is charged with something. The ring on the middle finger of my left hand starts to warm up, and the sensation pushes everything else out of my mind.

'Ouch!'

'What is it?'

The worry on Snake's face is the first thing I see as my eyes fly open. I glance down at my ring, then look up. 'It was...'

'Warm?' he asks, an excited smile forming on his lips.

'Ah, yes. How did you know?'

He reaches up to the neck of his T-shirt and pulls out a medallion on a leather thong. 'We are all given a token when we're young. It's a tool to help us learn to use magic. When your body senses or draws magic, it will warm up to show you're doing it right.'

I stare at the ring. I felt magic? For a moment, I'm not sure how I feel about that. Actually, that's not quite right. My head is not sure, but my body is singing.

'Here is okay then?' I say, dumping my pack beside his and turning away to cover my confusion.

Snake steps up beside me, his green eyes dark with concern as he flicks his fringe out of the way. 'Here should do fine.'

I take a deep, shuddering breath, surprised to find I'm more nervous than I was when sitting my exams. *You can do this,* I tell myself as I turn to face Snake.

'What do I do? Do I just call the goblin like you called the White Witch?' I try to ignore the tingle of magic I now sense all around me and focus on the task at hand.

'You will need to use magic to contact him. Are you okay with that?' he asks, unable to keep the worry from his voice. I glance away, not wanting to see it written on his face.

'I am fine with it,' I say, my voice flat and even— controlled. My stomach, on the other hand, is churning like a washing machine on spin cycle.

'If you're sure....'

His tone telegraphs his doubt, and this ignites my anger. Good. Anger is better than a fear of failure.

'What is his name?' My voice is harsher than I mean it to be.

'Grossman Green.'

Laughter bubbles its way up from the pit of my belly and rushes out. Once it escapes, I can't stop it.

'Please, don't say anything,' Snake says. 'He may be listening to us.' There is laughter in his voice as well, but he is doing a better job at holding it in than I am.

It takes a while, but finally, I am able to calm down. I close my eyes like Snake had me do before and reach out, letting the magic tingle over my skin. The ring on my finger warms up, and I start to call for the goblin, but then break down again.

I'm laughing so much, I can't stand. Dropping onto the log behind me, I draw in some deep breaths. I don't know why I find the name so hilarious—I just do.

'Are you going to be able to do this?' Snake asks. 'I mean, without cracking up?'

His face is so stern, laughter bubbles out again. I look away and nod, unable to speak.

'Sometime today?'

My shoulders shake. Then I can hold it in no longer. It feels good to laugh, and it is like all that tension that's been building over the last couple of days drains out of me. Wiping the tears from my eyes, I turn to Snake. 'Yes, today.'

He raises a single eyebrow, but the twinkle in his eye shows me he also appreciated the joke.

I gulp in some air. Giggle. Then take a few more calming breaths. I remind myself of what is at stake, and the urge to laugh disappears.

'I'm ready now,' I tell Snake as I close my eyes and allow the magic to flow through me again. 'I, Priscilla Crown, request an audience with Grossman Green.'

I slowly release my magic and open my eyes, prepared to wait, only to find a suited man standing beside Snake looking very out of place in the woods. Something in my face must have alerted my companion to the other man's presence, as he turns, stumbles over a root and face plants.

The suited man sneers at Snake, as if his actions are to be expected from one such as him. Looking down his nose, he turns to me and performs a sketchy bow. 'Princess Priscilla, I am here at your request.'

Without the supercilious twist of his lips, Grossman Green would be a moderately handsome man in his late thirties, perhaps early forties. He is dressed in a smart pinstripe suit that could be found in offices all over London but is completely out of place in the middle of a forest.

I watch Snake haul himself off the ground and move to stand behind me. Dusting leaves and forest debris from his clothes, he takes a position behind my right shoulder. The waves of distaste swirling around him are every bit as real as the magic in the air.

'Mr Green.' Too formal? The way Grossman stands a little straighter tells me I hit just the right note. 'I would like for myself and my bodyguard to attend The Court Below this week, and I was hoping you would do me the honour of endorsing us so we may do so.'

My eyes widen a little. Is he actually preening? Could it be this easy?

He clears his throat and says, 'I must respectfully decline.'

I do a double take. 'I am sorry. You decline? You are refusing me, a member of the royal line?' I try to sound as haughty as possible, which is actually quite haughty, but it has no effect.

'With respect, you may be a princess, and of royal blood, even, but there is nothing you can give me that would persuade me to endorse you. Not even your pet witch's familiar could do that.'

Pet witch? Familiar? What is he talking about?

'I came out of courtesy when you called, but now I must go. I was in the middle of a merger meeting.'

Before I can utter a word, Grossman Green blinks out of existence. I turn to find Snake with his jaw hanging open, as confused as me.

I had just walked almost five hours to spend less than five minutes with a goblin who never had any intention of helping us. Confusion is quickly replaced with anger, and my fingers curl into fists.

'What just happened here?' I ask.

Snake shakes his head, as if he can't believe what he has seen either.

'I'm not sure. The Greens always ally with the witches, who are second only to elves in the creature hierarchy. For him to have turned your request down can only mean one thing—a powerful elf got to him first.'

I frown, trying to work out what elf might want to stop me from going to the World Below. 'You mean, someone like Giles Regis?'

Snake's laugh is tinged with bitterness. 'No, someone way more powerful than him.'

'But he called me a princess. I am of the royal line. Who is more powerful than that?'

'Exactly.' Snake moves to pass me, running his hands through his hair. 'I am starting to wonder if there actually is more going on here than our parents being taken before The Court to answer mundane charges.' He pauses. 'This isn't right. Something else is going on here, Pris.'

Snake is clearly upset, and with my lack of knowledge of the creature world, I have no idea what would rattle him this much. 'Like what?'

Snake's jaw tenses. 'I don't know. Come on. If we want to catch that lift, we had better get a wriggle on.'

I don't move. Is he really going to drop a bomb like that and then leave? He turns away from me, and I realise that is exactly what he is going to do. No way am I going to let that happen.

I move to follow him and trip, grabbing hold of a tree to stop myself from falling. What the...? I stare down at my feet —well, down at the vines covering my feet and winding up my ankles.

Anger is replaced by confusion. 'Snake? What's happening?'

I look over to find my friend struggling with his own problems. The tree behind him has reached out and wrapped its limbs around Snake, who is frantically wrestling, trying to get free.

'Green. GREEN. Get back here,' Snake growls as the branches grip him more tightly.

Nothing happens other than the forest pulling us in further to its clutches.

'Mr Green, please,' I beg.

The goblin appears, his face a mask of concern, but the hard look in his eyes tells me he knew this would happen.

'Oh dear. I do apologise. This is Wistman's Wood, and I thought you knew that no one leaves without sacrificing something.' He smirks. 'Oh, I see you didn't know. How remiss of you not to do your research. The forest needs something of yours—any trinket will do.'

I smile sweetly at him, and my voice is sugary as I say, 'I have nothing on me, and we are unable to get to our packs.'

'I guess I could pay the price for you, but that would mean each of you will owe me a favour.'

Grossman Green's smile is oily, and my stomach heaves in revulsion at the thought of owing this creature anything. I want to howl in frustration, but I am aware the vines have reached my thighs and Snake is turning a strange shade of grey. He wants to negotiate. All right, I can do that.

My minds starts ticking over what I can offer him in the real world, Nothing, I suspect, because whoever is pulling his strings is likely in the World Below.

'Time is ticking,' he reminds me.

I don't know much about the creature world, but Giles Regis's reaction to my threat gives me an idea; I may have something he wants or might need.

'Here is my proposal. If we get to the World Below, and the plot against our parents fails, I will put in a good word with the Queen for you—tell her how you helped me out of a bind.'

Grossman Green smiles, and I think I have misjudged the situation. Then, as the grin widens, I start to wonder if I have offered him more than he could have imagined.

He reaches into his pocket, takes out a couple of pound coins, and tosses them in the air. 'Deal,' he says before they land, and disappears.

Snake falls to the ground as the trees release him, and it takes a moment for him to start breathing normally. The vines slowly leave my body, taking their time, almost caressing me as if they are reluctant to let me go.

I shudder as I am finally freed, then rush to Snake and help him to his feet. As he brushes himself off, I say, 'I feel like I gave away the house when he only wanted a room.'

He shakes his head. 'No, the bargain was fair, though it was more than the sneaky bastard deserved.' He picks up his pack, slings it over his shoulder, and adds, 'Come on. We were already late for our lift before this.'

He strides off, not even waiting to see if I'm following. I grab my pack and take a more sedate pace, wondering if he is annoyed at me or at Grossman.

I am well out of the oppressive air of the woods when I realise what Snake probably already had the moment Green turned us down—we're one step closer to needing to visit the gnomes if we want to attend court.

CHAPTER 8

What Now?

Putting one foot in front of the other, I ignore my bruised ribs and the pain stabbing my chest each time I draw a breath. I can't believe how that smug prat played us. It wasn't enough to turn us down; he had to profit from our visit as well.

Targeting my anger at Green allows me to hide from the one thing I don't want to think about. If I allow my mind to go there I might fall apart, and I can't do that.... Not yet anyway.

With each step I take, my heartbeat slows, and my anger slowly drains away until I can think clearly again. I mull over our options and realise that the goblin's refusal to help doesn't necessarily mean we will end up in Mawnan. I'm sure there's time to go to Bodmin and then up to Conway to the fairies.

As I begin to relax and breathe normally, something slowly dawns on me. Only a highborn elf would have enough pull to lure the goblins away from the witches. So, why is a high elf trying to prevent us from rescuing our parents from the World Below?

Gathering endorsements will be difficult enough without

someone actively working against us. Do we even still have a chance?

Our next visit is to the sprites. Would they give in to a high elf's request to refuse us? They are mercurial creatures, so it is difficult to predict their reaction.

Gnomes will never side with elves against me, a voice inside my head whispers. I shut it out. I'm not ready to go there yet.

The fairies in Conway also have no allegiance to any particular higher race, and.... It hits me like a sledgehammer. I swing round to find Pris is a long way behind me, and my face colours in shame. We are supposed to be in this together, and I took off without her. I stop and wait for her to catch me up.

When she finally joins me, I know I should apologise for my bad manners, but I can't find the words. Instead, I say, 'Pris, did you take our itinerary to bed with you the night before last, or did you leave it in the dining room?'

For a moment, I think she is so annoyed with me she isn't going to answer, but then her eyes widen. 'You're wondering how whoever is working against us knew to apply pressure to the goblins. Do you think they broke into my home?'

'Yes, I do. And maybe my thinking someone has been watching us isn't too far off the mark.'

Pris twists the ring on her finger as she says, 'This is not good.'

'No, it isn't,' I agree. 'I am now wondering if continuing with our current plan is such a great idea.'

Her shoulders drop, and I see how weary she is. 'Sorry. I'm so tired I can't think straight. Let's just make it to the train station in Plymouth. We'll have time to talk then.'

She's right. We're in the middle of nowhere. Once we are at a train station, we will have options. I nod. 'Okay.'

This time when I start off, I make sure I am walking at a pace Pris can manage. I am still in no mood to talk, and I get the impression Pris is none too happy with me, because she is unusually silent. The air around us is so tense that I am somewhat relieved when we arrive at Two Bridges to find a car waiting for us.

'I am pleased you made good time,' Mrs Wilson says as she opens the boot for our packs. Pris's fits inside, but she tells me to squish mine into the back seat.

I stick my head inside and find Mrs Wilson's black cat stretched out on a rug, taking up half the space. He looks up laconically and makes no attempt to move. Sighing, I wonder how much worse this day can get.

As I push my pack into the well behind the driver's seat, the cat narrows his eyes. I try to ignore him and concentrate on bending my frame into the small hatchback, folding my legs into the least uncomfortable position before I do up the seatbelt.

'Right, are we all in? Goodness, this is a bit of a squish. Fortunately, Portsbridge is only about twenty minutes away. Was your walk productive?'

What an odd way to phrase that question, I think as Pris starts chatting away. I pull out my phone and start doing some checking. We can definitely make it up to Conway and back to Godalming and still fit in Bodmin. The only problem is, if the sprites decide not to help us, we will have to go to the gnomes in Mawnan. I put my phone back in my pocket as the car slows down.

'The bus to Plymouth goes from just over there,' Mrs Wilson is saying. 'And if you need something to eat, the cafe inside does amazing toasted sandwiches. And a pretty good coffee, too, as I remember.'

'Thank you so much, Mrs Wilson. You are a godsend. I am not sure I could have walked all that way to here,' Pris gushes.

I mumble my thanks and earn a frown from my travelling companion. I hide my embarrassment by hauling my pack out over the seat, taking care not to disturb the cat. He glowers at me anyway.

'Thank you for the lift, Mrs Wilson. It was a really nice thing for you to do,' I say, pulling my pack over my shoulder. After all, she was being kind, and it's not her fault my day has turned to crap.

'You are most welcome, young man. Oh, look, that is your bus heading this way. You had best hurry, or you will miss it. Happy travels.' Mrs Wilson slips back into the car, and I shut the door as she pulls back into traffic.

'I'll sort our tickets if you can buy us a couple of toasted sandwiches and coffees,' Pris orders as we cross at the lights.

We manage to make it to the National Express terminal just as the bus pulls in. Pris does not wait for me to agree. She heads straight for the ticket office without even telling me how she takes her coffee.

Mercifully, the line is so short, I barely have time to scan the menu before a cheery voice asks what I will have. I freeze.

'Two ham-and-cheese toasties, please. And two cappuccinos.'

'Any sugar with those?' the girl asks as I hand over my card.

'Um, no, thanks,' I respond, hoping Pris takes her coffee the same way she takes her tea.

I arrive beside the bus in time to load my pack underneath before slipping into the aisle seat beside Pris. She takes her meal without saying a word. I guess she's still not happy with me.

The bus eases into traffic, and I place my food and drink on the pull-down table and grab my earbuds. Staring at the screen of my phone, I flick through my playlists until I find Mum's. I feel less alone listening to some of her favourite songs while I eat.

Tears form in my eyes as Stevie Nicks sings the lyrics to "Dreams", and I remember Mum singing along to it as she cooked dinner just a few days ago. My appetite is gone, and I wrap the remains of my sandwich back into the bag before grabbing our rubbish and heading down the aisle to place it in the bin.

By the time I return, the song has changed, but I am still wrapped in sadness. I close my eyes, shut out the world, and pretend to sleep for the rest of the trip.

When the bus pulls into Plymouth train station almost an hour later, my mood has not lightened. I am pulled between wanting to rescue my mother and not wanting to ask my family for help.

My body protests as I stand and make my way off the bus. It protests even more as I grab our packs from underneath as Pris goes to buy our train tickets. She is so quiet as we walk to the platform, my guilt gets the better of me. I mean, I was a little, well, childish, taking off before, and I have been Mr Grumpy ever since.

'I am sorry I walked away from you at the woods,' I offer as I lean our packs up against the edge of a bench on the platform.

Her blue eyes search my face, as if looking for something. I turn away and stare at the opposite platform.

'Are you ready to talk about why?' she asks.

My stomach clenches and I shake my head. 'No. I'm still processing.'

'That's what I figured.'

I slump onto the seat.

'Do you want a tea or something?' she asks.

'Another coffee would be great.' I fumble in my pack and pass her my clean mug for life.

Just like that, things are back to normal between us. We still sip our drinks in silence, but it is more companionable this time. I stand and stretch out my back before taking our mugs to the drinking fountain to rinse them out.

As I amble back to our seats, I catch a movement from the corner of my eye, and all of a sudden, I am running, but I am too late. A woman in a black hoodie, jeans, and Doc Martens is already striking at Pris, her wicked-looking hunting knife glinting in the evening sun.

Pris moves so fast, my brain takes a while to process what is going on. The result is clear though. The knife clatters to the ground, and Pris kicks it off the platform and then turns on the woman, who jumps to her feet and takes off through a startled crowd.

The woman turns as she reaches the stairs, says something and waves her hand, and immediately, it is like she was never there. People stop staring at her and Pris and return to what they were doing. I reach Pris seconds later.

'What was that?' I ask. Then think to add, 'Are you all right?'

'I'm fine. I guess muggers venture out of London as well.' She shrugs.

I search her face for any sign she is hiding her real feelings, but she actually appears to think this sort of attack is normal. First the mugging in Wimbledon, now this, and she is not even a little concerned. I sit and put our mugs back in my pack.

'Pris, how often does this sort of thing happen to you?' I ask.

'I don't know, about once or twice a month, depending on how often I am out alone.' She carries on flicking through her phone.

'And why do you think that woman chose you to attack out of all the people here?' I gesture to the busy platform.

She shrugs again. 'Perhaps because I look like I have money, or I guess I am just unlucky....'

As her voice trails off, I can see her mind working as she slowly looks around at the busy platform. When it hits her, her eyes widen in surprise. 'Do you think that had something to do with us and all... well, this?'

'Maybe.... Or—'

She tilts her head to the side and studies me. 'Dad always calls me unlucky, says I'm in the wrong place at the wrong time. But you don't think these attacks are random, do you?'

I shake my head.

'You think this is something to do with your... our world?'

What should I tell her? I have no idea why she would be a target, but whoever just attacked her was definitely a creature. Only a creature with magic could cast a forgetting spell on humans.

She drops her head into her hands, and I can almost hear the cogs of her mind working. When she raises it, her eyes are clear and her voice decisive. 'I can't deal with this now, not with everything else going on, and not when I can't talk to my parents about it. In the meantime, solving the why won't stop these attacks from happening. I'll continue to simply face each one as it comes as I've always done.'

The stubborn set to her jaw tells me her mind is made up. I am amazed at how easily she can compartmentalise things. Still, it's her business, so who am I to challenge her? Besides, the train to Bodmin pulls in, and we are otherwise occupied finding seats.

We arrive at Bodmin Central just after six. I'm so tired, I can barely walk, and Pris is not much better. We must look like a couple of old codgers as we leave the station.

She leads us to a motel across way, and manages to arrange adjoining ground-floor rooms for us for the next two nights. As I fumble with my key, Pris asks, 'Do you mind if we do room service for dinner? I can't bear the thought of going out, or doing the restaurant here.'

I wonder if this is because she doesn't want to risk any

more attacks, but I don't bring the subject up. Instead, I say, 'I'm fine with that.'

Very fine, in fact. I would go as far as to say I am relieved not to have to face anyone else tonight. Listening to Mum's music has left me a little down, and we will be talking about where to go next. That is best done away from strange eyes.

'All right. I shall order it for about seven-thirty in my room. Do you want to take a quick look at the menu and tell me what you want?'

'Nah,' I say. 'Just order me a burger and chips and a ginger beer, or sparkling water if they don't have any.'

She slips inside, so I don't catch her answer. My room is serviceable and looks like commuter hotels on TV and in the movies. I sit on the bed to take off my boots. The bed is a bit soft for my liking, but I'm so tired, it probably won't matter.

The shower, though—the shower is perfect. As hot jets of water soothe my aching body, I groan out loud. I would stay here all night, but of course I can't. At some stage, I will have to face Pris. Besides, I am more than hungry.

I drape myself in a towel and use the sink to wash out some clothes before dressing. I resist the urge to lie on the bed for a while because once I do, I won't be getting up until tomorrow. Instead, I walk stiffly to the door between our rooms and lean my forehead against the cool surface.

There is a lot for us to talk about if we are to move forward from here, some of which will not be easy for me to say. Still, Pris deserves the truth. She has come this far with me on trust, so the least I can do is tell her why I can't go to Mawnan. I knock on the wood—time to face the music.

Swinging open the door, I let Snake in. He seems clean and refreshed, but the haunted look in his eyes that appeared when the goblin turned us down is still there.

I return to my bed and the laptop that is already open. Snake swings the armchair around, sits down, and puts his bare feet on the end of the bed before resting his head against the chairback and closing his eyes.

'There is some time before the food arrives,' I say. 'Shall we do some planning?'

He shakes his head, and I swallow my frustration. Then he surprises me with a compromise. 'After we eat dinner. I'm too tired to even think now.'

I have a Plan B. I always have a Plan B.

'All right, I've been looking at the second part of the riddle, and I'm pretty sure the golden token is supposed to be a golden coin.'

Snake doesn't even open his eyes. 'I think so too. Only it can't be gold coloured, like a pound coin. It must contain actual gold.'

A smile tugs at my lips as he confirms my thoughts. Perhaps I am not so useless at this World Below stuff after all. However, I keep my voice even as I say, 'That's what I thought. A pound coin would be too easy. I searched online for places we might buy gold ones, and there are a few coin dealers in Southampton. We need to factor in a stop there on the way back. That is, unless the coins should be something special.'

Snake's chest rises and falls a couple of times before he answers in a heavy voice. 'No, I think from my knowledge of creature law, they just need to be actual gold coins.'

'And you're sure you can't just turn a normal coin into gold?' The comment is intended to illicit a reaction, to lighten the sense of gloom he has brought into the room.

Snake bites. His eyes fly open, and he snaps, 'Do you think my mother and I would live like we do if I could make gold?'

I try not to smile, but I can't help it.

A sheepish grin replaces Snake's sullen look. 'You're joking, aren't you?'

I'm saved from answering by a knock on the door. The waiter puts the food on the dresser by the television. As I let him out, Snake takes the covers off the dishes. I return to find him looking at the two chocolate brownies with ice cream I ordered for dessert.

'After that walk today, I think we deserve a treat,' I say.

He grins for the first time since we left Wistman's Wood. 'I'm not complaining.'

We eat in companionable silence. Well, I eat. Snake inhales his burger and chips, then decides to make a hot drink while I finish my main course.

He takes my plate and hands me dessert before placing a tea on the bedside table. With his drink on the floor, he settles back into the chair and starts playing with his brownie.

'The senior gnome, he's my dad's best friend, and he's family,' he says before shovelling a spoonful of brownie and ice cream into his mouth.

'But that's good, isn't it? I mean, he is unlikely to refuse to endorse us if he's a relation.' I am struggling to work out what the problem might be. Is it because of Snake's mother?

'He would never refuse us even if we weren't related.... He is one of the good guys,' Snake admits.

Instead of looking happy at this thought, his eyes are more haunted than ever.

'Still sounding good to me,' I prompt, worried he might leave it there.

Snake takes a deep breath, then places the rest of his brownie on the floor. I tense. What could make Snake upset enough to put him off his food?

'It's what he will ask in return that worries me.'

He sounds so bleak, I want to wrap my arms around him

and tell him it will be okay, that we don't have to go to Mawnan. But he is no fool, and we both know we might well have no option but to go there if we want to rescue our parents.

So, I remain where I am and force myself to ask, 'And what would that be?'

Snake does not answer immediately. I am about to repeat the question when he says, 'He'll want me to speak with my father.'

The words come out in a rush, and I glance up from my food, sure I could not have heard correctly. Snake won't look at me as he continues.

'It's what he always wants. Every time he's met with Mum and me since Dad left, he's begged me to speak with him. He will use this as an excuse to force me to do it.'

'You're telling me that the last time you spoke to your father was eight years ago?'

I can't imagine going a week without speaking with my dad. I mean, he's often distant, and quite strict, but he loves me. The thought of not speaking with him for years is unthinkable. Then I realise that may be exactly what will happen if I don't make it to the World Below and free my parents. The thought takes my breath away.

Snake stares out the window and says nothing.

'What does your mum think?' I prod.

'She says I shouldn't let what happened between the two of them get between us, that I have a family below....' His voice tails off.

When I realise he isn't going to add anything else, I ask, 'Wouldn't you do it if it meant rescuing your mother?'

A tear forms in the corner of his eye, but he says nothing. I am dying to know the rest, but I don't want to push him. It was obviously difficult for him to tell me this much. He will tell me the rest when he is ready.

I take a mouthful of brownie and chew thoughtfully before flicking the screen on my laptop to my notes. 'If the sprites endorse us tomorrow, we can go to Conway, then come back to Southampton to get the coins before going to Godalming.'

Snake doesn't move.

'Snake, are you listening?'

He turns around slowly and nods. 'Yes, I am.'

'Do you also realise that if the sprites turn us down, we will have no option but to go to the gnomes? If we go to Cornwall, we will still make it back in time if we rent a car and drive through the night. It will be tight though.'

'If you can drive, why have we been taking trains?'

Really? That is what Snake takes from this conversation?

I suppress the urge to shake him. 'Because what I would have to pay for insurance would be horrendous. Besides, I haven't ever driven outside of London. A car is a last-resort option.'

He nods. 'Oh, right.'

'Does that mean all right about the car, or all right we will visit the gnomes if we don't get the sprites onside tomorrow?'

'Both, I guess. I did the calculations as well. This is how it has to be.' He still will not meet my gaze.

Snake's sadness fills the room, and I decide we can plan the rest tomorrow, after we visit the moor. I change the subject. 'Shall we go back to the last bit of the riddle?' I ask.

'Sorry, I'm tired. I can't do this now.' Snake stands abruptly and strides to the door. 'Goodnight,' he says as he closes it behind him.

Funny, what strikes me is not his abrupt departure, but the fact my usually almost compulsively tidy travelling companion has left his half-eaten dessert on the floor.

I scooch off the bed, grab his plate, and add it along with mine to the tray before placing the remnants of our dinner outside. I walk across to the window. I pull the curtain aside and take a surprised step back as I come face-to-face with a black cat sitting on the rubbish bin outside.

What is it about black cats on this trip? I seem to be seeing them everywhere. I draw the curtains, still a little unsettled. I'm not sure whether it's by the appearance of the cat or by Snake's behaviour. I decide it is the latter. What did Snake's father do that was so bad, he would not talk to him for eight years?

The room is less welcoming without Snake's presence. In fact, if I'm honest, I have felt alone since he began withdrawing this afternoon. Alone and, for the first time, scared.

Until this afternoon, this whole adventure was like some sort of treasure hunt. I had managed to push the fact that my parents are being held somewhere, probably against their will, to the back of my mind and concentrate on our plan.

Until now, everything had gone according to that plan, and it lulled me into a false sense of security. Then the goblin turned us down, the forest captured us, and Snake withdrew to balance his fear of facing his father against the need to rescue his mother. Suddenly this was all very real.

When Snake pointed out that it is not normal for someone to be attacked so frequently, it almost undid me. Of course, I had thought about this before, but Dad had always smoothed things over, and I had no real basis for thinking I was different to anyone else.... Well... apart from the colour of my skin. Now? Now I knew there was more to this. My parents have plenty to answer for when I free them—*if* I free them from The Court.

Is the black cat I keep seeing an omen? Is it telling me we are doomed to fail? No, I refuse to think like that. We still have time, and we still have options. We will bring our parents back from the World Below.

I wander back to the bed, close down my browser, and

click on the Netflix app. It automatically goes to the next episode of a fantasy series I've been watching. I can't face others failing in their quests tonight. I scroll through and stumble on a rom-com. Just what I need: bubblegum TV to take my mind off everything.

·· * · ·🌙· * ··

I jump down from the rubbish bin and join Eleanora and Eugenie in the car.

'How are they doing? Have they decided to go to Mawnan yet?' my mistress asks.

I shake my head.

'We cannot interfere anymore, Eleanora. Percival could not persuade the goblin, not in your name or mine. I cannot believe my longtime ally, Goodman Green, would do this.'

'I know, Eugenie. Remember, your connection with the goblins is the only reason we could talk to him without it getting back to the council. I am afraid they are on their own with the sprites. At least *they* will not be persuaded or scared in this matter by any of the higher races.'

Pesky sprites, I think as I curl up on my rug on the back seat. They respect no one, not even their betters. At least I won't be sent to deal with them. Perhaps now I can return home to my rightful place.

'Have you found out any more about who is pulling strings behind the scenes?' Eugenie asks.

'I visited Giles Regis, but he was tight-lipped. His wife, now, she was a different matter. Her ambitions have long outweighed her abilities, and I got the impression she is in this up to her neck.'

'Amandine? I am not surprised. She married above her

station when she wed Giles. Who would she work with to raise her husband's status? Her family has some unsavoury connections....'

'Whatever is going on here is not criminal or related to the upper world. This started below, sister, and we need to find out what is going on.'

'Did I tell you my invitation to the next court came from Elias, not the Queen?' Eugenie asks.

'Elias standing in for the Queen? Now, that is interesting. I wonder what has happened to Bernais. Isn't he her First Minister?' Eleanora muses and shifts position in the front seat. 'That seals it. We really do need to find out what is going on in the World Below.'

I hide my face under my paw so she will not be able to see me.

'Maybe we should send Percival there to do some digging?' Eleanora muses.

I stay very still. If I don't move, they might forget I am here.

'Who will keep an eye on our friends?' Eugenie asks.

'I can stay here for a couple of nights, just to make sure no one interferes directly with them. Well, not me, but Annie can.'

A strange energy fills the car, and I risk raising my head. My mistress is now a slip of a girl with long blonde hair and large brown eyes. She is dressed in jeans and a sweatshirt displaying the University of Portsmouth insignia.

I am shocked into sitting up. It is so long since my mistress has changed appearance, I had almost forgotten she was capable.

'Annie is here to study The Tor on Bodmin Moor for her thesis. She is around their age, and they will not suspect her.' My mistress smiles at her sister before turning back to me.

'In the meantime, Percival, go visit the sprites and ask if

they will let you below. We need to find out what is going on there and why someone is interested in the Crown and the Fieth families.'

The door beside me clicks open, and I stare at it before glaring at my mistress.

'Yes, now. I need you back tomorrow afternoon. I will pick you up from the Tor.'

I stretch, arching my back. With one last accusatory glare at my mistress, I jump down and take a couple of steps from the car before casting a transportation spell to Bodmin Tor.

CHAPTER 9

The Phantom Cat of Bodmin Moor

S huffling into the lobby after an early wake-up call, my mind is still replaying last night's conversation for about the hundredth time. I slept very little last night. Fear and worry over whether or not we will be forced to visit the gnomes still gnaws at my stomach. For Pris's sake, though, I try to put on a bright face.

I mean, her parents are being held too. And she has every right to force me to ask the gnomes for their endorsement. The fact that she didn't endears her to me more than her willingness to launch herself into a strange, unknown world ever did. I appreciate the fact she didn't push me to make a decision last night, that she gave me space. It isn't her fault that I wasn't able to sleep as I tired to convince myself it would be okay to go to Cornwall.

Watching her at the desk, organising our transport to the moor, brings a smile to my lips. Part of me understands that controlling the small things helps keep her mind off the bigger issues, but she is just so good at it. *A future Prime Minister*, I think to myself, *or a drill sergeant.*

Pris hands over her credit card, and it is returned with a

pamphlet and some tickets. She thanks the woman behind the counter and turns. Upon seeing me, she smiles. 'Good morning, sleepyhead. Everything is sorted. The bus arrives in an hour, and I ordered walkers' packed lunches. They'll bring them to our table after breakfast.'

'You have been busy,' I say, leading the way down the corridor to the dining room, her energy making me feel all the more tired.

We load our plates from the buffet and find a table in the corner, away from the other early risers so no one can overhear our conversation. A waiter fills my cup with coffee and Pris's with tea. I tuck in to my bacon and eggs, and I half expect Pris to bring up last night's conversation once we are alone.

Surprisingly, her first words are, 'Tell me about the sprites.'

'Political or in general?' I ask, not sure how much detail she wants.

'I guess I need to hear it all,' she responds, resignation laying heavy in her words.

A twinge of guilt twists my gut. She is being so brave. If only I could do the same when it comes to my family. Pushing that thought down, I try to formulate an answer that won't freak her out.

'Sprites are part of the fairy class of creatures. Like all fairies, they're considered lesser beings, although don't ever say that to their faces, as they are fiercely independent and have never bought into the whole class system.'

Pris grins. 'I like them already.'

She seems quite excited, and I find myself lifted by her mood. 'I thought you might. They have a reputation for being mischievous, but they aren't, not really. They use tricks and scare tactics to keep people and other races at bay. Our biggest problem today may be getting them to even appear at all.'

'So, we can't call them with magic?' she asks before taking a sip of tea.

'We can try, but they're not compelled to answer in the same way other creatures are. I mean, they will respond to any of their own who call, but they don't recognise any obligation to other creatures.'

The waiter approaches to refill our drinks, and we are silent until he leaves.

'Yesterday I read about the Phantom Cat of Bodmin Moor. Is that anything to do with the sprites?'

She has been doing her research. If she ever becomes a lawyer like her mother, I pity anyone who comes up against her.

'People have lots of theories about the cat. There are even some who believe it's an escaped puma from a private zoo, but I am pretty sure it is the sprites' way of keeping people away from Bodmin Tor, which is their gateway to the upper world.'

Pris nods and is about to ask something else when a figure appears beside our table.

'Two packed lunches?'

'Ah, yes, thank you.' Pris takes the two bags and hands them to me.

I stow them in my small backpack as Pris checks her phone.

'Just enough time for a quick toilet stop before we are expected in the lobby,' she says, gulping down the last of her tea.

I look sadly at my half-finished meal, then at her empty plate. How had she managed to talk and eat at the same time? I shovel a couple of quick mouthfuls down, drain my coffee cup, then follow Pris back to the lobby. After a quick trip to the men's room, I wait by the check-in desk while she goes to the ladies'.

A slim, attractive girl is standing nearby. She turns as I approach, and I see she is wearing a Uni of Portsmouth sweatshirt, and her long blonde ponytail is threaded through the back of a university cap. She smiles tentatively as I approach.

'Are you taking the tourist bus to the moor?' she asks.

I nod.

'Me too. I'm doing a study of the rock formations around the Tor for my thesis.'

I nod again, but I don't say anything else. She is very friendly, and normally I would be happy to chat, but my mind is on our meeting with the sprites and the consequences should we not be successful today.

'Oh, hello,' the girl says again.

I turn to find Pris approaching.

'Are you two together?' she asks. 'I was just telling your boyfriend I'm going to the moor too.'

An intense heat rises to my cheeks, and I open my mouth to tell her Pris and I are just friends when Pris says, 'That's nice. Are you walking anywhere in particular?'

I zone out from their chatter. Pris didn't correct the girl. I sneak a look at her. She is totally comfortable with us being seen as a couple. I don't really do the boyfriend/girlfriend thing but, if I'm completely honest, the thought isn't totally repellant to me.

Pris and the girl, who introduces herself as Annie, talk the whole way to Bodmin Moor. My input is not required, so I stare out the window at the bleak scenery. I understand now why so many horror movies and books are set here. Although the sky is bright blue, a wind sweeps across the almost barren terrain. Only occasional small copses of trees or outcropping of rocks break up the monotonous vista.

Finally, the bus comes to a stop, and we tumble out. Annie and Pris are still talking, and I wonder how we're going to extract ourselves from the girl. I mean, we can't go calling magical beings with a human tagging along.

I need not have worried. As the bus pulls out and Pris says,

'Are you sure you're okay waiting here alone for your guide? We can stay with you, if you like.'

I frown at her. *No, we can't.* Then we would have to find a way to ditch two humans.

'He shouldn't be long. You guys head off and enjoy yourselves.'

'If you're sure....' Pris chews her bottom lip.

'I'll be fine. See you back here at three for the pickup.' Annie shoos us away with a flick of her hand.

I entwine my fingers through Pris's and tug her towards the path. She glances reluctantly over her shoulder. 'Do you think she'll be all right?' she asks. 'I mean, it *is* quite isolated, and there are horror stories about the moor.'

'If she wanted us to stay, she would have said,' I say to soothe her, but a part of me is wondering whether we should leave her by herself. I don't want to hear of her disappearance on the news tonight.

Now I'm torn. Is there anything I can do? I reach out and find a faint tingle of magic. Under my breath I say, 'Local guardians, please look out for Annie until her friend comes.'

'What was that?' Pris asks, twisting her ring.

Suddenly embarrassed, I say, 'Nothing. Come on. It's a bit of a walk, and we don't want to miss our pickup.'

Pris tugs at my arm, stopping me in my tracks. 'No, you did something. I felt a tingle in the air and my ring warmed up. Tell me!'

Heat rises to my cheeks, and I mumble, 'I... um.... I asked the local guardians to protect Annie.' The words tumble out, and I quickly walk away before she can see the blush that is surely colouring my face.

Pris soon catches me up and says, 'Why, Snake, I didn't know you were so sweet.'

My face heats even more as I stride ahead. Annoyingly, Pris keeps pace.

'You have to teach me how to do that,' she says, the words breathless as she pushes herself to keep up.

I slow down, and she falls into step beside me. 'Will you?' she asks.

I shrug. 'Sure, if we get a chance.'

We make good time to the Tor. Although my body is tired from yesterday, it isn't too sore, and I'm invigorated by the fresh air. I'm also grateful for Pris's fathers' jacket, which helps considerably with the wind.

Pris herself is dressed more for walking today. Her purple tie-dyed fleece comes halfway down the thighs of her black-and-purple animal-print leggings. She is snuggled into a down parka and is wearing her beanie again, but today I suspect it's more to combat the wind than to hide a hair disaster.

Finally, the Tor appears on the horizon, a fact I am pleased about because Pris says we should wait until we get there before breaking for lunch, and I am starving. As we approach, my medallion warms, which is odd because I am not reaching for any magic. Pris glances at me and fiddles with the ring on her finger. She must be feeling it too.

'Ouch,' Pris says, reaching a hand around to rub the back of her neck. Something pulls at my hair, and I turn my head just as something pinches my earlobe. Damn sprites! I resist reacting because a reaction is what they want.

'Ignore them,' I say, and carry on towards the Tor.

The closer we get, the harder the pinches become, and I begin to make out small figures in the air. Finally, the torment stops, and the figures buzz and coalesce into an enormous black cat. No, it's a panther. I break into a grin as I realise this is the mysterious panther of Bodmin Moor.

'Cool,' Pris says and pulls out her phone to take a picture.

I laugh as she frowns at the screen. Leaning over, I see exactly what I expect—rocks and grass and sky, but no cat.

'You can only photograph a creature if they want to be seen,' I explain.

'What do you want here, gnome?' the cat says.

'Wow, mega cool,' Pris says. She is clearly too starstruck to take the lead here, so I step forward.

'I am Snake Fieth, and my friend is Priscilla Crown.' Pris flinches at the use of her full name, and my lips twitch upwards.

'Yes?' The panther's voice reverberates.

'Our parents were taken to stand before The Court Below, and we would like to attend to help free them. We were hoping you would endorse an invitation for us so we can be admitted to the realm.'

The panther flicks its tail. 'We don't care for The Court and rarely attend.'

'You don't need to attend. We want to go so we can save our parents from an unjust punishment,' Pris says.

The panther turns and pins Pris with its gaze. 'I hope you are not suggesting our brothers and sisters took your parents under false pretenses.'

'They think you just accused the Bad Fairies of unfairly taking our mums and your dad,' I whisper. 'Can you let me handle this so we don't insult them even more?

Pris ignores me. 'No, you have it all wrong. I think your brothers and sisters did what they were asked to do. But maybe the charges against our parents are not quite what they seem.'

I groan at Pris's attempts to smooth the situation over, but I know there is no stopping her.

'If the Bad Fairies took them below, they must have done something really bad,' the panther insists.

Pris balls her hands by her sides, ready to defend her parents. My stomach sinks as I realise we will now have no option but to head to Mawnan, and I brace myself for Pris's outburst. However, when she speaks, her voice is controlled. 'We believe the charges might have been overstated, but that is not the point. They are our family, and we want to be there for them when they face The Court.'

The panther drops his head to the side and stares at Pris as if seeing her for the first time. 'Family is important.'

Buzzing fills the air. The panther comes apart and reforms into a human.

'I thought all creatures take human form while in the world above,' Pris whispers.

'They do, but for some reason, sprites and fairies do not feel compelled to follow the rules, and no one has ever had the guts to force them to.'

'If you are truly here to support your family, we think that admirable, but some of us are not sure of your intent,' the form bellows.

'Tell us how to prove ourselves, and we will do it,' Pris says.

I groan again. Has she still not grasped the idea that you never make such an open bargain with creatures?

'What she means is, I am sure we can come to an agreement about how we can prove our intent to you,' I amend, trying to put some limits on what she has signed us up for.

Pris frowns at me, clearly not liking being corrected, but I don't waiver. She has no idea what the sprites might ask for, and I am definitely not committing to some of the things my imagination conjures.

'Here is our offer. You will each let one of our kind walk inside you to assess your intentions.'

Pris blanches and I chuckle. I bet she is pleased I intervened now.

'Possession is illegal,' I counter. 'Find another way.'

'There isn't, one that fits within your timescale. Possession for a limited time in cases of emergency is allowed.'

'So, what is your full proposal?' I ask, trying hard to keep the fear from my voice.

'One of us sits inside your head, looks through your eyes, and thinks and hears what you do until you arrive at the road of men. They will then either grant you our endorsement, or not. Either way, you will leave our lands.'

I want to reject the idea. Every fibre of my being wants to run from anything getting inside my head.

'We will consider your offer,' Pris says, taking my hand and leading me over to the rocks.

'What?' I say as I stumble after her. 'Have you gone completely mad?'

'We need to weigh up our options,' Pris says in her don't-argue-with-me voice. 'Let's eat some lunch. Perhaps you will be less grumpy when your stomach stops rumbling.'

I still owe her for being so understanding last night, so I can let her have this. We sit, and I pull out our lunches. The sprite figure also sits, cross-legged, watching us but giving us space to talk.

My appetite deserts me, but I eat anyway because my body needs energy. The ham sandwich tastes like cardboard, and the crisps are too dry for me to swallow. Pris finishes off my bag as well as her own. I wash the meal down with water, and zone out while she finishes eating.

'Aren't you freaked out by the thought of someone being inside your head?' I finally ask.

'A little, but I can't see another way around this. The alternative is that we give up on the sprites, and that makes our job all the harder.'

'Mmm,' I respond noncommittally.

'Besides, the way I see it, I genuinely want to help my parents. I have no ulterior motive. I'm sure that for the short trip back to the road, I can concentrate on the scenery and not let them into any of my juicy inner thoughts.'

I dwell for a moment on what her juicy inner thoughts might be and whether they include me before pulling my mind out of the gutter and back onto the task at hand, and my real concern over why having a sprite in my head for even a little while would not be a good idea.

All day I have been debating over whether or not to go to Mawnan and the gnomes. Can I concentrate on something else for the couple of hours back to the road? Perhaps I can if it means we won't need to go visit my uncle.

'All right,' I say, sweeping our rubbish into a single bag and putting it back in my pack. 'Let's do this.'

Pris's lips break into a grin, and she almost claps with excitement. Even while my stomach knots with worry over being possessed by a sprite, her obvious enthusiasm brings a smile to my face.

She stands and takes a step towards the sprites. Two lights break away from the human form and flit around her head, and a look of pure joy crosses her face as she says, 'We agree to your terms.'

Seconds later, something that feels like a cool knife slices into my scalp. I shiver, repulsed by the thought of anything being in my mind. I concentrate on the scenery and Pris, and my stomach settles. The sprite presence is still there, but it is more like a stray thought. If I ignore it, I don't even notice it—well, not too much.

The other sprites disperse as I stand and pull on my pack. If I concentrate, I can block the slightly odd sensation in my head, and I head back to the bus pickup point with a little more confidence.

As we walk, the silence between us is peaceful. When my mind starts to wander, I replay the story line of Daphne du Maurier's *Rebecca*, thinking of how this windswept moor fitted the tone.

About halfway back, we pass Annie. I am relieved to find her all right. Then I stop walking, seeing that she is alone. As I open my mouth to ask her where her companion is, she yells, 'My guide couldn't make it today. We rearranged for tomorrow. I'm just getting a quick look at the Tor from a distance before the bus comes.' She rushes by us at a jog, and we continue on.

A little while later, I catch a glimpse of the road. This is almost over. I relax and a pressure pushes its way to the front of my mind.

'Your love for your mother is true, and your desire to help her is very real. For that I must endorse you.' I almost sag with relief before being overwhelmed by a sharp pain, and I fall to the ground. 'Yet, you will not go to your family for help, not even to save her. For that I must penalise you.'

The presence is gone, and cold seeps through my clothing. By my nose I make out a quarter coin, the sprite's endorsement. I reach out and grab it. As I do, the world goes black as pain engulfs me.

I roll over to my side, keeping my leg as still as possible. Pris drops to her knee, her face a picture of worry.

'Ankle?' she asks, and I nod.

'How did it happen?'

I almost tell her the truth, but I am too embarrassed at being outed by a sprite that I only tell her part of it. 'I tripped as the sprite left me.'

I slip the pack from my back and put the endorsement in my pocket before trying to stand. It takes a couple of attempts, and Pris's help, before I make it to my feet.

Once I am upright, I wait for the wave of pain to pass. I test my weight on my ankle and attempt to hide the agony I am in. Come what may, I must make it back to the bus. The road that looked so close only moments ago now looks unreachable.

'Did you get your token?' I ask, trying to keep my mind off the pain.

'Yes,' Pris tells me.

'I thought you would be happier about that,' I say, sensing a little anger in her tone.

'I'm pleased, yes... but the sprite said I was true to my family, even though they weren't always true to me.'

When she doesn't continue, I ask, 'Are you angry at the sprite because of what they said, or because they're right?'

'Humph. Let's just get to the road.'

I don't say anything else. If she can give me space to deal with my family issues, the least I can do is repay the favour. I hobble on, leaning on Pris and concentrating on not passing out.

'So, did you get your endorsement?' Pris prompts.

'Aw, that doesn't look good,' Annie says, bouncing up beside us. 'Oh, here's the bus. Hold on.'

She rushes ahead while we wait. I sense Pris looking at me, waiting for an answer, but it is all I can do to stay upright. Moments later, the bus driver is beside me, helping me to the bliss of a seat inside the safety of the vehicle. Toasty warm, with my foot raised and throbbing, the motion of the bus rocks me to sleep.

Back at the hotel, Pris orders me to my room while she sorts everything out. I use the wall for support as I make my way down the corridor. By the time I arrive at my door, I'm in a lather of sweat and shaking all over.

I resist dropping onto the bed and make my way to the bathroom. After showering and dressing in pyjama bottoms and a T-shirt, I collapse onto the bed. Curling up the duvet to make a bolster, I close my eyes, exhausted... defeated.

⋅⋅*⋅◟⋅*⋅⋅

'Are you decent?' I ask as I knock on the door. A mumble comes from within, and I take it to mean yes.

Snake is lying on the bed, almost as white as the sheet. At least he has had the sense to raise his foot up. It's already beginning to swell, but there is no bruising yet. Experience tells me that is not a good sign. The longer the bruising takes to come out, the longer the recovery, unless gnomes are blessed with some sort of super-healing powers.

I want to ask Snake the question that's been preying on my mind since I asked it on the moor, but it can wait. I head to the minibar and remove a bottle of water before taking my bag of goodies to the bed. I hand the water to Snake and pop a couple of ibuprofen with extra paracetamol out for him.

While he downs the painkillers, I reach into the bag and pull out a box of ice packs. Opening one, I crack it, and when it turns cold, I place it on Snake's ankle. He winches. I head to the bathroom, grab a clean towel, then use it to hold the pack in place.

'You're pretty good at this,' Snake says.

'I play tennis. I'm forever doing my ankles,' I tell him, trying to hide my worry. 'Are you comfortable?'

He shrugs and winches again.

'Perhaps we should take you to the hospital. It might be broken.'

'I can move my foot and place a little weight on it, so it's probably just a bad sprain,' he says.

I want to insist, but I can't force him to go. My concern must have shown on my face because Snake places his hand over mine and says, 'If it's no better in the morning, we'll get it seen to.'

'All right.'

His touch is comforting, and I reluctantly withdraw my hand so I can finish getting him settled. From the closet, I grab a couple more pillows. One I put under his ankle and the other I use to prop him a little higher on the bed.

'The painkillers will kick in soon,' I reassure him.

'Yep.'

'If you're all right for a bit, I wouldn't mind a shower.'

'I should be fine, if you could just pass me the remote.'

I do as he asks and then head for the door. As I reach it, he says, 'Thanks, Pris, for all this.'

I grin, then turn away, hoping he hasn't seen how stupidly pleased I am at his praise. I leave the door open in case Snake needs anything.

The shower is magic and, in spite of Snake's mishap, I'm feeling pretty good when I return to his room with my laptop and my coin, the three quarters now joined.

Snake is dosing with the TV on in the background. I settle into the armchair and rest my feet on the end of the bed. Snake's eyes flicker open and focus on me. I breathe more easily; there's a little more colour in his cheeks.

'Are you up for some planning?' I ask, then mentally kick myself. Why can't I ask how he is? Does his foot still hurt? Does he need anything else? I'm clearly not a natural carer.

'In a minute. My jeans are in the bathroom. Could you please get my endorsement? It was hard won, and I want to put it with the rest before I lose it.'

Well, that answers my first question, I think as I ask, 'Can you lose it? I mean it's magical, so I kind of assumed it would stick with me.'

'That's a good question. I'm not sure, but I am not going to risk it.'

I retrieve his quarter from the bathroom and hand it to him. He leans over to the bedside table and opens his e-reader.

He picks up the half coin and joins it with the new piece before shutting the cover and putting it back.

Turning back to me, he says, 'Thank you. I feel better now it's all together.' He blows out a breath and says, 'And thank you again for all this. Without your help, I think I would have wallowed in self-pity, but you have me feeling better already.'

'You're welcome,' I say as I walk back around to the chair, allowing my hair to fall forward to cover my smile.

'So, where do you want to start?' he asks.

'Can you tell me where to find the fairies in Conway so I can plot a new route?'

'Easy. The Fairy Glen is reached by a walk from Betws-y-Coed station along the Afon river.'

I pull up a map of Wales and the route planner. Flicking through our options, I say, 'That's definitely doable. If we travel to Birmingham tomorrow, we can find a coin dealer there. Then the day after, we could drive to Betws-y-Coed.'

I pause and do some calculations in my head. 'Can we do the walk in one day and head back to Birmingham? If we can, we can still make it to Godalming the following day in time for midnight.'

Snake sighs. 'Normally, we'd be able to do it in a day. But I checked the walk last night, and the trek to the Fairy Glen is two and a half hours. I can't walk it like this.'

I won't be defeated. 'You would be travelling most of tomorrow, and you can rest up in a hotel while I buy the coins.'

'Lovely idea, but this is quite bad, and gnomes don't have super healing or anything.'

Damn, there goes that idea. Potential super healing aside, why is Snake being so negative?

'Don't you want to go to the fairies?' I ask, trying to keep the exasperation out of my voice. I clearly don't succeed, because Snake jerks like he's been slapped.

'No. I mean, yes.' He runs a hand through his hair. 'I don't know what I mean.'

He looks up at the ceiling, then back at me. I wait for him to speak.

'I think the sprites gave me this handicap for a reason—'

'Hold on—I thought you said you tripped.'

Snake blushes but still holds my gaze. 'I wasn't sure at the time, but there was pain, and the sprite told me this was because I wasn't trusting my family.'

My jaw drops, and I stare at him. Then I close my mouth and swallow my exasperation. 'Why didn't you tell me before?'

The tension around his mouth signals his anger before I hear it in his voice. 'Perhaps because I was in a world of pain, and it was all I could do to get back to the bus.'

I don't back down. 'Or perhaps it was because you didn't want to think too much about it.'

He glares at me, then his face relaxes into a wry smile. 'Perhaps that too. Anyway, because Earth, the head gnome, is family, I think my ankle injury is supposed to force me to go to Mawnan and face my fears.'

Snake lies back and closes his eyes. I sit statue still. He takes a deep breath, as though setting his resolve, and says, 'Tomorrow, we go to Mawnan.'

I don't respond yet. This is hard for Snake, and I want to give him time to come to terms with his decision. Secretly, though, I'm pleased. We'll definitely get an endorsement from the gnomes because by Snake's agreeing to meet with them, he is also agreeing to do whatever it takes to get that piece of coin.

As I tap queries into the browser, some show's theme music plays in the background, followed by ads.

'Okay, it's two trains and two buses, but not much walking, and we can be set down outside the Red Lion in Mawnan within a couple of hours of leaving here. Is where we are going too far from the pub?'

'I've never been there, but I looked at a map last night. It's about five minutes' walk. Or ten, in this state,' he laughs.

'Sooo, we can stay the night in Truro, then make it to Southampton in time for some coin shopping before heading to Godalming.'

'Then that's the plan. I hope I'm up to the walking.'

'I also bought an ankle brace. If you're careful, you should be all right.' I frown, suddenly worried. 'Are you sure you didn't break it?'

'Pretty sure, and besides I don't think the sprite wanted to hurt me, just force me to face the gnomes.'

'Family counselling,' I say, trying to lighten the mood, and Snake smiles ruefully.

'Yes, I guess so.'

'And you're okay with it?' The question rushes out before I can stop it, and I immediately wish I could take it back when Snake stops smiling and his eyes darken with pain.

Impulsively, I lean forward and squeeze his hand. 'We don't need to do this. We can find another way.'

His smile is back. 'The pain of facing Earth won't be as bad as facing the walk to the Fairy Glen. Besides, it's past time I faced him.'

'If you're sure....'

'I am. Now, I must ask one more thing.'

'Sure.'

'Are you okay to do room service again tonight? I think I am beyond going to the restaurant.'

I laugh, perhaps a little too much for the weak joke. But I feel like a burden has been lifted from my shoulders and I am giddy with the lightness. The end is in sight, and I will see my parents soon.

'Anything in particular?' I ask.

'I saw they had a butter chicken on the menu. That would be nice. And... I didn't get to finish dessert last night.'

I order two curries and two brownies and curl up in the chair to wait. Snake flicks through the channels until he finds a binge session of a crime show. We pause it for food, then lose ourselves back in the plot again. With both of us mentally and physically exhausted, it's nice to switch off for a bit.

Snake falls asleep at around nine. I take the plates out and find a blanket in the closet to cover Snake. I reach out to push his fringe from his face, and I quickly withdraw my hand. We may have pretended to be a couple today, but we aren't. I head through to my room, leaving the door open in case Snake needs anything in the night.

As I slip between the cool sheets, I listen to Snake's even breathing, and relax. Tonight I don't feel so alone.

···•···

I curl up on the end of my mistress's bed. It is not home, but it is warm, and my belly is full. And at least I am no longer confined in that smelly bag she put me in when she picked me up on the moor.

Now that we are relaxed, Eleanora closes her eyes and casts the spell that will allow her to understand my language so I can report.

'It is chaos, mistress. The Queen has not been seen in public for some time, and Elias is organising the spring court, just as your sister said.'

'What happened to Bernais?' Eleanora asks.

'None of our friends know. He was beside the Queen one day, and the next he was banished from her home. Not long after, the Queen retreated from public life.'

Eleanora strokes my fur as she digests my words.

'I wonder how this relates to what is going on with Snake and Priscilla,' she muses.

I am reluctant to offer my opinion. It has been so long since I have been a part of creature politics, and I am not sure I want to become embroiled again. Finally, the silence forces me to speak. 'Perhaps it has to do with the past? With all that trouble when we fought the blight, and the backlash after?'

'That was centuries ago. Besides, Pris's and Snake's parents weren't involved.' My mistress runs her fingers through my fur, and I can almost sense the thoughts rushing through her head. 'Though their families were affected by the outcome, I suppose.'

I sigh. I must tell her all I learned, even though I know it will drag up unpleasant memories. 'There is a rumour that Snake's family are to be elevated to elven status at The Court.'

My mistress's sharp intake of breath tells me she understands why this is important. 'Bernais and his family would be livid. They would do almost anything to stop that from happening.' She pauses. 'And... if he is behind this... then perhaps it is to do with the past. Pris's family have never been fond of Bernais and his ilk.'

I wait. I can almost hear the cogs turning. 'If the Fieth clan become elves, there will be one more family supporting the Queen. If they are discredited because of the actions of Ginth, Snake's mother, then that is one less family to oppose Bernais.'

I lean my head into my mistress's hand so she can better scratch behind my ears.

'And if he discredits the Crown family.... I wonder.... I think perhaps Bernais Regis is making a bid for the throne.'

'I do not believe he is strong enough to do that yet, mistress.'

Her petting stops at the use of the word mistress. She does so hate it when I use that word. 'What makes you say that, Percival?'

My mistress runs her fingers around my ears. The pleasure is so intense, I forget the question for a moment. It is too much. I move away and shake my head. The question comes back to me. 'If he were strong enough, he would not have had Ginth and the Crowns arrested. He would not have needed to neutralise their threat,' I explain.

'Of course, Percival. There is that.'

I watch Eleanora pace around the room, turning everything over in her mind. I leave her to it. Creature politics is no longer my concern, and I have given enough tonight. I close my eyes, hoping that we are done and I can get some sleep.

'Why try and stop Pris and Snake from going below?' I open an eye, hoping the question is rhetorical. Unfortunately, it is not. Eleanora is looking directly at me, expecting an answer.

'I do not know, and there was no talk about them while I was below.'

'All they can do is plea for clemency for their parents... and if they don't make it to The Court, then that is one less risk. Mmm.... I believe Bernais might have overplayed his hand and moved too soon. He does not have these trials sewn up as tightly as he would wish.'

There is more coming. I feel it in my bones, and I am not going to like it.

'We must do what we can to see Pris and Snake get below. Once they are there we will see how Bernais reacts.'

And there it is. My chance of going home vanishes, because by 'we' she surely means me. I sigh as Eleanora carries on with her planning.

'With his sprained ankle, I believe Snake will now be forced to go to Mawnan. Quite handy, that little trick of the sprites.'

'Mistress, is that why you did not fix Snake's ankle? Because he would have no option but to go visit his uncle?

'Partially, and partially because it would have been rude to mess with the sprite's lesson, especially as it is one I agree with completely. It is past time Snake Fieth faced up to his family.'

'Still, could you not heal it a little for him?'

My mistress carries on as if I had not even spoken. It is so frustrating when she does that.

'They will be safe from pursuit in Mawnan. The only other place Bernais may try to stop them is on the way to the meeting place. You must stick with them, my lovely, and thwart any attack.'

'What can I do against a greater being?' I ask grumpily. Surely, she cannot expect me to do more?

'Come now, Percival. Bernais will not send a greater being to do them harm. That would be too obvious. No. He will send a lesser creature who owes him a debt.'

'I am sure Snake can handle a lesser creature's magic.'

'Now, Percival, you know some of the smaller creatures can be quite creative with their tricks, and Snake might not even realise he is being hoodwinked. And as for Priscilla, she is as defenseless as a newborn babe.'

I sigh. She is right, even though I don't want to admit it.

'But you can stay with me in the warm tonight, little one.'

I curl into the heat of her leg, grateful for this respite. I sleep, dreaming of my bed by the fire and fish—lots of fish.

CHAPTER 10

The Owl of Mawnan

I lean my backpack against the whitewashed wall of the Red Lion as the bus pulls away. It's a shame we can't stop for lunch in the picturesque thatch-roofed pub, but we're on a tight schedule.

Beside me, Snake takes care to make sure he is braced before hauling his pack into place. Even though I took some of the heavier items from him, he grunts with the effort of standing with the extra weight.

He glances at me, and I avert my face, hoping he didn't catch my worried frown. Even with the strapping I helped him put on this morning, and dosed up with painkillers, walking is a struggle for him. His foot should be propped up, but we don't have the luxury of time.

Snake pulls his phone from a pocket and checks his map of Mawnan.

'This way,' he says, hobbling along at what is really a snail's pace.

A little ways in front of him is a signpost indicating we're heading to the local church. I easily catch Snake up. He is walking so slowly, there is time to turn and take a photo of the pub and send a snapchat to my friend Amalie.

As I swing round to continue, I pull up quickly before I bowl Snake over. He has stopped walking and is watching me, raising a single eyebrow in query.

'I told my friend I was visiting family. She'll think it's strange if I don't send her anything, and she would love this pub.'

He shrugs and carries on, and I realise I haven't seen him contact anyone this whole time. I want to ask him about it, but given what he is preparing to face today, I don't want to upset the apple cart.

'My friends are all living it up in France. They won't be back for a couple of weeks,' he says out of the blue.

'You didn't go?' I ask.

He shakes his head. 'I was going to work the holidays before starting uni.'

As I think about his friends, I wonder if he has a girlfriend. Or boyfriend? I sneak a glance at Snake as I put my phone in my back pocket. His lips are pressed together as he concentrates on putting one foot in front of the other—or more accurately, one foot forward then shuffling the other to meet it.

The thought of Snake having someone he is that close to tugs uncomfortably at my heart. I do a mental eye roll. It was one thing to pretend we were together with Annie yesterday, but I need to remember it isn't real.

We make slow progress along the quiet country lane, and there isn't even anything to look at, as the hedges are so high I can't see over them. Then Snake stops abruptly, and I pull up beside him. Is his ankle bothering him? I follow the direction of his gaze.

A man has exited a thatched cottage opposite. He walks to the car parked in the driveway, gathers some grocery bags from the boot, then heads back towards the door. It is surreal, like I am looking at Snake in thirty years' time.

As if he senses he is being watched, the man turns his head and stares. The bags drop from his hands, and I hope he hasn't any eggs inside because they are surely scrambled now. He ignores the spill of groceries as he literally runs towards us. One moment he is in his garden, and the next he has enveloped Snake in a hug.

'My goodness, Snake, you've grown so much, it took a moment.... I am so happy you came. Glisth and I have been looking for you since we heard about your mother. Oh my, what am I doing, standing here blathering for? Come inside. Tell me where you have—'

I watch Snake as the man wraps his arm companionably over my new friend's shoulders. His expression goes from embarrassed to sheepish to sad all in a few microseconds. Tears glisten in his eyes as his shoulders relax.

As if this is some sort of cue, the man stops midsentence and turns his head to look at me, as if he suddenly realises I am there. 'Oh, excuse me. My manners, I don't know where they disappeared to. I am Earth Fieth, Snake's uncle. Well, his father's uncle really, but we grew up together, more like brothers. And you are?'

I paste on my best polite smile and offer my hand. 'I am Priscilla Crown.'

Earth blushes from the tips of his ears. 'My goodness, Snake, why didn't you warn me you were travelling with royalty? I am so embarrassed.'

'If you had let me get a word in—'

Earth's arm drops from Snake's shoulders, and he turns to me, then back to Snake, and then he gestures to the house, his hands shaking. 'You must both come inside. Glisth is making tomato soup for lunch.' He frowns and shuffles a little, then adds, 'You will join us, won't you?'

He manages to bundle both of us towards the cottage, and I catch Snake sending a fond smile his uncle's way as he hobbles forward.

'Oh goodness, look what I did,' Earth says, spying the grocery bags laying on the ground. 'I will never hear the end of it if I have broken anything.'

He bends to gather the items back into the bags, and in his excitement drops almost as much as he manages to get in. I slip off my pack and join him.

'Oh no, Princess Priscilla, I can't allow—'

'I don't mind,' I say, unable to stop myself grinning at the flustered man who looks so much like Snake but is so different.

'Oh, if you insist, then thank you very much.'

I pick up a couple of the bags and follow Earth into the cottage. Snake follows us in and props our packs by the door. The door leads directly into a flagstone entrance. To the left is a living room, and to the right there is a table down the end of a short hallway. The smells drifting towards me tell me this is likely the kitchen.

Earth heads along the corridor. I wait for Snake to take the lead, and as he passes me, I ask, 'Is he always that... effusive?'

Snake's chuckle comes from deep inside. 'This might be hard to believe, but he is one of the finest political minds in the World Below. So don't be fooled by that bumbling exterior.'

'Don't tell me he is faking it?'

He shakes his head as his gaze slips past me to his uncle. A tender smile curls his lips. 'No, we have thrown him off his game, and he really is that pleased to see me. Come and meet his wife. You'll find they love nothing more than having family to fuss over.'

The flagstone floor continues on into the most perfect country cottage kitchen. Earth takes the shopping bags from me, and I hang back by the doorway as Snake hobbles over to the petite dark woman busy putting bake-in-the-oven rolls onto a tray. She pauses when Snake approaches, and the joy on her face lights the room as he hugs her.

'You naughty boy. Why didn't you at least ring? Earth was so worried. When we heard about your mother....'

'I am sorry, Glisth. It was a little thoughtless of me, But—'

The woman holds Snake at arm's length and frowns. 'You don't think we had anything to do with your mother being taken, do you? Your uncle has been working night and day for her return.'

Snake takes her hand in his. 'Of course not. I know I have been... distant... but I never doubted you and Earth were there for us.'

'Good. Now tell me, who is your friend?' Glisth turns her beaming smile my way, and I bask in its welcoming glow.

It is Earth who steps round Snake and introduces me to his wife. 'Oh my. Glisth fo Dnat, may I formally introduce Princess Priscilla Crown.'

I can't believe my eyes when Glisth actually curtsies. 'Welcome to our humble home, Princess.'

Snake is choking on his laughter and wiping tears from his eyes as my face heats with embarrassment. I'm so shocked, I don't know what to say. I mean, what is the protocol when you are introduced as royalty in someone's home? Hearing creatures tell me I am of the royal bloodline is one thing, but being called Princess not as a joke is a whole other level.

'Um, please call me Pris,' I fumble, wondering how I might tell them to treat me just like anyone else.

Snake comes to my rescue. 'Guys, Pris is travelling incognito. So, a little less of the royal treatment would be great.'

He winks at me, and my bones melt. I must have overdone the walking the last two days for him to affect me that way.

'Well, if that is what you wish, then it shall be our command,' Earth says.

'It is my wish,' I confirm, relieved not to be feted as apparently befits my royal heritage.

'You will stay to lunch?' Glisth insists. 'I always make plenty.' She wipes her hands on a dishcloth and appears nervous as she adds, 'It isn't anything fancy, though, just plain old soup.'

My stomach rumbles at the thought of a homemade meal. 'Soup would be perfect, thank you,' I say.

Earth seats us at the table and makes hot drinks while Glisth puts the rolls in the oven.

'These are the people you were afraid to visit?' I whisper.

'Don't get me wrong, I love them to bits. They have not yet been blessed with a child of their own, and when I was younger, they treated me like a son. To be honest, I've missed them terribly.... Catching up with them is not what I am afraid of.'

I wait for him to continue, but we are interrupted as Earth sets the table before joining us.

'I am sorry about your mother, Snake. I have been doing what I can for her. She is being held in a state room, not a cell, and is allowed time outside. But I am blocked at every turn when I try to argue for her release.'

Snake sits forward and covers the man's hand in his. 'That is why we are here, Earth. We need your help so we can help her.'

Before Earth can answer, Glisth takes a seat. 'Eating first, business later. Surely you have not forgotten the house rules,' she admonishes, and both Snake and Earth mumble apologies.

The meal is relaxed as Earth quizzes Snake about how he did in his exams, what his plans are for university, and how his band is going.

I look at Snake in a new light. 'You didn't tell me you're in a band,' I say.

'Oh yes, and they are very good. Snake sings and plays guitar,' Earth says.

'Are you musical?' Glisth asks.

I grimace as I think of my piano lessons. I enjoy music, but musical talent bypassed this body. 'Not in the slightest.'

Glisth pats my hand. 'Me neither. But my Earth, he can sing the birds out of the trees. That was how he stole my heart and lived up to his name.'

She winks at me, like she is sharing a secret. As I eat my soup, I roll her words around in my head. Stole my heart and lived up to his name. Earth? And anagram Heart. Fieth? Hold on. His name is Heart Thief.

I smile to myself. That means Snake's name is... 'Sneak Thief.' The words pop out, and Snake claps a hand over my mouth. 'We don't say our true names out loud. It's bad luck.'

Great. Another faux pas. I wonder how badly I transgressed this time. My gaze meets Snake's, and he is clearly amused, perhaps because it took me this long to figure out gnomic naming conventions.

'We are with family, Snake, no harm done,' Earth says, smoothing over the situation.

Snake removes his hand. 'Sorry, Pris. I'm just not used to hearing anyone but my mum call me that.'

I touch his hand as it rests on the table. 'No, Snake. I'm the one who's sorry. There's so much Mum and Dad haven't taught me....'

'I grew up with your mother, you know, and I met your father once. His brother is surely one of the great leaders of our age,' Earth interrupts, his tone solemn as if he is speaking about someone famous.

I look at Snake, who appears as surprised by this revelation as I am. Glisth stands and starts picking up dishes.

'It seems it is time for business. I will clear away while you all go into the lounge.'

'Can I—'

'No, dear. You have things to discuss, and I prefer to keep out of the business side of Earth's life.'

I follow Snake along the corridor and into the cosy lounge room. The walls are covered in shelves of books, and there is no television. This room is designed to shut out the world.

Earth crouches by the fireplace and points at the logs as he whispers something. I eagerly lean forward, watching him use a spell to light the fire. I have to restrain myself from clapping my hands—this is real magic, like something from the movies. The gnome mutters a few other words, and the fire is blazing.

Earth takes an armchair on one side of the fireplace, and I join Snake on the couch opposite. As we sit, I whisper to Snake, 'Can I do that?'

He grins. 'We can all do that.'

My excitement simmers down as the fire settles. Watching the dancing flames, I remember the question that had formed in my mind as we entered the living room. I lean in and ask, 'Snake, who is my uncle?'

He shrugs. 'I've no idea. All I know is, your mother is one of the Queen's cousins, but I don't know anything about your father's family.'

I mull this snippet of information over as Earth relaxes back in his chair and places his hands in his lap. 'So, what can I do for you?'

'Who is my uncle?' The words are out of my mouth before I even realise I have spoken.

Earth freezes for the merest second, then recovers with the smile of a consummate diplomat. 'My dear, I am sorry, but I don't really feel comfortable being the one to provide you with that information. Perhaps that question is best asked of your parents.'

'Is he some sort of criminal? Is that why you won't say anything?' I blurt out.

Our host blinks a couple of times, as if my question startles him. 'No... no... Quite the contrary. Oh dear. I fear I have made matters worse.' Earth wrings his hands. 'Yes, I think it would be all right for me to say that he is not well thought of by many in the World Below, but to many others, he is a hero. You should ask your father for his story.'

He turns to Snake, and I get the impression he has said all he is going to. 'Now, is there something I can help *you* with?'

A little bubble of anger is forming inside me as Earth glibly moves on. I was so close to learning something more about who I am. Shutting my eyes for a moment, I remind myself that this is an important meeting for Snake, and not everything is about me. I turn to Snake.

'Are you okay?' he asks.

I shrug. 'I guess.' I nudge him, signalling that it's up to him now. We need to focus on getting our final endorsement.

'I would like you to endorse us so we can attend the Spring Court,' Snake says.

'Straight to the point, as usual.' Earth smiles. 'And why does a princess need an invitation to attend court?'

Snake takes my hand, and Earth's eyes fixate on our entwined fingers. He seems disturbed by the action. Sooo, it's okay for us to be friends, but nothing more than that? I decide to ignore the look.

'Because my parents were taken to stand trial with Snake's mother,' I say. 'I was not invited to attend The Court, so I must go through the same process as Snake to speak for them.'

'Interesting. I expected Snake's request, but not yours.' He taps a finger against his lip. 'I guess it doesn't make any difference. I will clearly support you, but it is creature law that I cannot do so without exacting a price.'

I squeeze Snake's fingers, knowing this is the bit he has been dreading.

'I will give you my endorsement after you spend a night in the church.'

'What?' Snake says. 'Is that it? Then we ag—'

'Wait a moment.' I turn to Snake. 'If we stay here the night it is going to give us less time in Southampton tomorrow. We need to at least get back to Truro today.'

'If time is the only thing stopping you, I am sure it is not against any rules for me to take you to the nearest form of transport in Truro tomorrow morning. You will be at the station in time for the first train, the one you would be taking anyway.'

I can think of no further reasons to object, except that my gut is saying Earth's task is more than it seems. Snake's eyes meet mine, almost begging me to agree. He is totally relaxed for the first time today. How can I refuse him? I nod.

'Agreed,' he says.

···•᠕·•··

Earth slots a large antique key into the opening, and it turns smoothly in the lock. The door is heavy as he pushes it, but it opens silently.

'How do you have a key to the—?' I start.

'My human job is caretaker and tour guide of the church,' Earth says with a smile. 'St Mawnan and St Stephan's church has a long history and a long association with our kind.'

Inside, the late afternoon sun streams in through the lead-light windows. For a moment, Pris is caught in the coloured light, and she glows—luminescent. My heart reaches out of my chest for her, like she is a missing piece of me.

I turn away to find Earth watching me thoughtfully. Heat prickles my skin. I know exactly what he is thinking—elves and gnomes do not mix. It doesn't matter what my heart might want; my head is calling the shots.

'What do we need to do?' I ask, getting down to business.

'Just stay here the night.' He hands me a couple of quilts. 'It can get a little cold. Behind the altar are some candles and matches if you want some light later on.'

'And that's it?' I can't help feeling there is more to this, but Earth is being cagey.

'Yep. That simple. I will lock the door, though, just to be sure you keep to our bargain.'

Definitely something else going on. Even so, I nod my agreement. Earth hugs me, which is a little odd given we are just staying here for one night. Rather than comforting me, the action feeds my fear. I'm still searching for the catch when Earth lets me go.

Hobbling to the closest pew, I drop down with a thud. The door bangs shut as my uncle leaves us alone. Moments later, Pris slips into the pew behind me with her phone in her hand.

'Do you think our staying the night here has something to do with this?' she asks, handing the device to me.

Her browser displays references to the Owl Man of Mawnan. I flick through some of them.

'Sounds like this was some sort of local legend, perhaps even some of my ancestors playing tricks to keep people away from something they didn't want them to see.' I hand the phone back.

'Are you sure? I'm not great with anything reeking of horror. Movies with jump scares are a complete no-no.' She laughs, but it sounds hollow and nervous in the empty church.

In light of the frequent attacks she endures, I am sure she doesn't need any more scares in the rest of her life.

'I can't be totally sure it won't appear, but I am here to

protect you if anything scary happens.' I laugh to show her I'm not serious.

'My hero.' Her chuckle this time is genuine, dispelling the tension in the room. I can barely walk, and she's some sort of karate super ninja. I'm well aware of who would be protecting whom should anything nasty appear.

'We may as well make ourselves comfortable,' I say as I hand her one of the duvets.

She makes a nest on the floor between the pews, using her backpack as a pillow. Having made her bed, Pris heads to the altar and grabs four candles. She sets them on holders at the end of the two pews we are using, ready to be lit when it turns dark.

Having organised us, she lies down and picks up the book she bought at the train station this morning and opens it. She's already halfway through. Glancing up, she catches my eye and asks, 'E-reader?'

I nod, and she reaches into one of her pockets and pulls out my device. I prop my ankle up on my backpack and roll my duvet to make a back rest before opening an old favourite, the *Dune* trilogy. I am halfway through book two and am soon lost in a faraway world.

As the sun sets, Pris rises to light the candles. She passes me one of the packages of food Glisth had given her, and I open it to find a roast beef sandwich in a crusty roll. I salivate as I take my first bite, devouring the pickles and cheese along with the thick slices of roast beef.

'There are worse ways to spend a night,' I say to Pris as I tidy the crumbs and open my book again.

'Apart from the floor being a little hard, this is better than I expected,' she agrees.

She smiles a sleepy smile up at me, and I briefly wonder what it would be like to curl up beside her. The moment is lost when she rolls over to carry on reading. I sigh. Well, back to *Dune* it is, then.

Some time later, the candles flicker, flames catching in a draft as the wind whips up outside. I look around to make sure Pris isn't freaking out to find her sound asleep. I glance around the room, which is shrouded in darkness outside our little pool of light.

Shifting a little in the seat, I make myself more comfortable, not in the least bit tired. My eyes flick back down to my book, only to swiftly rise again as the sound of scratching reaches my ears.

'Just the trees against the windows,' I say out loud, as if speaking the words makes the idea more real.

The flames dance in unfelt eddies of air, and the scratching becomes more persistent. The hairs on the back of my neck stand on end.

I place the book on the pew beside me and slip around for a better view of the back of the church. Waiting for my sight to adjust to the darkness, my gaze roves the shadows. Nothing there. I drop my foot to the floor and turn slowly back to the front. My heart freezes and my mouth opens, but no scream escapes, even though it is rising in my throat.

Looming over the altar is the silhouette of the largest owl I have ever seen, and it is growing. I swing my head back and forth, trying to identify what is casting the shadow. I can't find anything.

The air is freezing, and my stomach clenches as a deep voice booms. 'If you want to leave here tonight, you must feed the Owl Man. You must feed him your fear.'

'What?' My voice is thin and reedy in the cavernous space compared to the deep timbre of the Owl Man's.

'If you want to live through the night, you must tell me your greatest fear. If it satisfies my appetite, you may leave.'

Really? That is it? This is almost the same question

Eugenia asked. My heart slows down and my ears are no longer filled with its pounding. I have got this.

Pushing myself into a standing position, I shuffle away from the pew. As I straighten my shoulders, I reel off my answer. 'My biggest fear is being like my father and letting my family down when they need me most.'

'Oh.'

The response sounds choked, and the Owl Man begins to shrink, then crumples to nothing. The church is silent and still for a moment, and I wonder whether or not I have passed the test. Then the sound of footsteps comes from the front of the church.

'Hello?' I say, and the word echoes in the night air.

The shadows behind the altar shimmer, and a figure emerges into the light, forming into a man.

'Oh, Snake, what did I do to you?'

My jaw drops. I take a step back and collapse into the pew.

'Dad?' I whisper.

Silence hangs in the air between us as we both regard each other. He is just the same as he is in my memories. I peer a little closer. No, there are more lines on his forehead, and he looks... sad.

Part of me longs to run to him, to have him wrap his arms around me like he used to when I was little. The more rational part of me wants to rail at him, ask him why he left me, and why he has come back now.

I do none of these things. Instead, I say, 'It was too easy. I should have known Earth would do something like this.'

Surprise flickers across my father's face before it settles into resignation. 'Don't blame Earth. When I heard rumours of what you were doing, I hoped you would come to him for help. So, I arranged this meeting as the price for your endorsement. I am selfish. I wanted to see you. And I wanted to help you help your mother.'

So many emotions chase each other through my head, I can't settle on one. For a moment, I can't respond. Finally, anger wins the battle and I spit, 'What do you care about me or Mum? You abandoned us years ago.'

'Oh, Snake.' My father takes a step towards me, and I hold up a hand before he can take another.

'Stay where you are.'

Surprisingly, he does as I command.

'Your mother—'

'If you're going to say my mother poisoned my mind, you're wrong. All she ever said about you is that you did what you had to. My contempt for you is of my own making, born from abandonment. We barely survive up here, and you didn't even care enough to check in or support us.'

Years of anger and bitterness fill my heart, and it is all I can do to stop myself from rushing at the man in front of me and pummelling him to a pulp. I expect him to defend himself, but all he does is stare at me, tears streaming down his face.

'You are right. I deserted you and your mother. We argued. She thrived above ground, and you were happy there too. I had too much time on my hands. My jobs were few and far between, and I was restless and wanted glory. I wasn't a good husband. Rather than support Ginth, I tried to make her return below, knowing she would not be valued there.'

'I don't want to hear your excuses,' I say.

'Please, I am not trying to excuse my actions. I was proud, and young, and arrogant. After one particularly bad argument, I returned home without leave from our elders. It was stupid. I got caught and was sentenced to ten years below without any contact above.'

'So, you're telling me you couldn't even get a message to Mum? I don't believe that.'

'Earth acted as go-between. What those messages contained is between your mother and me. If she chose not to share the contents with you, then I will not betray her trust any more than I already have.'

For a moment, I don't know what to say. Mum and Dad had been speaking all this time? Although I know that changes things, I am not ready to let go of my anger.

'So, how come you're here now? According to your story, there is still a year and a bit to go.'

'I bargained an hour with you for another five years banishment from the World Above.'

What? My jaw drops again.

'You would not come to me no matter how often Earth or your mother asked on my behalf. So, I had to find a way to get to you. I am not asking you to trust me or forgive me. All I am asking from you is to let me help you help Ginth. She was taken below because she married me. I cannot let that act cause her any more pain than it already has.'

'Pris and I have that in hand. Earth will give us the last endorsement we need. We don't need your help.'

'What about the rest of the riddle? Have you solved it all?'

'Yes, we worked out we need to pay a gold coin for entry. Pris has a plan for that.'

'That reminds me.' My father reaches into his pocket and holds out his hand. 'Your grandfather asked me to give you a gift.'

I stare at two gold coins but make no move to take them.

'Are you allowed to do that? Isn't it against some sort of rule? Shouldn't we find everything ourselves?'

'There is no rule against a grandfather giving a gift to a family member. It is up to you how you choose to use them.'

I still don't move. My father spins the coins in the air and directs them to the pew beside me, where they settle next to my e-reader with a slight clink.

'Did you work out where the Spring Court is being held?'

'Yep, in the Underground Ballroom the night after tomorrow,' I say to prove I do not need his help.

My father shakes his head. 'The Court is held from midnight tomorrow night until midnight the following night. It is how it has always been. Those twenty-four hours above ground are the equivalent of one month in The World Below. One month twice a year when those above ground and those below congregate to make new laws, settle disputes, and confer thanks.'

My eyes widen. 'Are you sure?'

'Of course I am. I am to attend on behalf of the family, so I should know.'

My stomach lurches. We will be cutting it fine, but if we don't need to stop to find coins, we should make it. My mouth goes dry as I think about how we were so close to missing our chance to save our parents. Bending, I scoop the coins into my hand. Beggars can't be choosers.

'What about the word?'

I frown, trying to remember the riddle. A rustle from behind causes me to start as a hand pops over the back of the pew, waving the note. I wonder how long Pris has been listening. I'm not sure how I feel about her overhearing my reunion with my father. Then again, I'm not sure how I feel about anything at the moment.

'Thanks,' I mutter as I take the paper from her.

I read the rhyme: 'Speak the word to create that which needs our breath but cannot breathe.'

It still means no more to me than it did the other dozen or so times I've read it.

'I cannot tell you the answer, but I can tell you that those who enter The Court from the World Above for the first time must prove they are from the magical realm,' my father explains.

'I am so stupid.' I slap my palm to my forehead. It refers to the first spell we all learn, and one of the few spells all races can perform. In fact, Earth used it earlier today right in front of me. I hold out my palm and say, 'Lasair.' A small flame appears a centimetre or so above my palm.

'Perfect. You are set. What about you, young lady? Can you produce a flame?'

'What, me?' The pew wobbles as Pris bangs into it just before her head appears. 'Can't Snake just do it for the both of us?'

My father laughs. I'd forgotten how infectious his laughter is, and it takes my breath away.

'No, you must produce it yourself to show you are truly from the World Below.'

Pris uses the pew to push herself to her feet. 'I've never done any magic.'

'Yes, you have,' I tell her. 'You called a goblin, and you used your glamour.'

Her eyes lock with mine, her uncertainty and fear warring in their bright blue depths.

'You can do this,' I tell her, placing my hand over hers. 'Open your other hand. Now reach for magic like I showed you.'

Pris closes her eyes, and the ring under my fingers warms up.

'Good. Now imagine a flame on your palm.' She nods, eyes still closed. 'Now push your magic into the flame and say the word lasair.'

'Lasair,' Pris says.

A small light flickers over her palm, then fizzes out.

'Not bad for a first attempt,' I say. 'Maybe this time, you could do it with your eyes open.'

Pris's eyes flick open. 'Should it be hot? And does it matter what colour I imagine the flame to be?'

'You're overthinking this.'

I start at the voice, and Pris draws her hand back, as if suddenly aware of my father's presence.

'You almost had it, but you doubted yourself. Try again,' my father directs.

Pris stands up straighter, concentrates on her hand, and says, 'Lasair.'

Again, a little flicker of light, then the flame dies.

'I can't do this.'

'Yes, you can,' Dad and I say together.

'If you can start a flame, you can finish it,' I tell her. 'You just need practice.'

'And you also need to believe you can do it. But you will never be able to do that until you admit to yourself who you truly are.'

I swing round to tell my father he doesn't know what he's talking about, but I stop short. He is watching Pris with such compassion that I realise he understands completely.

His gaze lifts to meet mine, and I am blown away by the strength of the love his look conveys. The angry shell I have built around my heart to keep my father out cracks a little; not completely, but enough for me to recognise there will be more to our story when this is over.

'I appreciate your help and what it cost you to deliver it.' Okay, it's not forgiveness, but it is a start.

Tears leak from his eyes. 'I know it is too little too late as far as you are concerned. But I will do all I can to save Ginth fo Drefin, and not just because she is your mother, but because she does not deserve this.'

He draws in a breath and says, 'Just seeing you for this short time... I would have given much more.'

I lurch forward and hug him. 'I have not forgiven you, but thank you.'

From far away, a bell tinkles. Dad holds me tight, as if he doesn't want to let me go.

'This has not been nearly enough time,' he says as he releases me. 'I will be there to support you when you make it below.'

Then he is gone. My heart is breaking into pieces, just like it did the first time he left me, and I want to curl into a ball and cry.

Pris's voice fills the room as she says, 'Well, that was all completely unexpected.'

I whip around to tell her exactly how hurtful and unsupportive her comment is, to find she is right behind me. A moment later, she gathers me into a hug.

I want to collapse into her arms, but I remain stiff, trying to maintain my facade of nonchalance. Then I can be strong no longer, and it all comes out in a rush. I turn into a howling baby. She rubs my back and croons something by my ear. I am not sure how long we remain like that, me releasing years of hurt and her letting me. Finally, the tears stop, and I raise my head.

'Better?'

I nod, unable to speak.

'Uhm.' The voice comes from the doorway. 'There are comfy beds next door if you would rather spend the rest of the night inside.'

I want to yell at Earth. To tell him he is a sneaky no good... whatever he is. I cannot think of the word. My mouth opens to do just that, only to find all my rage has disappeared. Suddenly I am weary and drained.

Earth looks past me at Pris. 'Take him inside. Glisth has hot chocolates with marshmallows ready for you. It should help with the shock. I'll bring your gear.'

I am sitting in front of the fire, allowing the sweetness of the drink to do its work, half listening to Glisth give Pris tips on how to produce her flame when Earth sits beside me.

'You all right?' he asks, placing his hand on my knee.

'I will be,' I say as warmth radiates down my leg. It reaches my ankle, and I tense as the pain lessens. 'Did you just—'

He chuckles. 'If you hadn't avoided me all these years, I could have taught you a thing or two about what we gnomes can actually do.'

'But that's an elven power,' I hiss under my breath.

'So many believe.' Earth's lips curl into a half smile

There is more to this conversation, and I sense Earth willing me to ask the questions forming in my head. But I am emotionally drained, and my mind will not take any more in.

My gaze wanders to Pris, and I have a new respect for how she has dealt with the upheaval I brought into her life.

CHAPTER 11

The Final Leg

The cold morning air clings like a limpet, and I pull my jacket more firmly around my body. I am grateful for the beanie Glisth insisted I take, as it helps keep the warmth in.

Earth leads me to the car, and I dump my pack in the boot. Although my ankle twinges a little as I walk, it is way better than yesterday. After this is over, I must return so I can learn about how gnomes can heal. I can hardly believe that two days ago I was reluctant to come here. Now I don't want to leave.

As I take my place in the front seat, I breathe in the smell of the straight-from-the-oven cinnamon scrolls Glisth handed to Pris as we left. We did not have time for breakfast, but the ever-thoughtful Glisth made some for us while we showered and changed. I had forgotten how kind and loving she is, and tears had formed in my eyes as I hugged her goodbye.

Before we back out of the driveway, Earth turns on Radio 2, and I close my eyes to the sound of the golden oldies I remember my father listening to. The simple thought of him no longer tugs at my heart, or causes resentment to well inside of me. I have not forgiven him, but I guess I realise now that there is more to my parents' story than I had previously thought.

In my mind, it had been all about an upper-class gnome falling for a common girl. They married, moved to the human world, and he could not take the loss of status. He begged her to return, and she wouldn't go with him because here she was valued for who she was, not where she came from. Taking matters into his own hands, he abandoned his family, never to be heard of again.

As if guessing the train of my thoughts, Earth says, 'I am so happy you spoke with your father. Now I am free to talk of things I was bound by your parents never to discuss.'

'Parents?' I raise an eyebrow.

'Yes, I am afraid neither of them have been very fair to you while they sorted out their marital issues, but it is not my place to say more than that about them.'

'What things?' I prompt.

'Things? Oh, we can talk about that when this is over.'

Sometimes Earth can be exceedingly frustrating to deal with.

'After I drop you off, I will be returning to the World Below to see what I can do to help your mother. It may not be much, I am afraid, because the family is treading a very dodgy political path at the moment, which I suspect is why your mother is facing these charges.'

'We thought something else was going on,' I admit to Earth. 'Are you able to tell me anything more about what it is?'

Earth does not take his eyes off the road as he shakes his head. 'I am sorry, but I think in this instance, you will be more effective freeing your mother if you stay well away from the politics. Creatures are more likely to be persuaded by you if they think you have nothing more to gain than your mother's freedom.'

When it comes to creature politics, there is none better than Earth for forging a path without setting off any major explosions. I heed his advice and don't ask any more questions.

The sun is just peeking over top of the Victorian brick frontage of Truro station when we pull up. He takes off to buy us tickets for the 6:40 to Reading while I sort out our packs. Leaning them against the building, I turn to wait for Earth, only to find him standing in front of me, two steaming mugs of coffee in his hands. 'Glisth made me promise to set you on your way with a proper breakfast.'

Emotion clogs my throat again over my aunt's kindness as I take the cups. With such a strong family standing with me, how can I help but rescue my mother? Pris appears by my side, taking her cup so I can hug Earth.

'We will meet again at court, my friends,' he says through the window as he drives off.

We make our cumbersome way to the platform and wait patiently for the train, which seems not to want to appear. I check my phone. It's ten minutes late. I stand up and look down the track, then sit again.

'Chill. Trains run from Reading to Guildford every twenty minutes or so,' Pris tells me calmly. 'And there are plenty of trains from Guildford heading down to Godalming.'

I try and relax, but I can't. 'I thought we had more time,' I say. 'Dad pointing out that The Court starts on midnight the day of the full moon rather than the evening... well... I just thought we had more time to prepare.'

Pris chucks her empty coffee cup into the bin beside her and shrugs. 'We would have spent most of today getting our golden coins, so we really are no worse off,' she says, ever the practical one. Then she mumbles under her breath, 'And at least you don't need to learn how to cast a spell before midnight tonight.'

I open my mouth to reassure Pris, but the train chooses

that moment to finally arrive, and we are distracted with making our way through commuters and finding spaces to sit. Because we spend time putting our backpacks in the luggage racks by the doors, we are the last to find seats, and there are no two together.

At Exeter the woman beside me leaves, and I shuffle over to make room for Pris. Her face is pale, and she is unusually fidgety. I sense she wants to talk, but the packed train carriage is not the place to discuss magic.

Finally, she says in hushed tones, 'If I can't do it, will you speak for my parents as well?'

I want to tell her this is unnecessary, that she'll be able to make a flame. The fear I read in her eyes stops the words in my throat. 'Of course I will,' I say instead. 'But we will have time for you to practice once we are at the conference centre. We should be able to find somewhere to rest and to perfect your flame.'

'It may still not be enough,' she says.

This is unlike her. She is normally so positive, or at least focused on a way she can achieve her goals. Is she really that worried about calling fire? About actually admitting she is a creature? Or is something else going on? I smile in what I hope is an encouraging fashion, hoping to talk some more about it.

She doesn't smile back. Opening her book, she mumbles, 'Okay.' Her eyes drop to the page in front of her and the discussion is over.

I study her profile for a while, wondering how I can help her. Over the last few days, she has been so supportive of me, and I'm pretty sure I wouldn't have had the courage to face my family alone. Now she is troubled, and I want to offer the same to her.

She can make the beginnings of a flame, which means she can use magic. Is my father right? Does she need to accept who she is before she can use her powers? And if he is, how do I help her accept her elven heritage in half a day?

I pull my earbuds out of my pack and click on my classical playlist before immersing myself in a piano version of Satie's "Gnossiennes" on continuous loop, hoping for divine inspiration.

⋅⋅∗⋅ ☾ ⋅∗⋅⋅

Trains are such dirty, smelly things. Humans jam themselves in like fish in a can, and it makes the smell even worse. I wrinkle my nose and slip back under the luggage rack to avoid trampling feet.

From my hidey hole, I can protect Snake and that elf. They are fully endorsed, and I can smell the gold they carry. And they are travelling in the right direction to attend The Court. Why are they not happier? Have they had an argument? Surely, I did not miss that.

All right, I did delay a little in Glisth's kitchen. It was warm, and she made me a very special breakfast. Even so, I made it to the station just as they did and have been tailing them ever since.

No, there is something else going on. I slip forwards a little and check the carriage. There is nothing obvious, but an air of doubt hangs heavy, and it is centred around Snake and her.

Whoever is doing this is well hidden, and I cannot cast a spell to seek them out without drawing attention to myself. I settle back down. I will bide my time.

The next station is announced, and the girl and Snake make their way towards me. I ensure I am well hidden before they arrive to gather their bags. They stand by the luggage rack, waiting for the train to stop.

At first, they don't say anything, then the elf says, 'Glisth told me last night that most creatures cast their flame spells almost before they can walk. I think she meant to demonstrate how easy it is, but it isn't easy for me. I start out okay, but I can't make it form completely. I can't do this.'

Stupid elf. I can make a flame. Even most humans could make one if they slowed down for long enough to sense magic in the air.

'You can do this, Pris. We will practice this afternoon.' Snake glances around. 'When we are alone.'

He is far too nice to her. The elf girl sighs, and I resist the urge to swipe her with my claws. She is a *princess,* for goodness' sake. She should start acting like one!

The doors open, and my quarry disappear amongst the commuters. I wind my way through legs and dodge feet to catch them up. There they are, heading for another platform. Seriously, someone should tell them they *can* use other forms of transport.

They reach the platform just as a train slips away. Shoulders slumped, they take a seat to wait for the next train to their destination. I take up a post beside a dispensing machine and scan the area. No obvious creatures here, but there are three people who were also in the carriage on the other train. It could be any one of them.

I hunker out of the wind and fight off a sudden urge to pop home. Whoever is doing this is throwing everything at Snake and the elf. Snake is giving the girl a pep talk. He fumbles in his pack, and his hand comes out with two mugs. He stands up and heads to the kiosk. The girl looks around forlornly, twisting the ring on her finger, and I realise she is on the verge of leaving.

Snake is nowhere to be seen. I don't like elf girl, but Eleanora will be displeased if I let her get away.

I force myself to my feet and out into the cold, blustery wind sweeping the platform. No one gives me a second glance as I pad over to her and rub against her legs. Immediately, I am swamped with self-doubt. How can I, a lesser creature, ever believe I can help a princess of the crown?

As Pris leans down and rubs a hand through my fur, I feel the heat in her ring. There is a spell, and it is directed at Pris. That was why she was twisting it.

It cannot completely dispel whatever the other creature is doing, but as the princess continues to pat me, I cast a spell of lightness and well-being. As I do, I sense the elf girl relax.

'Oh, aren't you a handsome fellow,' she says as her fingers find the sweet spot behind my ears, and I lean into her. Perhaps she isn't so bad after all.

Familiar trainers enter my line of vision, and I slip under the seat and away before he catches sight of me. The air is a little clearer after my spell, but it won't be so easy to thwart the creature once we are in the confined space of a carriage.

The elf girl leads us on to yet another train, then one more after that. During each leg of the journey, she sinks more and more into herself, and I worry. I fear she will not make it to The Court tonight if this carries on. The only small ray of sunshine is that Snake is so intent on keeping elf girl's spirits up, he does not appear to be as affected by the spell, but it does worry me that he has not sensed what is going on.

By the third train, I have narrowed the culprit down to two men. One is wearing a business suit, and the other is clearly a tradesman of some description. It is obviously the suit —never trust anyone in a suit.

Snake stands up. We are clearly changing trains again. I wait until everyone departs, then dash out before the doors close. Turning my head this way and that, I cannot find Snake or elf girl. Finally, I spy them on the other side of the barrier.

He and the elf are arguing about something. I walk by them. Are they really fighting about clothes? I slip in behind a fence and survey the area. Suit man and tradesman are both waiting by the station entrance. Are they in this together?

While I keep an eye on Bernais's henchmen, I fail to notice Snake and the elf begin walking into town, meaning I have to rush to catch up with them. Then I almost get caught by Snake as he turns to glare at a garden. His figure blurs, and the elf turns, her eyes widening in surprise.

I am close enough to catch the girl's words when she says, 'What did you do?'

'If people persist in thinking gnomes look like those abominations, they deserve all they get.'

'So, the urban legend of garden gnomes moving by themselves is true?' The elf girl's laugh must be infectious because Snake's face loses its grouch, and he grins.

'You could say that. Come on. If we really must buy suitable clothes for tonight, let's get it over and done with.'

As they walk off, I jump lightly up onto the stone wall to survey Snake's handiwork. I am shocked, to say the least. Snake had been very inventive with the poses he had placed the gnomes in—inventive enough that I am surely blushing under my fur.

I find Snake and elf girl wandering the high street. Snake is pulled into a clothing shop, and I park myself in a doorway to wait for them.

The spot I chose is cold and dank, and it smells faintly of human functions that should not be done in such a public place. Some people have no shame! My nose wrinkles and I shuffle forward to get some fresh air, and then I spot him, the tradesman, two doors down, leaning against a store window.

Peeking around the doorway, I check the rest of the street. Suit man is nowhere to be seen. I have my culprit. Leaving my post, I walk past the man, giving him a sniff as I pass by.

'Leave off, you eejit.' A foot kicks out at me, and I dash away to save myself from injury.

I sniff again. Leprechaun. Really, have they no imagination? He could have disguised himself as anything—a tradesman is way too stereotypical. And Bernais, of all the low tricks, sending a leprechaun to do your dirty work. They should not even be above ground in England, let alone allowed to practice magic here.

I double back and return to my hiding place. Even the smell of urine is preferable to being near a leprechaun. They are tricksters and make sprites and fairies seem like amateurs.

Moments later, Snake and elf girl reappear, carrying bags. I slip in behind them as we head away from the leprechaun. Raising a shield of air to dispel any spell sent our way, I am confident in the knowledge that the henchman could not call enough power to break through it, not this far from his native land.

A few doors on, the girl heads into a food shop, returns a couple of minutes later with some extra bags, and they carry on down the road. Snake checks his phone, and they turn a corner and stop outside a small, nondescript building. He waits outside with the bags while elf girl enters. Before she returns, a car pulls up and a man jumps out.

'You the party for Whitley?'

'We are,' the girl says as she reappears behind Snake.

Their bags are loaded into the back, and in less time than it takes me to lower the shield protecting them from evil thoughts, they are gone.

'Bloody hell, I'm for it now.' The voice comes from behind me, followed by a rush of air, and the leprechaun is gone.

My job is done. Time to wait for the ballroom to open so I can join Eleanora.

·*·🌙·*··

The taxi pulls up outside the gates of the conference centre, the nose of the car pointing directly at a sign telling us it is closed for a private function.

'Are you sure this is the right place?' the driver asks, not moving to open the boot.

'I am,' Snake says from beside me. 'We are part of the function.'

In the rear vision mirror, I see the man raise bushy grey eyebrows.

'I mean, we're here to help with the catering,' Snake explains, realising we are not the type of people normally attending private functions here.

'Okay, then.'

The boot lock clicks, and I open the door beside me. The man doesn't even leave his seat to help with the bags. Given the exorbitant amount I prepaid for this trip, I'm about to give him a piece of my mind. Snake places a hand on my arm, and I turn to find him shaking his head.

'It's not worth it,' he says as he slams down the boot.

He's right, it isn't worth worrying about given the task ahead of us. My stomach sinks at the thought. All day I've had this overwhelming feeling of futility, wondering why I am even trying to get into the ball.

When we were at Guildford, I had almost told Snake to go on alone. I was heading for the platform to Waterloo when Snake grabbed my arm and virtually dragged me to the Portsmouth Platform as if he had read my mind.

Nagging doubts about my magical abilities still eat at my stomach, but I'm resolved to at least try and see this through.

'Hey, what about my tip?' the driver leans out of the door and yells, bringing me back to the present.

'Here's one for you: next time get out and help,' Snake says before turning and walking up the path.

'Bloody kids today.' The response follows Snake and me up the driveway.

'Shouldn't we be hiding, or at least be careful no one sees us?' I ask as I catch him up.

His shoulders rise in a shrug. 'Earth said court entrances are owned by creatures. They will be expecting a number of our kind to be arriving today, so they won't be worried.'

'This early?'

'Probably not, but there doesn't appear to be anyone about. Come on. Let's go round the back. Maybe I can find a window or door to let us inside.'

'I'm not sure about this, Snake. I mean, not only will we be breaking and entering, but isn't using your magic for personal gain wrong?'

Snake turns the corner, and we're faced with a series of French doors opening into various conference rooms. Reaching into his pocket, he pulls out two long pick-like things, and moments later, the door swings open.

'Firstly, I don't propose to use magic, and secondly, I never break anything.'

I hesitate in the doorway.

'Come on. We won't be damaging anything, and we will leave it as we found it. We just need somewhere to eat, and rest, and for you to practice your magic in private.'

And there it is, the real reason why I don't want to go in. I remain where I am, not yet ready to face the fact I can't even produce a simple flame, something children can do.

I take in a gulp of air. This person who is afraid to even try is not who I am. Besides, I have come too far to turn back now.

Snake has arranged the deli food I bought on the table, and is busy piling some onto a plate. That boy's capacity to stuff food down his face no matter what is going on around us is amazing. I am surprised he isn't the size of a house. He catches me watching him, and grins. 'It's good food. Aren't you eating?'

I close the door and join him on the other side of the room. The food does look good. I drop my pack and bags to the ground before loading my plate with a pork pie, some coleslaw, and potato salad. Taking a seat opposite Snake, I dig in.

'These pies are the best,' he says, leaning over to add another to his plate.

I open an iced tea and take a gulp before sitting back in my chair, unable to eat anything more. Wearily, I close my eyes. We have been on the go for a week, and, more than anything, I would love to spend the evening curled up on the couch at home watching crap TV before hauling my tired body upstairs and sleeping in my own bed.

I must have dosed for a bit, because when I open my eyes, the table is clear, and Snake is standing before me with a steaming mug of tea.

'How?' I ask.

'I assumed conference centres must be able to provide refreshments, and I was right. I found a bar outside with a fancy coffee machine and a great selection of teas.'

I wrap my hands around the mug and take a sip. Tea soothes the soul, my mother always says, and it does exactly that for me. Snake takes a seat on the floor and pats the carpet in front of him. I sigh. I can't put this off any longer. Sitting cross-legged in front of him, I take another sip of tea before putting the mug down beside me.

'Do you do any breathing exercises when you do karate?' he asks.

I frown at him. 'Yes, but what's that got to do with my making a flame?'

'You're as stiff as a board. This is never going to work when you are so tense.'

My head tips to the side as I consider his words. 'When you learned to make a flame, did you do any drills or anything beforehand?'

'Of course. I was given my medallion, and I had to practice reaching for magic until I could sense it and hold it without having to think too much.'

I rise to my feet. I think I need to relax and allow magic to flow through me as if it is a part of me. Taking up a position in the middle of the U of tables, I begin running through my karate kata. At the same time, I reach out and touch the magic in the air.

The first time, there is no flow to my movements because I am concentrating too much on feeling the magic. By my third run through, I am moving from memory, and the magic, which began as a slight tingle, flows through my body almost as if it has always been there. I am ready.

Snake is leaning back against his pack. His eyes are closed, but I had sensed him watching me as I practiced.

'Ready?' he asks, moving his body to sit up and opening his eyes as I join him.

I nod. Holding out my hand, I do not need to call magic this time, as it is pulsing through me in time to my beating heart. The flame forms easily, but I still cannot grow it or hold it. It simply slips away.

'What do you think of when you lose it?' Snake asks, after my tenth attempt.

'I don't know.' I chew on my lip while I start over, concentrating more on when the flame disappears. 'I see the flame form, and I.... It's like I can't believe it is me making it.'

'Like something inside of you is blocking your magic?'

'No,' I snap. 'I can't describe what happens. It's like I can't believe *I* am making the flame.'

'But it is you,' he says, stating the obvious.

'I know,' I shoot back, frustration bubbling over. I rise to my feet and pace, too agitated to try again.

'Maybe what you can do will be enough,' Snake says. 'We have a few hours before we need to get ready. Perhaps we should rest for a bit. It might be a long night.'

I humph, aware that Snake is being amazingly supportive and I'm acting like a spoilt brat. While Snake pulls a jumper on, I continue to pace. He lies down and drops a cap over his eyes to block out the light.

I place my pack down beside his, pull out my denim jacket, and use it as a blanket as I rest my head on my bag. My mind is buzzing with pent-up energy and frustration. Too restless to sleep, I roll on my side and stare out the windows. Snake is snoring gently, and this only frustrates me more. I'm not going to be able to sleep like this.

Being as silent as I can, I put my jacket on and let myself outside. Pulling my phone from my pocket, I slip in my earbuds before scrolling through my playlist. I start listening to "She Speeds" by Straightjacket Fits, but quickly change it. It may be one of my current favourites, but it doesn't suit my mood. Then I spot "Mascara" by Killing Heidi. The kick-ass female anthem is exactly what I need.

As I sing along to the chorus, I think of the number of times Mum has told me you can put lipstick on a pig, it is still a pig. Killing Heidi and Mum have hit the nail on the head. Deep down I'm afraid calling myself an elf doesn't make me one.

I walk over to the lake in front of the manor house and stare at the dome of the Underwater Ballroom. As the sun begins to set, I find a seat nearby and skim a few pebbles across the water before sitting down.

I remove my earbuds and put them and my phone back in my pocket, happy to sit here and listen to nature and the faint rumble of cars in the distance. Snake's father said I need to accept who I am if I'm to make a flame. But how can I do that when I don't know anything about being an elf?

'I'm an elf,' I say out loud, as if the words will somehow make it more real. Instead, I just feel stupid. I swing my legs, admiring my purple Converse high-tops before dropping my feet to the ground and scuffing the gravel.

What more can I do? What if my beginning of a flame is not enough? What if they won't let me into The Court? I can't let Snake face this without me. He said he will speak for my parents, but we started this together, and we should finish it the same way.

I kick out again, and a spray of gravel spatters into the water, causing droplets to disturb a cat sleeping in the last of the sun. It turns its head accusingly towards me.

'Sorry, puss—my bad.'

It lazily stands and moves until it is directly in front of me. I reach down to pet it, wondering what it is about black cats and this trip. The cat avoids my touch and pads towards the water. Halfway there, it pauses and glances over its shoulder. In international cat language, I am pretty sure this means 'Follow me.'

Rising to my feet, a smile tugs at my lips. If attempting magic is not bad enough, now I am following a cat. How strange my life has become in less than a week.

My feline friend stops at the water's edge and looks down, as if staring at its own reflection. I drop to my knees on the grass beside him and lean over so I can see what he is staring at. In the water is an image of me... and the cat, of course.

My face reflects how weary I am. I run a hand over my eyes, and as it drops back to my side, the image shifts and ripples, like someone dropped a stone in the water. When it settles again, the person staring back at me still has my blue eyes, but my face is longer and thinner, my hair is silver-white, and... oh my god, my ears are pointed! I reach up to check, but the tips of my ears feel as round as they ever were.

I turn to the cat, and it meets my gaze. I swear his look says, 'See, this is who you are.'

Thinking I must have dreamed it, I drop my gaze back to the water. The silver-haired me is still staring back. Is this the real me, this strange, alien creature? In this moment, my world completely shatters, and yet, somewhere inside, I know this person in the reflection is more me than I have ever been. For a moment, the image shimmers, and then my usual face is back. The cat nudges me.

'What now?' I ask, still reeling from the undeniable truth that I really am an elf.

It sits in front of me like Snake had, waiting patiently.

'Oh, I get it,' I say, holding out my hand. It's time to make a flame.

I take a deep breath and let the magic flow through me. Before I form the flame, I give myself a pep talk. 'Right, elf girl. If you are going to do this, you are going to do it Pris style.'

In my mind, I envisage *my* flame. 'Lasair,' I whisper. A glow starts to form on my hand, then I allow it to take shape. The flame grows, flickers, and almost splutters out. 'Not this time,' I tell it. 'You are mine,' I say, forcing it to appear as it did in my mind. It holds for one... two... three seconds before it disappears.

'I did it,' I tell the cat, and it simply stares at me, as if it knew I could do it all along, before standing, flicking his tail, and sauntering over to the bushes.

'Thank you,' I yell after him, not worrying how crazy I sound talking to a cat.

Standing up, I do a little happy dance. I just cast my first honest-to-god spell Harry Potter style, and it was incredible!

Once I calm down and return to the conference centre, I walk as if I'm floating on air, with a stupid grin plastered on my face. I did it. I cast a spell and—I pause midstep—I am a freaking *elf princess*.

CHAPTER 12

The Underground Ballroom

Pris snores. I would like to say it's a delicate sound befitting someone of royal stature but, quite honestly, a freight train is what comes to mind. I force myself to my feet and stretch out the kinks. The room is all shadow and moonlight. It is late, but my alarm hasn't gone off, so I still have a bit of time.

I creep out into the reception area to make some coffee to wake me up, then have a better idea. I wonder if this big old building has somewhere to shower.

The toilets off the reception area are just that. I wander along the corridor and spot what I'm looking for: a sign for a gym. It is in an annex, and I find showers in the changing rooms, along with a good supply of large, fluffy towels.

Standing under the steaming hot water, all the knots and strains leave my body. I am fresher and more awake, and I smell pretty damn good as well, all pine and sandalwood. I wrap myself in one of the complimentary robes, roll my dirty clothes into a ball, and head back to the conference room.

By the time I get there, Pris is awake and rubbing sleep from her eyes.

'Your alarm went off and I couldn't stop it.' Her tone is accusatory, and I grin at her.

'Not a morning person?' I ask.

She glares back and snaps, 'This is not morning.' Her eyes widen as she takes in my attire. 'What are you wearing?'

'Would your evening start a little better if I tell you I found showers?' I tease.

She rises gracefully to her feet and says, 'I would kill for a shower, and I will kill you if you don't give up their location immediately.'

I grin as she gathers her toilet bag and clothes, and I point her in the right direction. Once she leaves, I go about dressing. The moon provides enough light to pull my clothes on, but I use the bathroom mirror to shave and tidy my hair.

I stare at my reflection in frustration. The black open-necked shirt with a subtle purple stripe is perfect for an evening function, and I definitely look ready, except for my damn hair. No matter what I do, it keeps flopping over my forehead. My mother would have something that would sort it for the evening. My heart wrenches at the thought of her.

'I'm coming, Mum,' I say to my reflection as I flick my hair out of my eyes. I sigh. It will have to do.

Returning to the conference room, I tidy up and look around for somewhere to secure our packs. The only place to leave them out of sight is behind the coffee bar next door. I remove my token before I haul mine around the back, leaving Pris's behind, not sure if she is finished with it yet.

As I check to make sure no one can see my bag from the reception side of the bar, a noise from behind startles me and I turn, ready to confront the intruder. I stop dead in my tracks. My jaw drops, and I close my mouth again quickly, not wanting to appear like an idiot.

I have dated girls, and have even taken them to some

swanky places. But I swear none of them have ever taken my breath away as Pris does now.

She wears a simple shift dress with purple and blue flowers growing up it from the bottom, leaving the bodice white. Her hair is pulled back into a loose plait, but she has left tendrils hanging down around her face, and they dance with some fine silver earrings she has threaded through holes in her ears I didn't even know she had. She must also have done some sort of makeup thing because her blue eyes almost leap from her face, and her lips glisten as she smiles shyly.

'Do I look okay?' she asks as she pulls a midnight-blue shawl from a shopping bag.

I want to tell her she has almost stopped my heart, she is so beautiful. 'You.... Um... yes.' Not my best work, but quite honestly, I can't think straight, let alone form a complete sentence.

'I'm still a bit worried. I mean, we look pretty good, but this is a ball. I'm pretty sure we will be underdressed.'

I shrug. 'We were not able to buy tuxes and ball gowns in Godalming. Besides, I think we did pretty well to remember not to turn up in jeans and tees.' I run my hand through my hair, pushing my fringe out of my eyes again. Pris frowns.

'Here, let me sort that,' she says as she pops the bag containing her old clothes onto the floor. Rummaging in a toilet bag the size of my day pack, she pulls out a container. Before I am able to tell her I'm fine, she is in front of me, rubbing something on her hands. Reaching up, she runs her fingers through my hair.

My senses overload. I smell roses and spring air, and the touch of her fingers on my scalp sends a shiver down my spine. I close my eyes and lose myself in the sensation. If my night ended now, I would be in heaven.

Looking down, I find two startling blue eyes staring up at me. I give myself over to the moment and lower my head, pressing my lips to hers. They are soft and taste faintly of strawberries. As I deepen the kiss, Pris responds, and I wrap my arms around her, pulling her body against mine.

Electricity runs through me, and the touch of her hands down my back increases the sensation. I shift so I can fit her closer to me. I run my tongue along her lips, and she sighs, leaning into me. Everything except for the taste, the smell, and the touch of her is driven from my mind. Have we time before the....

I freeze. The Midnight Ball. I take a step back. This is not just Pris, my friend. This is Princess Priscilla, cousin to the Elven Queen. Could there be a more forbidden fruit?

With swollen lips, Pris looks up at me, confusion written on her face. Every fibre of my being wants to pull her back into my arms, but I take another step away.

'Um... we'll be late if we....'

She does not move, her eyes searching for an answer to the unasked question hanging between us—why did you stop?

She has no idea what other creatures would say about my being friends with her, let alone... this. I have so much to say, but I can't find the words to smooth this over.

Turning on her heel, she gathers her gear and leaves me standing alone. I stand there a while longer as I wait for the aftereffects of our kiss to become less noticeable. Taking deep breaths, I remind myself that this is not a date. We are here to rescue our parents, and that is the only reason an elf would go anywhere with a gnome like me.

I follow her into the conference room. The air is charged and awkward. I watch her for a moment, both wishing our kiss had not happened and perversely wanting it to happen again. As she goes to pull her backpack over her shoulder, I move to her side.

'Let me,' I say, taking it from her hand before she can refuse.

By the time I return, her feet are encased in some strappy blue sandals, her shawl is around her shoulders, and there is a small blue drawstring bag hooked over her wrist.

I hold out my arm and ask in what I hope is a dashing way, 'Are you ready, Princess?'

Her nose wrinkles, and I'm not sure whether it is because she doesn't like the formality or isn't comfortable with my escorting her as though this is a date, especially after the last few minutes. The moment passes, and she slips her arm through mine. I'm careful to not hold her too close as we take the short walk to the lake's edge. Even this small contact threatens to weaken my resolve.

When we find the round entrance to the Underground Ballroom, I blow out a breath, not realising how worried I still was about making it here. The door is open, and I lead Pris through.

The narrow stairway is not wide enough for two people, so I let go of her arm and allow her to descend the circular wrought-iron staircase ahead of me. I take it again as we reach the bottom.

In front of us is a corridor which must go under the lake. At the end is a... the only way to describe it is a shimmer. It isn't a door, but we can't see anything through the throbbing, thickened air.

'What do we do now?' Pris asks.

'I don't know. Perhaps—'

The sound of footsteps above stops me midsentence, and we duck into the shadows under the stairs. In silence, we watch a short, dark-haired man in a tuxedo and two women in glittering ball gowns sweep along the corridor and disappear from view.

'Should we...?' Pris's voice drifts off as more people arrive and follow the others through the entranceway.

'Right, let's do this,' I say once they have gone.

Pris slips her hand through the crook of my arm, and we walk along the underwater path and confidently step... into a wall.

'OUCH!' Pris exclaims, hopping on one foot as she rubs the toe of the other.

'Excuse me,' a voice says from behind, and I help Pris out of the way to allow two besuited men past.

'Is it because we don't pass the dress code, do you think?' Pris frowns as another group of spectacularly dressed people are admitted through the barrier. 'Or maybe we're doing something wrong,' she says. 'Perhaps there's a lever, or a magical word they say—'

The rest of her words are drowned out as a bell tolls, filling the space with its vibrations. As the sound dies away, a tall man dressed in red livery, complete with a white wig straight out of Eighteenth Century England, walks through the barrier and stands, holding out his hand.

I look at Pris and she pushes me forward. Great, I love being a guinea pig.

I slip my fingers into my pocket and pull out my endorsement, then I place it in the white-gloved hand. The man takes it between two fingers, turns it from side to side, then presses his fingers together, and I stare open-mouthed as my hard-won coin turns to dust and disappears.

The footman extends his hand again, and I place the gold coin on his palm. He doesn't even look at it. He simply slips it into his pocket. His hands drop to his sides, and he tilts his head as if waiting for something. I pause a moment, at a loss, then I remember. Holding out my palm, I speak the word, and a flame appears.

The footman takes a step aside, extends an arm, and ushers me inside. I step forward and my foot easily passes through the barrier. Rather than stepping all the way through, I turn to wait for Pris.

To my surprise, she confidently steps up, hands over her coins, then extends her hand and says, 'Lasair.'

On her palm appears a small, perfectly formed purple flame. I hide my surprise as she raises her eyes and grins at me before closing her fingers and extinguishing the light. The footman moves aside, and Pris steps forward and clasps my hand.

'How did you manage that?' I ask.

She winks at me. 'A girl's gotta have her secrets.' Then she pulls me through the icy cold barrier into the World Below.

The Underground Ballroom is a circular dome of windows rising above us. It is already crowded with bedazzled creatures standing around, chatting and eating canapés. The amazing array of otherworldly creatures is jaw-dropping, and I attempt to guide Pris around the edge of the assembled crowd without staring like a shell-shocked tourist.

When we are a couple of metres from the door, I turn to see if Pris is as stunned as I am at the spectacle, and for the second time today, my heart stops. Pris had been beautiful before, but in her elf form, she is breathtaking.

Moments ago, she had been as tall as my shoulder, but now her piercing blue eyes stare directly into mine. While her skin is still a warm brown, her hair is silver-white, framing an elongated face with slightly tilted eyes. And she glows. I mean, there is a shimmer of power around her, forming a glowing aura. In spite of her transformation, she nervously scans the room.

'You look every bit the Elven Princess you are,' I reassure her, offering her my arm.

· ·✦· ◗ ·✦· ·

Snake extends his arm, and I clutch at it, feeling disoriented. I knew the World Below would be different, but it is like we walked into a movie set where the makeup and special effects team have been having a field day. Snake is my only constant, and I cling to him like a lifebuoy.

I lean into his shoulder. His warmth and strength steady me. I'm pleased he hasn't turned into a garden gnome. In fact, he has hardly changed at all. No, that isn't quite true. Here he is more—more of everything.

His eyes are greener, his skin is more olive than it was, and he emits a definite calming energy. Above ground, he was good-looking enough in a boy-next-door sort of way, but down here, he is supermodel good-looking. Other than that, he is reassuringly the same.

'What?' he asks.

I must have been staring. Trying to ignore the heat rising from my belly, I say, 'It's just, you look surprisingly normal. You've hardly changed at all.'

He turns to catch a glimpse of himself in the window, and I stifle a giggle as he does a double take.

'Dang, that's an improvement,' he chuckles.

Tearing my eyes from him, I remind myself that I'm still annoyed with how he treated me earlier. I allow the hurt and rejection I buried for the sake of tonight to resurface, and it makes Snake instantly less appealing. I turn away to survey the ballroom and its surreal occupants.

It is difficult to fathom that this circular room is actually underwater. In the dead of night, the windows are ink black, so the effect is kinda lost. If the place is disappointing, the inhabitants are not.

There are tall, angular creatures whose ears come to a point. Their clothing is understated but still dazzling to the eye. There are equally tall, but not quite so lean, creatures whose clothes are a bit more sparkly, as if to make up for not being so gaunt. Their groups stand close together but slightly apart.

Every creature here is light skinned and almost human in appearance. There are no hags, or sprites darting round, or anyone with green skin, or gold skin, or dark skin like mine. I glance at Snake and notice him taking in the crowd.

'Is this it?' I ask. 'I mean, this could simply be a dress-up party in the World Above.'

Snake continues to study the assembled creatures. 'There are a smattering of goblins, and obviously a lot of elves.' He pauses. 'There are the gnomes. They're never far away from the elves, just in case one of their betters might ask them for something.' Bitterness laces his voice.

'Are you sure they're not enslaved?' I ask, the note of disgust clear in my voice.

He shakes his head. 'Quite sure, but our families are bound by history. And there are many gnomes who crave to be elevated to the same status as elves.'

'Can that actually happen?' I am not sure whether or not he is joking.

'Not often, but yes.'

Laughing, I say, 'So, what do they do, make your ears more pointy, or something?'

'Well, yes, sort of.'

I turn to check he isn't pulling my leg. A ghost of a smile tugs at his lips, and he cannot contain it any longer. 'Centuries ago, gnomes rebelled against elves. As a punishment, their power was bound and they were bonded to elven families until they proved their loyalty. When a gnome family is elevated, their bonds are removed, and I believe there are cases where their ears regrew after.'

He is too serious. This must be a joke.

'You're kidding, right? Snake?'

My partner is no longer listening. He is peering over my

shoulder, and I turn around to find a tall dark-haired woman walking towards us. Her emerald-green velvet dress clings to her body like a second skin, emphasising her curves as she saunters over. At first, I think Snake is leering, but the smile he sends is open and full of welcome as he mutters to me, 'And there are witches too. So, all the higher creatures are here.'

I raise my gaze to the woman's face and realise she is the Witch of Wimbledon.

'Princess, Master Fieth, welcome to the World Below. So pleased you were able to join us,' she purrs.

How had I not noticed how stunning she was when I first met her? The moment my mind flicks back to that first meeting, heat rises up my neck and I am sure I must be blushing. I am glad of my dark complexion as I hope no one notices.

'Good evening, um... Eleanora? Is that the correct title to use?'

Her lips curl into a smile. 'Ah, you have found your manners, little Princess. You may address me by my name, but here I am called the Protector of London.'

I duck my head, shame over my behaviour in Wimbledon curdling my lunch. She was gracious and helpful, and I was a spoilt brat. Now, finding she is more than a grandmother and a witch, that she has rank and status within the creature community, I feel unworthy of her kindness.

There is an awkward silence, which Snake ends. 'We wouldn't be here without you, Eleanora. We owe you our thanks.'

It is as if his voice releases something in me, and my words rush out. 'Yes, thank you. You set us onto the right path, and we owe you our heartfelt thanks.' I stop, trying to find the right words, then realise that sometimes the simplest words are the best. 'And I'm sorry I was so rude to you before.'

One of Eleanora's eyebrows arches elegantly. 'You *have*

had a change of heart, Princess Priscilla. You will need it if you are to help your parents.'

'Excuse me, mistress. They have arrived.'

I was so taken up with the presence of Eleanora, I had not noticed her companion. The man was barely five feet tall with slicked back black hair and the most amazing green, catlike eyes. As if he realises he is being scrutinised, his head swings around. I could swear I've met him before, he seems so familiar, but my mind is blank. I can't place him anywhere, and he isn't someone you would easily forget.

'Snake, Princess, this is my right hand and my oldest friend, Percival,' Eleanora says as her gaze sweeps past me and fixes on someone across the room. She frowns slightly.

Before I can find the source of her unease, I feel a hand on my elbow, and I shift to find myself face to face with... 'Earth,' I exclaim, pleased to see a familiar, friendly face.

He is handsome in a formal tuxedo with his World Below glow. He stands straighter and appears more in control than he had earlier today.

'Welcome,' he says, leaning around me to include Snake in his greeting. 'It is not long until the formalities start, and I am sure the two of you would like to spend a little time with your parents.'

My heart rate speeds up with the mention of seeing Mum and Dad, but I hesitate. So much has happened since I saw them last. What will I say?

Eleanora steps aside to allow us to pass. 'I will see you both later.'

I follow Earth across the room, trying not to stare at the variety of other races who have entered in the last few minutes: tiny delicate, ethereal beings, individuals who look almost human except for elongated fingers and ears, and square-looking people with almost black eyes. One thing they all have in common is the glitter of their clothing and jewellery. The other thing is, they are all white. It hits me that I am the only person in the room with dark skin.

My gaze slides over the array of creatures and rests on the man and woman on either side of the corridor directly in front of us. They are my height, dressed in severe black suits, their long dark hair pulled back into ponytails which emphasise their delicate faces. There is nothing delicate about their bodies though. They obviously spend a lot of time at the gym. My eyes almost pop out of my head when I spot gossamer wings rising above their shoulders.

They move to block the doorway as we approach. Earth shows them a piece of paper, and they move aside to allow us passage.

'Bad Fairies?' I whisper to Snake.

'Yep, they are the World Below's police.'

I can't help but chuckle. 'They aren't bad. They deal with the bad.'

Snake stops and stares at me. 'Isn't that what I've been saying?' he asks.

I realise that it is, but while he meant one thing, I read into it something completely different. This misunderstanding reminds me how little I still know about my homeland.

Earth stops in front of a door. 'Your mother is inside, Snake. I am afraid that because I am a member of The Court, I cannot join you for your reunion.'

Snake hesitates outside.

'Go on,' I urge. 'She'll be waiting for you.'

He smiles at me, and mouths, 'Good luck' before he disappears inside.

Earth leads me towards a room further down the corridor. We are stopped outside by a tall, incredibly handsome man, an elf by the shape of his ears, and an older one if the grey hair over those ears is anything to go by. He grabs one of my hands between both of his.

'Priscilla, I am so pleased you are here. I am Elias, your mother's cousin. I can only allow you a small amount of time with your parents because we are about to start proceedings, but you can speak more later. And when this is over, I hope we can talk, as it is past time for us to discuss your royal role.'

I am stunned. Royal role? I don't know what to say. It seems I am not expected to say anything, because he smiles a politician's shark smile that is all teeth and no substance, lets go of my hand, and heads down the corridor towards the ball.

Pushing the odd conversation aside, I turn to the door and go to knock, then pause. I understand now why Snake was reluctant to enter his mother's room. We worked so hard to get here—I can't believe I am actually about to see Mum and Dad.

'Go on. They are waiting.' Earth's hand is gentle on my back, giving me comfort and support, and a little nudge.

I take in a big breath, turn the handle, open the door, and enter. My gaze goes directly to the two figures standing in the middle of the room. They turn to me as one, and I stop dead in my tracks. These are not my parents, and yet, they are.

I take in the changes in their bodies, my father's silver hair and my mother's now auburn tresses. Then I look into their faces, and something clicks into place; I rush towards them, sinking into their embrace. I am home.

Strong arms hold me close, and teardrops dampen my hair as my father lays his cheek on top of my head. I find myself gripping my parents tight, reluctant to let them go.

Finally, my mother pulls away and leads us to the table at the back of the room. We sit, but I can't let go of their hands. I can't believe I am with them, and I am not sure they won't just disappear.

I blink a couple of times, as if to clear my vision. 'It's so strange, seeing you look like this,' I say. Everything about them is elongated, giving them a regal appearance, in spite of the fact they are still wearing casual human clothes.

Dad is in chinos and a white open-necked shirt, and Mum is wearing capri pants and a floral top. This was not what they were wearing when I last saw them, and their clothes look clean. Do people here wear similar clothes to people in the World Above, or are my parents trying to make some kind of a statement?

'For you to be here, in your true form, it's something we were never sure we would see.' My father's teeth flash white against his dark skin.

'Why didn't you tell me?' I blurt out. 'Why didn't you prepare me for... for... this?'

Neither of them speaks. Their eyes meet, and I imagine some sort of wordless communication passing between them. My mother brushes a stray strand of hair from her forehead and pins me with eyes that are mirror images of my own.

'It was not an easy decision, Pris, and we don't have much time to go into the ins and outs of it, but we felt your life was in danger, so we decided to distance you from our families,' she said, squeezing my hand.

I frown, thinking of the number of times in my life I had to deal with muggings and attacks. My parents' decision for me to train in karate so I would be safer. Snake forcing me to admit it is not normal to be attacked a couple of times a month and hinting at another reason.

My head swings from one parent to the other. 'Are you telling me the random attacks I have faced my entire life are not bad luck, but creatures wishing me ill?'

My father nods. 'We always believed so.'

My jaw tenses. 'But you didn't think you should tell me?'

How could they believe I was better off not knowing I was being personally attacked? Why had they believed not accessing my magic was a good idea, or that not helping me to understand my abilities was for the better? They had forced me to fight with one hand behind my back.

A knock at the door jolts me. My father grabs my hand again; when had I let go of him and Mum?

'There is not much time left, and we can explain everything to you later. What is more important at the moment is that you believe the charges against us are false. They've been trumped up as part of some political machinations down here. We are fighting them as best we can. If you want to help, you can try appealing to everyone's sense of fairness and decency. The vote is close, and a plea from you may just sway some in our favour.'

'How?' I ask. 'What should I say?'

Mum laces her fingers through mine. 'Use all those skills you learned from debating. Listen to the arguments and use what you know to refute them.'

'We believe in you,' my father adds.

My stomach clenches. His eyes are bright with fear, and my father is never afraid of anything.

'What will happen if you are found guilty?' I ask.

I understand now that feathering your own nests while working above ground is frowned upon, but it isn't murder or anything. How bad could this be?

Dad runs his thumb over the back of my hand. 'Best case, we will be banned from returning above ground for a time.'

'It is time we treated her like an adult, Malachi. Pris, there is a chance we will be banned from returning above ground —ever.'

The door opens, and one of the Bad Fairies who has been guarding the hallway enters. 'It is time,' she says. And just like that, with the threat of never being able to return to our old life hanging over my head, our reunion is cut short.

W alking behind the Bad Fairy, I resist the urge to touch the wings gently swaying in front of me. My hand reaches out as if of its own accord, only to be grasped by my father's large brown one.

'Don't. Touching them is a very intimate act.'

My hand drops down, and I am sure my face turns beetroot red. Before I have time to compose myself, we are led back into the ballroom.

Is it just my imagination, or has the room grown larger in my absence? On my right, a dais has appeared, and most of the creatures gathered in the rest of the room are turned towards it. On the stage itself are three chairs, only one of which is occupied—by a woman in a bright, loose-fitting dress with brown wavy hair tumbling free down her back. Her dark brown eyes are fixed on someone in the crowd. I follow her gaze and find Snake standing beside Earth and his father.

Dad folds me into a hug as my mum's hand cups my face. 'Here goes,' he says as he lets me go. 'Time to face the music.' My gaze trails after them, wanting to follow, but I know I can't.

'Good luck, I love you,' I whisper, then make my way across the room, slipping between creatures as I head towards Snake. Whispers follow my progress, and heads turn to stare at me.

By the time I make it to Snake's side, I'm sure the whole room is talking about me. I sweep my gaze around the gathered creatures, holding my head high and taking them all in. Snake's fingers entwine with mine, and at his touch, the confidence I am displaying becomes real.

As we wait for proceedings to begin, a group of severely dressed muscle-bound creatures enters the ballroom. They are similar to the square creatures I noticed before, but in amongst the glitter and dazzle, they alone stand out as drab. My eyes follow them as they span out around the edges of the crowd.

'Who are they?' I ask.

'Dwarves,' Earth says, his brows drawing together in a frown. 'Few of them ever attend court. Too busy amassing their fortunes and disdaining decent folks.'

Snake leans into me, and his breath tickles my cheek as he says in a low voice, 'Dwarves will do anything for gold or jewels. I wonder who here is paying them?'

My senses reel at his being so close, and my eyes are drawn to his lips as I remember our kiss. I close my eyes to shut out the distraction and consider his words. When I open them again, I find myself scanning the crowd, trying to work out who might be behind this display of force.

My gaze finally settles on my parents as they take their seats on the dais. As they settle, the man from the corridor steps in front of them and waits for the room to fall silent before speaking.

'Elias, the Queen's Prime Minister,' Earth tells us, just as a hush falls over the crowd.

'On behalf of Queen Anastasia, welcome to the Spring

Court. The Queen is a little indisposed and will join us for some of the later events. In the meantime, I will be chairing this evening's proceedings.'

The crowd murmurs. Someone behind me says, 'When was the last time anyone saw her?' And another adds, 'I doubt she will be here tonight or any other night.'

'Our first order of business is to deal with some terrible accusations levelled at three members of our community who carry out work for us in the World Above. They are charged with using their magic for personal gain.'

The room gasps collectively.

'It isn't like they didn't already know. They have been talking of nothing else for the last couple of days,' Snake's father says through gritted teeth.

'I am sure many of them thought the charges would be dropped before it was taken to full court,' Earth said.

'How can you impartially oversee this trial when one of the accused is your beloved cousin?' a voice shouts from the floor.

Elias squares his shoulders and stares down his nose at the man in the crowd.

'I will refrain from getting into an argument about *our* cousin, Bernais. As always, if you are not happy about how I carry out my duties, you are within your rights to appeal to the Queen. Now, if we are ready.'

I crane my neck, trying to catch a glimpse of the man speaking from the floor. He is almost an exact match for Elias on the dais, except his hair is lighter, and more auburn like my mother's. Looking from one to the other, I see the family resemblance. *So, this is what having family is like*, I think as I wonder if I might have been better off not knowing.

'Many of us would prefer this matter to go before the Queen herself. We are prepared to wait,' Bernais says.

The crowd shuffles restlessly, and I can't tell whether it is because they support this man, Bernais, or whether they are annoyed that he is causing a scene. Whatever the reason, the air thrums with tension. I catch movement out of the corner of my eye as some Bad Fairies move to place themselves in front of the dais.

Bernais opens his mouth to continue his argument, a few more Bad Fairies appear, and he steps back. When everyone settles down, Elias carries on.

'Now that is settled, I call upon Ginth fo Drefin's accuser to present their case.'

As the crowd parts, I quickly shuffle the letters of Snake's mother's name. 'Finder of Things,' I mouth and smile as Grossman Green moves to the middle of the dais. My smile freezes.

'What's that slimy creature doing here?' I mutter, sneering at the goblin.

'I've no idea, but it can't be anything good,' Snake answers.

One of the creatures in front half turns and shushes us. I am about to give them a piece of my mind, but then Grossman starts speaking, and I find I have bigger things to worry about.

'I, Grossman Green, Senior Goblin in the World Above, accuse Ginth fo Drefin of profiting from her skills while living amongst humans. I have received reports from our kind who have seen her using her gifts to steal from shops and pick pockets.'

There is a collective gasp from the room.

'Her own kind turn a blind eye to her transgressions, and this must stop. She must face up to the consequences of her actions.'

'Bloody goblins. They have always resented us.' Snake hisses.

'Why?' Pris asks.

'Because we are close to the elves, closer to the power they desire,' Earth says.

'You have evidence to back your claims?' Elias is asking as Pris's attention returns to the front.

'Not specific evidence—'

'You mentioned reports?'

'Um... they were verbal.'

'But you can produce witnesses,' Elias prompts.

'Of course, given a little time.'

'Give him enough time, and I am sure he can bribe as many witnesses as it takes to convict my mother,' Snake mutters.

Not put off by Elias's requests for proof, Grossman carries on. 'I can work out what she earns from her work for us, and I cannot believe she can afford to live in London without helping herself to things she shouldn't,' Grossman says, searching the crowd for support.

'Okay.' Elias draws the word out. 'In that case, will anyone speak on Ginth fo Drefin's behalf?'

There is movement beside Snake as Earth steps forward. He is beaten to the dais by Eleanora.

'I would like to speak for Gin. Since her husband has been unfairly held in the World Below, I have given comfort and support to Gin in my role as Protector of London. Ofttimes, I provide food and money when the powers that be below stop family funds from reaching her. Other times, I give her and her son little gifts and luxuries to make life more bearable. Perhaps it is these items Goodman Green is referring to.'

Elias smiles. 'Thank you, Eleanora, and thank you for the work you do for our people above ground. I know many would not be able to cope without your generosity.'

The witch lowers her head as she accepts Elias's thanks and steps back. As she does so, Earth makes his way to the front of the gathering.

'I, Earth Fieth, speak as the Senior Gnome in the World Above. My nephew's disappearance left Ginth struggling, and she was initially too proud to ask for help. A few years ago, she was caught stealing food for herself and her son. We brought this matter before our own council and agreed that as she only took what she needed to survive, making this a minor transgression. We placed Gin on probation, and since then, to the best of our knowledge, she has not strayed again.'

'Thank you, Earth. If this is all, then I propose we drop the charges against Ginth fo Drefin as already dealt with by the Gnome Council,' Elias says.

Grossman Green moves as if to step down from the dais. I watch in stunned silence as he catches Bernais's eyes and stops. Bernais shakes his head, and Grossman lets out a sigh. So, it is this elf, Bernais, pulling Grossman's strings.

Grossman clears his throat, then says, 'The original accusations were never brought before the full court. How do we know Earth is telling the truth and the charges were dealt with fairly—after all, Ginth is married to his nephew.'

Grossman is clutching at straws. It is written on the faces of the crowd around me, and even I can sense most creatures have no appetite to uphold the claim. Unfortunately, it appears he has struck a chord with Elias.

'I will need to check the fine print of the laws governing lesser council's dealings with offences under their remit. In the meantime, we will suspend Ginth fo Drefin's trial.'

Grossman steps down from the dais, and before Elias can release Snake's mum and announce the details of the next case, Giles Regis leaps onto the platform. He is followed more sedately by his wife, Amandine. The pair stare expectantly at Elias.

'Oh, um... I guess you are here to present the case against Princess Cecily and Malachi Crown.' Elias appears to be a little flustered by the influx of elves, but he soon regains his composure. 'Princess Cecily and Malachi Crown are accused of using their position and skills above ground, specifically their glamour, to benefit themselves at the expense of humans. Giles Regis, if you would like to state the case against them.'

Amandine virtually pushes Giles into centre stage, leaving no doubt about who is behind these accusations.

'Hm. Although the Crowns hold prestigious positions, their income from those roles does not explain how they can afford their house, private school fees for their daughter, regular overseas trips, designer clothes, high-end cars....' His voice drifts off, as if he has run out of steam.

'How can Amandine Regis stand there, dressed in something so obviously not off-the-rack, and accuse my parents?' I fume.

Snake's fingers reach for mine, and I gratefully grab hold of his hand.

'Our time will come before the vote. Just keep it together until then.' His breath tickles my ear as he leans in to whisper. He moves closer, and I lean into him for support.

'Have you specific evidence, or just suspicions?' Elias asks.

'You only have to look at what they own,' Amandine spits.

'Says the woman who lives in Grosvenor Square,' I murmur.

'All right, who will speak on behalf of Princess Cecily and Malachi?'

My father stands up to respond, and a voice from the crowd yells, 'Outsiders cannot speak in the court.'

'What the?' I ask, thrown by the vehemence of the accusation.

Snake turns wide eyes towards me. 'I have no idea.'

My mother rises gracefully. She may not be decked out in designer clothes, she may not glitter, but she is every bit a princess as she takes centre stage.

'That was a mistake,' I say. 'They obviously have not seen my mother in court.'

Mum clasps her hands in front of her and gazes around the room, meeting the eyes of all those judging her.

'Many of you know me. You grew up with me, or you oversaw my education. I would love to believe that was enough for you to judge my honesty, but there is something else going on here, and I am forced to open my life to your scrutiny to meet some political objective.'

A wave of whispers goes round the room. Some creatures shuffle uncomfortably, others cannot not meet her gaze, but quite a number stare openly at her. I cannot tell if that is because they are offering support or because they are revelling in her embarrassment.

'It is a matter of public record that my husband's family has amassed great wealth in the World Above over the centuries through legitimate means. Prince Malachi's brother offered us the use of one of his London properties while we live in the city. When our daughter began experiencing frequent attacks on her life, he also offered to pay for her to attend a private school. This was discussed in the Elven Court, and it was agreed that we would accept the offer. Everything was open and above board.'

Now the muggings have grown into full blown attacks on my life? What is going on here? My parents have a lot of explaining to do when this is over.

Snake squeezes my hand. 'We can sort this later,' he whispers, his words mirroring my own thoughts.

'Our frequent overseas trips are for work purposes. We do sometimes add on a holiday at the end, paid for by ourselves. The rest of our luxury items are bought with our salaries. We work long hours, often at the expense of family life, in jobs that help the world become a better place. Do you begrudge us these small pleasures?'

The crowd falls silent as Mum's gaze roams the room and finally falls on Bernais. I shiver at the intensity of it, but she doesn't say anything as she turns and takes her seat.

'What? Is that it?' I ask. 'Why doesn't she mention the fact that she had Dad make large donations in cash and give time to many charities, and that they make me work half of my holidays volunteering for various organisations?'

'Perhaps that will sound better coming from you when you make your plea to The Court,' Snake offers.

The room is humming with low conversations as Giles and Amandine step down to rejoin Bernais and Goodman Green. That man is at the centre of this, I am sure. But what has he to gain from all of this? He turns, as if he senses I am watching him. His eyes meet mine and he smirks. Fury wells up inside me.

'Before we vote, is anyone here to make a plea on behalf of the accused?' Elias asks, raising his voice to be heard over the crowd.

Snake and I go to step forward, but I find myself taken in a gorilla grasp from behind as a hand clasps over my mouth. Turning my head, I find Snake in a similar position. Where are Earth and Snake's dad? I try to catch a glimpse of them through the dwarves, who have made a tight circle around us. I just make out someone hauling Earth to the back of the room. There will be no help from that quarter.

I am turned so I can watch Bernais step onto the podium and shove Giles out of the way. 'Let us vote and get this trial over and done with.'

The anger that has been slowly boiling inside me since this farce began threatens to explode. I struggle against the strong arms, but my efforts are futile. My captor tightens his grip, and I almost suffocate as the hand extends over my nose.

That is it! I did not spend all those hours training in karate to escape this very sort of situation for nothing. Sensei's voice sounds in my head. 'Channel that anger, use it to sharpen your attack.'

I close my eyes and assess the situation just as she taught me. My attacker is taller and wider than I am, and his centre of gravity is lower. I will not be able to take him off his feet. What I can do is attack his weak points.

Shifting my weight slightly so I can breathe, I force my teeth to clamp down on his hand. He grunts and his grip slackens imperceptibly. Reacting immediately, I stomp down on his toes, making full use of the sharp point of my heel and, at the same time, swing back with my elbow, taking him by surprise.

He lets me go, and instead of moving away like he expects me to, I turn and bring my left knee into his groin with all my force before stepping back and punching him in the jaw.

I am in ready stance, breathing heavily, waiting for him to retaliate, when a Bad Fairy slips in between us. I'm not sure whether he is protecting me or the dwarf. I don't relax yet because I am not sure what is happening. The room has divided into two, with a small clearing around Snake, the two goons who held us captive, and the Bad Fairy.

I swing my head around, taking in the shocked expressions on everyone's faces. Then I find what I am searching for. My parents are standing on the dais, restrained by fairies, but the pride on their faces makes me stand taller and hold my space, meeting the glare of the dwarf over the shoulder of the fairy.

'That was awesome,' Snake says from beside me. 'Is it bad that I found you taking down a dwarf superhot?'

Laughter bubbles out, and the last of the tension leaves my body. I lean into Snake, and he wraps an arm around my waist in support. When I have composed myself, he asks, 'Are you okay now?'

'Yes,' I say.

'Are you ready to fight for our parents?'

I nod. He releases me and takes hold of my hand. We turn and face the stage.

'We would like to speak on behalf of our parents before any vote,' he says, his confident voice filling the room.

· · * ◡ · * · ·

Pris and I stand together in the middle of a sea of creatures. I feel their stares, but I focus on my mother. A smile curves her lips as her gaze drifts to mine and Pris's hands. My collar is tight around my neck as I realise everyone can see us together. I resist the urge to let go of her hand, but I am reluctant to show any weakness.

Pris was awesome as she took out that dwarf goon. If she can fight someone twice her size, surely I can stand in front of the whole court and show that Pris and I are here to free our parents—together.

You want more than that though, a sneaky voice in my head says. I want to shut it down, but it speaks the truth. At the moment, though, as much as I want to be with Pris, my focus is only on getting our parents back and away from whatever force is manipulating this court and using our parents for their own ends.

'All right,' the Prime Minister says. 'But you do realise, young man, that if we vote on your mother's case before I have the chance to check our laws, the verdict will stand?'

I look at my mother, and she nods. We had so little time together before the court began, but she had told me she trusted me, and to follow my gut. Now she is reminding me of her parting words—that she will support me whatever I choose to do this evening.

'I do,' I say.

'Which one of you wants to go first?' Elias asks.

'Wait!'

I had forgotten the other man on the dais, the one who had stood with Grossman and the Regises.

'Our laws allow for another way to resolve this... ah... situation.'

'They do?' Elias appears skeptical, and I trust him more than I trust the man who stood with my mother's accuser.

'Our laws allow for anyone to undertake a trial. If they succeed, then they may ask anything of the court.'

'How does that help us?' I ask, not able to understand why he had brought this up, but sensing a trap.

The creature's head pivots around, and he glares at me. I straighten my shoulders. I will not be bullied by this elf, not when my mother's freedom is at stake. His mouth pulls into a sneer.

'Why, gnome, if you were successful in your quest, you would be able to petition for the charges against your mother to be dropped. Surely that is better than a guilty verdict.'

His superior tone rubs me up the wrong way, and I bristle at the implication that my mother is likely to be found guilty. What is he seeing that I am not?

'Is this true?' I direct the question at the Prime Minister.

'Well, it is not what the trials were designed for, but I guess it is possible. Yes, indeed, it could work the way Bernais says.'

'What would it entail?' I ask.

'If you choose to go down that path, the Queen's advisors would meet tonight and set you a task to complete. If you accomplish what is asked of you, you may ask for your parents to be released.'

It could not be that easy. Nothing is ever that easy.

'Can you give me an idea of some potential tasks?'

Giles frowns, and my stomach clenches. Why is he so worried?

'The rules forbid me from giving you details, but I can tell you that many of our great sagas tell of past trials and quests.'

I stare at my feet, trying to remember the details of the stories my mother used to read to me as a child. All that comes to mind are half-formed images of rescuing treasure from dragons or fighting sea monsters. I'm no hero to be taking on such things.

'Thanks, but I will take my chances with the vote,' I say, and my mother smiles her support.

I expect Bernais to argue, but he simply shakes his head sadly. 'Of course, The Court might find for your mother on this charge. But ask yourself if this is truly the worst she... or you... can be accused of?'

Fear roils in my stomach as I catch my mother's stricken face. She searches for and finds my father, and the look that passes between the two of them feeds that fear. What is it that I don't know? What can be worse than this?

I raise my head and glance around the room, hoping to find Earth or someone else to tell me what is going on. While we have been talking, the room has divided.

On one side stands the dwarves, Grossman and his cronies, the Regises, and a number of other creatures. Their faces are fierce, and determined, and scornful. They are looking at my mother as if she is... trash. What exactly have they all banded together to fight against?

On the other, standing behind a line of Bad Fairies, were my family, Eleanora and her sister, and the rest of the creatures. They stand tall and proud, facing down their opponents across the room.

Then there is a third faction. Some of their faces show concern, some curiosity, and some are enjoying this battle. Can I convince enough of these creatures to back me? And if I do, what does Bernais have up his sleeve? It will definitely be worse than this. And will they still support Mum and me after that?

I swore to myself I would do whatever it takes to save my mother. Sucking in a deep breath, then slowly expelling the air, I make up my mind. 'All right, I choose to take on a quest.'

The room erupts before I complete the sentence.

'Silence. SILENCE!' Elias's voice booms, obviously boosted by magic. When the noise reduces to a few whispers, he speaks again. 'Are you—'

'They have chosen to undertake a trial,' Bernais declares. 'This court is over.'

'Hold on a moment! Wait!' Pris is saying beside me, but I think I am the only one who hears her as the noise level rises.

'I SAID SILENCE. WE ARE NOT DONE HERE.' The Prime Minister's voice shakes the room.

My father's face is stricken as he looks through a gap in the line of Bad Fairies. He tries to push through towards me. Others in his group are also trying to get free, and a scuffle breaks out. Suddenly, the fairies are pushed out of the way, and chaos erupts around us as both sides turn their frustrations into pushes and shoves and threats.

The sound of thundering hooves fills the room, followed by hushed whispers racing around. Finally, everyone is silent. You can hear a pin drop. I stand on tiptoe to see what could possibly make these enraged creatures pull back.

Centaurs. Unbelievable. Honest-to-god centaurs. In my head, I knew the Queen had chosen a troop for her personal guard, but I never expected to actually see one. Glancing at Pris, I wonder if my face mirrors the amazement and awe on hers. Two guards joined Elias on the dais, surveying the crowd, looking for any further signs of trouble.

'Please escort Princess Cecily, Prince Malachi, and Ginth fo Drefin to their accommodations and make sure they are comfortable. They are to remain there, safe, until the trial is complete,' Elias commands, breaking the spell.

My mother finds me in the crowd and mouths, 'I love you,' as she leaves the dais. Once a fairy guard has escorted them from the room, Elias continues, 'In light of that outburst, the rest of tonight's court proceedings will be delayed until after the trial.'

Grumbles and mumbles run round the room. I'm a little disappointed because Mum had told me my father's clan was due to be elevated to elven status this evening in recognition of their service to the crown. Then again, with my mother not completely cleared of charges, that may have sparked another outburst.

One of the centaurs moves restlessly on the stage, and the room immediately falls silent.

Elias turns his gaze to Pris and me. 'I invoke trial rules. You two will meet here at ninth bell tomorrow to receive your instructions from the council. Appropriate food and equipment will be provided. Until that time, you are free to enjoy the ball and the hospitality of your families.'

'Hold on,' Pris says, but people are already moving. She stamps her foot, and I hold back a smile. 'I said, wait.' Someone shoves past us, and I realise no one is going to listen to her.

Pris grabs hold of my hand and drags me through the crowd until we are face to face with Elias.

'I did not say I would do this,' Pris says. 'In fact, why would I? I'm sure my parents would have been cleared.'

Bernais sidles up beside the Prime Minister, and his smile is oily as he says, 'I am sorry, Princess. I thought the gnome spoke for you both.'

My fists clench. I really want to punch that smirk off his face. One look in his eyes tells me he would enjoy that, as well as the punishment I would receive as a result. This stokes the fire of my anger, and it is all I can do to not react.

'No one speaks for me. I want to speak on behalf of my parents and let the people decide their fate.'

'I am afraid our Prime Minister, who is speaking for our Queen, has already invoked the rules of trial. It is too late.'

Again, that smirk. Seriously, I want to punch him so badly.

'I think we can make an exception,' Elias says. 'After all, she did not specifically agree to participate. We have enough witnesses to that affect to make the change.'

I freeze, and then turn to Pris. I was prepared to do this alone, but I will admit I was pleased when I believed she would be coming with me. As Pris's eyes meet mine, I sense her internal conflict.

She leans closer and whispers, 'What made you choose to go on a quest rather than speak for your mother?'

Bernais is straining to catch our words. I shift my shoulder around to block him out.

'Bernais led me to believe that if I didn't do this something worse would happen to my mum, and my family. Besides, I did a quick count up of numbers, and I wasn't convinced we could win a vote. And with all the tension in the room, I was worried that if we voted tonight, we would start a riot. I wanted to buy some time. I didn't mean for you to be included, I mean, I said—'

'I heard what you said.' She leans in closer. 'I'm wondering if this was Bernais's plan from the beginning.' Pris scans the room and must see what I saw moments ago. Tensions have everyone on edge, and anything could spark another outburst. This was never going to end the way we wanted it to.

Keeping hold of my hand, she straightens up and faces the two men. 'Cousin Elias, I have changed my mind. Snake and I will undertake this quest together.'

I blow out a breath I didn't know I had been holding. Before either of the men can respond, Pris turns on her heel and leads me back through the crowd towards my family.

CHAPTER 14

A Deal is Struck

As the tension in the room disperses, I follow Eleanora and her sister. Near the door our dear friend Gin left through, they stop the Prime Minister.

'That didn't go well, Elias,' Eugenia says. 'We are left in limbo, and Bernais bought time to consolidate his position.'

'I am sure that is exactly what Bernais thinks as well.' Elias's smile raises my hackles. I am sure he planned this whole evening and is exceedingly happy with the result.

My mistress taps her lips thoughtfully with her index finger. 'I get the feeling you are not completely surprised by what happened tonight.'

A smile plays around his mouth. 'I'm not sure what you mean, Ellie.'

'So, Fairburn and his centaur guards just happened to be passing by the ballroom.... What are you up to, Elias?'

'I am not without eyes in Bernais's camp, and I had some inkling of his plan. It could have gone one of two ways tonight, and I believe I had both bases covered.'

Eugenie huffs. 'You are playing with fire... or at the very

least, two young creatures' lives. I fail to see how this outcome works in their favour, or in yours.'

'I have been talking with some councillors who are as concerned as I am over Bernais's plotting. We have some ideas on how this trial might work to our advantage.... With a little nudge in the right direction and a little bit of planning, Bernais will be sorry he ever pushed for this.'

Elias's smile is almost sinister, which is unnerving, because the man has a good heart and is one of the nicest creatures I know. When he was appointed by the Queen to replace Bernais as Prime Minister, many thought he would not be up to the job because he is too laid back.

Eleanora, though, said it was the quiet ones you had to watch, and that Elias plays a long game. She should know, since she was close to him once. Even now she is studying his face, trying to work out what is going on.

Chuckling, Eleanora asks, 'Tell me, Elias, did you actually ask the Chief Centaur to wait in the corridor just in case things went bad?'

'The centaurs are only interested in protecting the Queen's interests. They bow to no one,' Elias replies, quite serious.

'So, this has something to do with the Queen?'

'Eleanora, you know I cannot discuss state affairs with you.'

Eugenia smiles. 'You didn't answer her question, Elias, but no matter. If you do have a plan, what do you need from Eleanora and me?'

'Just for you to support my proposal in the council.'

'Of course,' Eugenia says, 'but that support might be more full-bodied if we knew what you have up your sleeve.'

'I cannot tell you yet, except perhaps that you are not going to like it because it will put the Princess and young Snake in harm's way.'

'I am not sure about this.' Eleanora frowns at Elias. 'I promised Gin I would look after Snake.'

Elias's eyes are troubled as he speaks. 'And I would not put Cecily's child in danger if I had a choice. Unfortunately, Bernais and his cronies will not agree to a token quest. It must be real. Please trust me, and trust my plan.'

'You will really be placing these young creatures' lives in danger as part of a political manoeuvre?' Eugenia asks.

Is that a flicker of uncertainty I see cross Elias's face? Or is it sadness? It is gone so fast, I cannot be sure exactly what I saw.

'Yes, I suppose I am, but I also believe they might be in danger already. Besides, after hearing reports of their recent activity, I believe Pricilla and Snake will come through this... perhaps not completely unharmed, but alive.'

Eleanora and Eugenia share a look, and the buzz in the air tells me they are speaking. My senses prickle. What are they talking about that they don't want me to know?

Eugenia nods, and Eleanora returns her gaze to Elias. 'We will support you on one condition: that you find a way to allow Percival to go with them.'

What? Hold on. Me? No. Definitely not!

I move around my mistress to catch Elias's attention so that I can object. I clear my throat, but the noise is lost as the Prime Minister speaks.

'I think that can be arranged. Both Priscilla and Snake are new to the World Below, and it would only be fitting to provide them with a guide, and one whose powers are not strong enough to materially assist them should be acceptable to Bernais.'

My head swings from the minister to my mistress. Have I just been insulted and hung out to dry all in the same sentence?

'But, Ellie....'

Eleanora reaches out and cups my face in her hand. 'Percival, I promised you could return home when this was done, but I cannot let the children go on a dangerous quest alone. They would benefit from your wisdom and knowledge.'

And I would benefit from time in front of a roaring fire and some tasty morsels of chicken. My sigh is deep. When she looks at me in that way, like I am the only one she can trust, I can deny her nothing.

'As you wish,' I say, all the while thinking, *This is not over yet*. The council might not agree to my going.

I follow Eleanor out of the ballroom towards the council chambers, wishing I could do more than hope for a council vote in my favour to release me from this commitment.

CHAPTER 15

The Midnight Ball

P eople stare at us as we walk through the crowd. All I want is to hide away and think through what just happened, but I'm stuck here. I don't even know where I'll spend the night. I stop walking, suddenly unsure about where to go. Can we leave? Stay the night at the conference centre? Or would that muck up the time difference thing?

Snake's hand cups my elbow, and he steers me towards his father, who is deep in conversation with a group of gnomes. I am shaking, and I pull my shawl around myself. Snake drapes an arm over my shoulder and pulls me close.

'Are you okay?' he asks.

I nod, but I am not, not really. Sensing this, he pulls me in closer, and I allow the warmth of his body to calm me. Snake's father and Earth draw away from their friends and join us.

'Agret and I are lining up votes on the council to stop this farce from going any further. We will present the paper-work absolving your mother, and that will be that,' Earth says, and I marvel at how businesslike the gregarious man appears now.

'No.' Snake shakes his head. 'If you succeed, Pris would be left facing this alone, and that is not right.'

'Son, we can clearly see that Bernais railroaded her inclusion, and so could everyone else. We want this whole thing to be called off.'

Again, Snake shakes his head. 'Something is going on in The Court. It is not of our making, but someone is using our families to make a point for some reason. At least at the moment, we are in control of what's happening. If we stop this, then we will be looking over our shoulders, waiting for the next strike.'

I feel in my bones that Snake is right. The tension in the room has lessened, as this was perhaps the only outcome that would not end in bloodshed tonight. I move closer to Snake, his presence calming me and boosting my confidence. We must face this quest head-on and end this nonsense. It is what my parents would do. They would never give in to bullies, and they raised me the same way.

'We agreed to do this, so please don't waste your political capital for us. I fear you would lose anyway. For some reason, Bernais, and many of his friends, want Snake and me out of the way.' I stand a little straighter as I voice my opinion.

Agret grunts. 'It was a long shot, anyway, but I felt we had to try. I cannot just stand by and allow the two of you be sent on some useless quest that could get you killed.'

I wiggle out from Snake's comforting arm, refreshed and ready to face whatever this was. 'You won't be standing idly by. While we are away, you'll be working to find out why Bernais wants us gone, what he wants with our parents, and what is really going on in the World Below. And you can start by telling me why my father is not considered part of this court.'

Agret looks at Earth, who shakes his head. 'But she deserves—'

'For reasons of their own, your parents did not tell you

about their past. I believe you have a right to know, but this is their story to tell.' Earth reaches out and takes my hand. 'What I can tell you is, I know them. As I have already told you, I met your uncle once. He is a kind and wise man, as is your father. You can trust their intentions were good when they decided to keep their history from you.'

I roughly withdraw my hand. 'I suppose you cannot tell me why people keep attacking me either.'

Earth shakes his head. 'That would be part of the same story, I am guessing.'

This skirting around the subject of my past is getting beyond a joke. My fists clench as my temper threatens to take hold, but I am suddenly overtaken by a deep weariness. It will do no good to rant and rave. If outright questioning will not gain me answers, then I will have to be more subtle... but not tonight.

Tonight, I'm exhausted and overwhelmed. To my shock, tears form in my eyes, and I resist the urge to brush them away. I am a mess. I want to appear strong, but at the moment, I have never been more lost and alone in my life.

'I worked out I am related to Elias, and I guess to Bernais too, but I don't want to stay with either of them. Do I have any more family here? I mean, I need to find somewhere to stay the night.' I know I sound forlorn, but I don't have any energy left to hide that that is exactly how I am feeling.

Earth again grabs my hand, and I see that underneath his facade, he is still the kind and generous creature I met in Cornwall. 'Of course, you will be staying with us. Agret already sent word for rooms to be made up.'

I sag with relief. 'Perhaps if we leave now, you can tell us something about what to expect on this quest.'

Again, Earth looks at his nephew, and a wry smile forms on Agret's mouth. 'We might have boasted about going on quests when we were youngsters, but truth be told, no one has been on one in generations.'

My stomach clenches. If I had not realised what a big deal this was before, it was made clear to me now.

'All we know is that it is likely to be dangerous, and you will need your wits about you to succeed,' Earth adds.

I am stunned into silence. Fortunately, Snake is not. 'Can someone go and fetch our packs from the conference centre behind the refreshment bar in the lobby? We may need some of our stuff for tomorrow.'

'Of course, I will arrange it now.' Earth departs so hastily, I believe he is relieved to be away from us.

Agret smiles at his son. 'I will look after your mother while you are gone. I will make sure nothing happens to her.'

'I trust you to honour that promise,' Snake says before turning to me.

'If we are to be sent to our doom tomorrow, we should enjoy a little of tonight. I believe we have earned it,' he says, grinning crookedly, a glint in his green eyes. He holds out his hand. 'Would you like to dance?'

I look around in amazement at the people swaying around us. I had been so deep into our conversation and my own misery, I had not even noticed the band take the stage, and they are singing music from home.

'Don't they have their own music?' I ask.

Snake smiles. 'They do, but the first night of the ball is always a mixture of songs from both worlds to celebrate people from the World Above coming home.'

As the band finishes off Fleetwood Mac's "The Chain" and the first notes of Chris Isaak's "Wicked Game" drift out, Snake takes my hand and leads me to the dance floor. He draws me into his arms and says, 'For a while, let's pretend we're just two normal people at a dance.'

Swaying to the music with Pris in my arms feels right, more right than anything has since the Bad Fairies took my mother. The music changes to Coldplay's "Trouble", and I can't help but chuckle as I start singing along under my breath.

'This should be our theme song,' I say. 'You've had nothing but trouble since I stumbled across your doorstep.'

She pulls away from me just far enough so I can look into her eyes.

'If you hadn't tracked me down, I would never have known what happened to my parents, and goodness knows where I would be now.' She smiles softly at me, her eyes warm, inviting me to move closer, and I oblige.

She is so beautiful, and I want nothing more than to lean forwards and brush my lips against hers. In her eyes, I see that she would not object if I did. I hesitate, and the moment is gone when, over Pris's shoulder, I catch sight of Bernais glaring at us.

He may not like Pris, but he would never stand for a mere gnome taking advantage of an elf, let alone an elven princess. My eyes flick around the room, and I realise he is not the only one.

Pris's face is now a picture of confusion, and the hurt I glimpse stabs me like a knife. I pull her back into the circle of my arms. She is not for me, not in the long-term, but we can have tonight, can't we?

'What's up?' Pris asks, her breath tickling my ear as she speaks.

Should I explain the social norms of the World Below to her?

'Is it because they are all staring at us?' she presses.

'Partially.'

'And they are doing that because gnomes and elves....'

I wait for her to finish, but she doesn't.

'Yes, because gnomes and elves don't mix,' I confirm.

'I deal with people treating me differently because of my skin colour all the time. You must know all that doesn't matter to me.'

She doesn't go so far as to say she likes me, but I hear the unspoken words, and a grin forms on my lips. I pull her even closer and rest my cheek against hers.

I finally admit what I have been trying to ignore for the last week. I want to be with her so much it aches, but this is all I will have. We might be able to overcome the race thing, but she is elven royalty, and I am a not-quite elf. We will never be able to overcome our different social statuses.

'If they won't accept us down here, we will be fine when we return home,' she says, snuggling closer.

I stop moving. She is so positive we will succeed. That we will go home and everything will be normal.

'Snake?'

'Sorry, got lost for a moment there,' I say.

I will not be the one to tell her nothing will ever be the same for us after this. Battle lines have been drawn in the World Below. If we survive our quest, the ripples of this war brewing around us will permeate into the World Above, changing the world as we know it.

The song changes to The Fray's "How to Save a Life", and I croon along softly as we sway to the beat. I close my eyes, blocking out the room, wishing we could stay like this forever.

Acknowledgments

It takes a team to produce a book, and I am very lucky to have a great support team.

To my arc readers, Sandy, Tracey and Laura. Thanks for reading this before it looked lovely and all your amazing feedback really made me think about how to make this story better.

Also, thank you to the team at Creating Ink, especially Sali Benbow-Powers, and the team at Hot Tree Editing and McKinley Hellennes Krantz with the help of Keeley Catarineau for improving my story telling and making it more readable.

As always, my love and thanks to my moral support Jim, and my son Sam for putting up with me when I hide away to finish a book. Without them I wouldn't eat and I would miss every deadline.

Finally, thank you for reading my musings. If you get a chance please let me know what you think of the book by leaving a review on your favourite site.

About the Author

Vivienne has been writing books since she was fifteen years old, but only friends and family were allowed to read them. Forced to give up work because of family commitments she was encouraged by friends and family to finally put some of her writing out there for others to read.

Born in Invercargill (New Zealand), she has lived in; Dunedin (New Zealand), London (England), Petersfield (England) and currently lives with her husband and son, their dog Trouble and cat Lola in North Sydney (Australia).

When not reading or writing she can be found walking, crocheting, knitting and watching movies.

For future releases and current news you can find Vivienne at www.viviennelfraser.com.au where you can also join my newsletter.

Also By Vivienne Lee Fraser

If you enjoyed The World Below, why not try The Guardians of Time Series Time Travel Adventures?

SWAGMAN

What if the Swagman did not die when he jumped into the billabong?

What if he ended up in medieval England embroiled in a plot to set a new king on the throne?

For once in his life Swagman John is lost for words. Accused of stealing the lamb he rescued fears being thrown in jail. But instead of protesting his innocence he backs into the waters of the billabong and falls. Certain he is dead, John cannot believe the lamb when he tells him he has been brought through a time and space portal to Medieval England. When Mistress Barabal and Squire Stanislaus stumble upon John in the New Forest he is taken back to Winchester Castle where he actually finds the King has been killed and his brother Prince Henry is about preparing to take his place and his new friends are assisting him.

Suddenly talking lambs are the least of his worries.

Caught up in political intrigues he does not fully understand, John finds dungeons and magic are not just for fairy tales, and that there are people prepared to go to great lengths to see William the Conquerer's other son crowned king—even as far as murder. Just as John wonders if going to prison for stealing sheep was not a better option all along, he finds there is an even more sinister foe meddling in with history.

Against such odds how can John set history straight so he can return home to his family?

ALCHEMIST

Would you Travel 900 years into the future to save the lives of some dogs?

Alain, Apprentice Apothecary and sometime Alchemist, is on a high after saving the life of his king. After all the excitement he is not content to slip back into everyday life. So when he is offered the chance to travel with his Master to the future and investigate a strange disease in dogs he leaps at the chance.

Taken through a portal to The New Forest in 2017, Alain finds life in Medieval England had not prepared him for a world full of machines where everyone lives in manor houses and there is no real magic. Uncomfortable and homesick he regrets leaving the comforts of home until his new friends decide to help with his investigation. Just when returning home is a real option, they uncover a sinister plot behind the animal illness that threatened more than just family pets.

Will Alain risk everything he holds dear to stop those who threaten the future of mankind?

https://viviennelfraser.com.au/time-guardians

· · ⋆· ◗ ·⋆· ·

Or if you enjoy Fantasy Adventure why not try

THE WIZARD AND THE WARRIOR?

Centuries ago prophets predicted the rise of a great wizard and a formidable warrior who would save the people of their land.

Now an invasion fleet is heading for Aria, is it time for the Wizard and the Warrior to arise and save them all?

Runaway bride Aliah wants to be more than someone's wife. Fleeing his destiny, Seamus has no idea what he wants from his future. Thrown together by fate, the two journey to the nation's capital; one to warn the king of an impending invasion, the other to do the unthinkable—train to be a wizard.

Their chance encounter takes them on a wild adventure where they must face their pasts and decide their future, all while helping Aria prepare to defend itself.

However, fate has not finished with Seamus and Aliah. In an unexpected twist, they are placed at the very centre of the conflict facing their home, and must decide whether or not to take up the challenge.

With the gods on their side, it should be easy for Aliah and Seamus to identify and locate the real power behind the invasion and find a way to defeat him; all while pulling together a support team and having mid-night lessons to learn how to use their newly acquired magical tokens. Well, it would be if the gods weren't hiding more than they shared.

Aria's future hangs in the balance, can two runaways tip the scales?

What one reader on Amazon said: Great book - it might be targeted at youth readers, but even as an adult, I was hooked on the storyline. Can't wait for the next one!

https://viviennelfraser.com.au/wizard-and-warrior-one